Battlescars

a rock & roll romance

Sophie Monroe

Sophie Monroe

The author acknowledges the use of the following:
Cover Photo courtesy of:
Will Ferguson- www.facebook.com/willfergusondrummer
Taken by:
Noelle Carina- www.facebook.com/artbynoellecarina

Adele, Age of Days (Daze), Brian Fallon-The Gaslight Anthem, Cartier, Chevy, Escalade, Faneuil Hall, Google, Granduca Hotels, Hard Rock Café, Hinder, Honda, In-N-Out Burger, Jameson, James Taylor, Juicy Couture, Kings of Leon, Lit, Los Del Rios-Macarena, Lucky Charms, Lucky Strikes, Marlboro, Millennium Hotel, Mini Cooper, New England Aquarium, Poison, Range Rover, Ray-Ban, Rod Stewart, Rock Band, The Golden Girls, The Rolling Stones, Three Days Grace, Van Morrison, Wii, W Hotels

Battlescars:
A Rock & Roll
Romance

Sophie Monroe

Thank you to my readers and fans for taking the time to read something that I wrote.
To my blog friends and friends that took the time to beta read and offer feedback THANK YOU!

To my husband who dealt with all my insanity while writing this story and for helping me make sure that it was the best it could be. I love you!

A special thank you to my friend Tara W. for helping me with the medical parts (and your advice and laughs along the way.)

A very special thank you to my friend Will Ferguson who's picture you're seeing on the cover and to his awesome girlfriend Noelle for taking the picture! (and for staying up until 2:30 in the morning helping to perfect it.)

Music gives a soul to the universe, wings to the mind, flight to the imagination and life to everything. ~ Plato

PROLOGUE
Jake Parker, circa 2007
Five years earlier...

"Jake." A voice whined.

Not again... I groaned.

I sat up and rubbed my hands over my scruffy face. Damn, I really needed to shave. I woke up with not one, but two girls in my bed. I always tried my hardest to get them out as soon as the party was over, and I had my fun. Obviously, last night was a mind eraser because I barely remembered any of it. I remember playing the show, but everything that happened after that is anyone's guess. I'm pretty sure the one is named Vanessa and the other one was Trixie, or was is Victoria?

Who cares? I couldn't even keep up with them anymore.

I rubbed my eyes willing the room would stop spinning. I looked over and noticed the pile of condoms on the floor. Thank fuck I've never be that stupid, even while completely inebriated. I tried to climb out of bed. Vanessa kept trying to push me back on the bed. I struggled against her and managed to get to my feet. She sat on the edge of the bed pouting with her arms crossed. *Awesome...* I walked out into the living room and saw my newly acquired bodyguard, Brett, sitting on the couch. I motioned with my head for him to take care of the disposal. He nodded in understanding and went to do this mornings tossing. The label really needed to give him a raise or something.

I stepped into the shower and turned the water on as hot as I could. My head was pounding something fierce. I wondered what the rest of the guys ended up doing last night after I left. I stayed under the water until I couldn't stand it anymore. Walking back into the room I noticed that it had been cleaned up a bit. All the wrappers were gone, as were last night's guests. I went over to the dresser and pulled out a pair of boxers and some clothes. I dressed in a haste and hurried across the hall to see the rest of the guys. We overslept and needed to be at the arena in an hour. I opened the door and started banging around.

"What the fuck man?" Derek grumbled.

"Come on we need to go." I said rolling him off the couch onto the floor.

We were a bunch of twenty-one year old misfits that met in Arizona as teenagers and took a chance on moving to LA last year. We were stuck playing small gigs when we were fortunate enough to found by Dylan Ryan, the lead singer of Crashing Down. A few weeks after his label approached us about signing. We jumped at the opportunity and have been on a small fifteen-passenger bus for the past three months opening up for Crashing Down.

We spent our days sleeping off our hangovers and our nights playing shows and partying. At the rate we're going I think I'm going to need a new liver soon. I went over to the bedroom and started shaking Blake. He was bitching to leave him alone when Kevin came out of the bathroom ready to go. Together we managed to get Blake to his feet. He was still feeling the effects of last night. Once everyone was ready we climbed into the van and headed over to the venue.

We lugged in all of our equipment since we weren't quite at the status of a headliner and didn't get roadies. After performing a quick sound check we headed over to the little closet that they called a dressing room. The groupies were already waiting there in the masses. I saw a cute little dark haired girl and decided she would be the bad decision for the night. I walked over and tapped her on the shoulder. She turned to look at me and gaped. She was cute, dark hair, big brown eyes with a hot little body.

"OH MY GOD!" She squeaked. "Y-you're Jake Parker." She stuttered.

"Last I checked." I smirked.

"I'm a huge fan." She eyed me up and down. "I'm Rachel."

"Nice to meet you Rachel." I grabbed a beer and walked over to sit on a folding metal chair. She came over and sat on my lap. *Yep, she's an easy one.*

We did the show and took the van back to the hotel. We had a little party in the room before Rachel and I retreated back to my room. I was definitely drunk, again. Rachel was more than willing and by the time I came out of the bathroom from taking a piss she was sprawled out across the bed naked. She offered me a condom, but I didn't trust anything that wasn't mine. I suited up and fucked her. I honestly don't know why I continued to do it night after night, especially since it was meaningless sex that meant nothing other then getting my rocks off. There was no emotional connection whatsoever and it was always unfulfilling. I pounded into her until I came and didn't give a second thought to the fact that she didn't get off. She was pouting her bottom lip looking annoyed. I chose to ignore her by turning off the bedside lamp and closing my eyes.

When I woke up the next morning, actually it was the afternoon I went straight into the bathroom. I showered and came out to get some clothes, but when I reached for my jeans from last night I noticed that my wallet was missing, as was my cell phone. I walked into the living area and asked Brett if he took them. He looked at me and shook his head. *Fucking bitch stole my shit!* I tossed everything in my suitcase and used the hotel phone to call and cancel all my credit cards. Brett's phone started ringing. He answered it and handed it to me. It was Ron. He was like my dad, the only steady adult figure I've had in my life.

"Hi, son. How are you?" He asked, knowingly.

"Alright." I tried to sound like I had my shit together. Though there was no fooling him.

"You sure as hell don't sound alright." He protested. "Listen, you are supposed to be on tour. Have fun. Hell, have a few beers here and there, but I know exactly what you're doing and that shit ain't right, Jake. You can't change your past. I know it's all fun and games getting your dick wet every night, but there's more to life than that. Get your shit together or I'm coming to take you home. I will not stand by and watch you dry up into another has been. Understand?"

"Yes, sir." I mumbled.

"Good. I'll check back with you in a couple days. Remember what I said." He said sternly.

He hung up the phone and I handed it back to Brett. I went back into my room and sat on the edge of the bed. Ron was right. I needed to get my shit together. I was using my fame and leaving a wake of destruction in its path. The media already had me pegged as being out of control after the whole Ashley Noelle episode, and then again with Lily Atlas. I wasn't even super famous yet and they wouldn't let me live that shit down. I vowed to give up the drinking, except for an occasional beer from time to time and the groupies needed to go. I was going to try my hardest to get my act together. I just hoped that I was strong enough to do it.

CHAPTER ONE
Everywhere I Go

"Aubrey!" My dad called waking me from a stupor.

I lifted my head off his desk and yawned loudly.

"Amen." I suppressed a giggle.

Someone once told me if you ever get caught sleeping with your head down to play it off like you were praying and hope for the best. I knew I wouldn't get in trouble and that my dad would find it amusing. Besides, it was his fault that I was exhausted from being gone so much this week. I had been to LA, NYC, Boston, and San Francisco just to name a few. I didn't go to visit. No, I spent my time playing stewardess to rich middle-aged men. They would hire my dad's commercial aircraft company to fly them to their destinations, and I was part of the deal. *Yay me!*

"Nice try kiddo." He beamed his crinkly-eyed smile at me. "Listen, I know you just got back, *and* you're exhausted, but I need a favor."

Not again... I was looking forward to going home and sleeping for a day, or several.

"I have a date tonight?"

"A date?" He choked.

I didn't date, and he knew it.

"Yeah, with my bed. We were totally going to sleep together." I said sarcastically.

He rolled his eyes and laughed. "Nice try."

"Ugh. What is it this time?" I asked, feeling slightly annoyed.

I already knew my answer, and it involved packing.

"We just got a call for a last minute flight and I need you to go. It could turn out to be a valuable client." He smiled, and I knew I was doomed. I may have been twenty-three, but I was still daddy's little girl and wanted to make him happy.

"What are the flight details?" I asked curiously.

"Well, this one is leaving from LA and heading to Manhattan. If this goes well, there could be several more."

"Who are we flying this time? It better not be that creepy Carter guy again. I left him walking funny for a week last time."

My dad flinched. "No, he's no longer a client here."

The "Carter Incident," as my dad referred to it happened three weeks ago. Carter Murphy is a pompous ass whose dad owns Murphy Enterprises, a Texas based textile-company. He thinks that he's entitled to everything he wants, including women. He learned the lesson the hard way with me that you can't always have what you want. We were flying from Houston to Dallas, a complete waste of fossil fuel, when Carter decided he wanted to cop a feel. Boy, was he surprised when I copped a feel of my own and twisted, *hard*. I wish I had a Polaroid of his face so that I could hang it as a warning to anyone else that wanted a try. No one touched me without my permission. Especially after what happened…

I knew that I was decent looking, and I've had my fair share of suitors. I didn't think it was a job hazard since most of our clients wouldn't be interested in someone that looked like me. I never liked to *blend* with the crowd, so I tended to stand out. Basically, I have black hair with hot pink highlights, a couple piercings and a bunch of tattoos. I'm a size six, because unlike most skinny bitches I want to eat things other than salads. I have a mouth that would make a sailor proud. I also never hold back what I want to say in order to avoid hurting someone's feelings. However, I am fiercely loyal and compassionate, just don't cross me.

"That's too bad." I said, not feeling guilty at all.

"Listen Aubrey, things have been slower than normal lately… with the cost of fuel going up along with everything else, we really need this client."

I recently noticed that things were slower than normal, but the edge in his voice told me he was worried. It was especially unsettling for me because this business was his whole life. It was built up from literally nothing by my Gramps with blood, sweat and tears. I would do whatever I had to, even if it meant making myself suffer to keep it afloat.

"Is it Channing Tatum? Please tell me it is…" I pleaded playfully.

"No, it's um," He put his glasses on to look at the post-it in his hand. "It's a Jake Parker."

I rolled my eyes. *Jake Parker, joy.* His name had been screamed and damned to hell by lots of women according to the gossip rags. Everyone under fifty, except my dad, knew who Jake Parker was. He was the uber-sexy lead singer of the band Battlescars. He was tall, handsome and covered in tattoos. He also had a reputation, one that I wasn't interested in knowing. *You just said you would do anything.* I told myself.

"Fine, I'll do it. But you owe me big time, and I mean BIG. I need to go home and grab some clean clothes. When do we need to leave?"

"Be back by two at the absolute latest. Can you tell mom that I'll be a little late for dinner tonight?"

I nodded and did a couple spins in the swivel chair before heading to my car, a beat up Honda Civic with a serious muffler problem. I put it in to first gear and headed home. I drove down Main Street and admired all of the families walking up and down window-shopping on the crisp fall day. That sort of thing would never be in the cards for me. I was almost at the point that I accepted it, almost. I was destined to be alone because of *him.* I pushed that thought aside and continued my journey home. Ten minutes later I pulled up to my parent's small ranch. It was white with gray shutters and a red door. The walkway was lined with red, orange and yellow mums. There were two pumpkins on either side of the stairs and a scarecrow planted in the bush off to the side. It was where I grew up, and I loved it.

I turned the key and pushed the door open.

"Mom, I'm home." I yelled.

"In here honey." She yelled back from the kitchen, which was a whole ten feet away.

The house smelled delicious. She was making beef stew. My stomach growled obnoxiously. I headed into my mom's charming little kitchen. It boasted original cabinets and appliances from the 50's, except the fridge. It was retro chic. I kissed her cheek and made myself a bowl. I crumbled up some crackers and dug in.

"That's very un-ladylike Aubrey Jean." My mom scolded.

My mom, Caroline was incredible. She was your typical all-American housewife, minus the Botox. She was the best cook and could easily give Paula Deen a run for her money. She was strong and witty. I admired her immensely. We were about the same height at five foot five and had the same honey brown eyes. Her hair was a light shade of brown, where mine was naturally a dark brown like my dad. I dye mine black because I think it compliments my skin better. I stuck my tongue out at her and grinned. I hated when she called me by my full name. My middle name was Jean after my Granny Jean who lived across the street. She's awesome. A total spitfire. I would make a point to stop by and see her before I took off again. I finished eating and rinsed my bowl. I headed to my room to pack.

As soon as I started down the hallway my cat, Mitsy, spotted me. She started going nuts and kept trying to climb in my suitcase. She followed me around as I went from room to room collecting miscellaneous crap. Most likely I wouldn't need any of it, but I liked to keep it handy just in case. I stopped dead in my tracks when I walked past the bathroom. I looked in the mirror and wanted to scream. I couldn't believe that I actually went out in public looking like this. My hair looked like the bride of Frankenstein, and my eyeliner looked like a scene from hooker meets pimp. I grabbed a washcloth and wiped my face. I reapplied my make-up and took a brush to my hair. I went back into my room and changed into a pair of black skinny jeans and a lightweight gray hoodie. I tossed the rest of my belongings into the suitcase and zippered it. I scratched Mitzy for a couple minutes before it was time to go. I hugged my mom goodbye and headed over to see Granny Jean. I walked across the street to her blue bi-level. I didn't bother knocking because she'd whack me with a wooden spoon if I did. She always insisted that her house was my house.

"Well, if isn't my favorite bran muffin." She was sitting at the kitchen table drinking a cup of coffee and smoking a Lucky Strike.

"If it isn't my favorite dinosaur." I teased back.

She stuck her tongue out at me like an errant child. "Roar!"

I sat at the table and stole one of her cigarettes. How she smoked those things I would never know.

"Looks like I'm off on another adventure. I don't know how long I'll be gone this time." I said somewhat sulking.

"Where to this time?" She raised a brow.

"We're off to New York carting around some rock star."

I waited for her reaction. Granny *loved* rock stars.

"Who is it?" She prodded.

"Jake Parker." I said with disgust.

"Oh, I'd like him to come clean out my cobwebs." She beamed.

I did not need the mental picture that followed.

"Granny, that's disgusting!" I shrieked.

"Whatever, it's true. That boy is a tall drink of water if I've ever seen one."

"Alright, I'm outta here. Thanks for the nightmares."

I snubbed out my cigarette and stood. I walked across the table and kissed her white fluff of hair before heading out the door. To an outsider she looked like a grandma that made apple pies and listened to gospel records. That was the farthest thing from the truth when it came to Granny Jean. She was spry and would much rather listen to The Rolling Stone's over gospel any day. I loaded my suitcase in the trunk and clambered into my car. I groaned as soon as I turned the key and the muffler sound radiated loudly throughout the car. I seriously needed to start saving up for a new car because this was getting embarrassing. I backed out of the driveway and started back to the airfield. When I arrived I popped the trunk and grabbed my suitcases. I leaned them against the passenger side and went to the office to get the flight details. I also wanted to say goodbye to my dad. I walked down the hallway and opened his office door.

"Hey kiddo, they're just finishing the last of the pre-flight checklist. Mark is going to be the pilot since I know the two of you won't kill each other. Especially, if you end up being gone for a long time." He sounded hopeful.

He handed me an envelope with some cash and the company credit card.

"How long is a long time, Dad?" I pouted.

"Three months… but before you go all drama queen on me we *really* need this Aubrey. Please be on your best behavior." He begged.

Three months!

"Fine." I relented.

He stood up and walked around to where I was standing and kissed my hair.

"Thanks honey, I love you. Any problems just call."

I stuffed the envelope in my back pocket and stalked out of the office cringing. I pulled a Marlboro Red out of my pack and headed outside to light up. I needed to mentally prepare myself for the long flight from Shitsville, I mean, Smithville, Ohio to LA. Then all the way back to New York.

Dave, who was one of the crew guys, was ogling my ass. "Hey Aubrey, looking good."

"If you'd like to keep your eyes I suggest you keep walking, monkey boy." I blew a plume of smoke in his face.

"Always the lady." He laughed and shook his head as he went inside.

I wasn't a man-hater. I just didn't think that I was put on this earth to be objectified as their piece of meat. A couple minutes later Ian came and told me we were ready to go. I walked into the cabin and stowed my luggage. At least my dad was right about being stuck with Mark, we wouldn't kill each other. I've known him since I was a kid, and he treated me as was one of his own. He also understood my twisted sense of humor and wasn't easily offended. Mark Wilson was in his early-forties, unmarried by choice and suffered from male-pattern baldness. He was an all around great guy, and it made me dread this adventure a little less. Unfortunately, we would have a different co-pilot for each flight. We would get "rogues" which was whoever was coming or going from other private airlines like ours. Today we got Scott, who was drooling after me like a total weirdo. I said a quick hello and went about my business. I was not interested in making another friend. Mark started hitting switches to prepare for takeoff. I plopped in one of the comfortable chairs and pulled out my e-reader. I started reading and hoped that the time would pass quickly. Once we were airborne I started to prepare the in-flight meal so that it would be ready for our guests. I sat back down and closed my eyes for a much needed nap. Unfortunately, Jake Parker was part of my very sex filled dream. *Ugh!*

I wasn't able to get any more sleep for the rest of the flight.

Four and a half hours later we touched down in LA. Mark lowered the stairs onto the tarmac. A blacked out Escalade was there waiting. A hulk of a guy that I could only assume was Jake's bodyguard stepped out. I groaned internally and went to make sure everything was in order. I was stocking up the bathroom when I felt someone breathing near my neck. Acting on instinct I quickly turned and kneed the guy right in the balls. He cupped his crown jewels. *Fuck!* I knew that I should apologize, but hasn't he ever heard of personal space?

"I'm Brett Barnes," He was unaltered by my attack, but spoke in an off-pitched voice. He proffered his hand. "Head of Mr. Parker's security. I need to make sure the plane is secure before takeoff."

I glanced up at the twenty-something beefcake with a buzz cut. He looked ex-military. If I had to guess, I would say he was six-foot-four and two hundred and forty pounds. He was broad shouldered and burly but looked clean cut in his black suit. I offered my hand in return.

"Aubrey Thompson. Sorry, by the way." I waved my hand in front of his package. "You shouldn't sneak up on people like that." I scolded.

I gestured my hand for him to have at it and walked out. It was going to be a long night. He looked through every nook and cranny of the plane before giving the go ahead for Captain Celebrity, I mean Jake, to board. Jake stopped at the top step and slid his Ray-Ban aviators to the top of his head. That's when I got my first real look at him. He was tall, at least six-two, tan and toned with a black Mohawk and intense, penetrating blue eyes. He had two piercings in his left eyebrow and a pair of spider bites on his lip. His face could make the Greek Gods weep with his square jaw and high cheekbones. Even his fucking nose was sexy. Then he smirked at me. *I hate rockstars!*

Dammit! He probably thinks I'm admiring him. I kind of was, but still.

"I'm Jake Parker." He winked and offered his hand.

"I know who you are." I replied bitchily.

Then I quickly remembered I was supposed to be nice. I offered my hand in return and noticed that I didn't start to feel clammy like I normally would by this time. He had giant hands. They completely enveloped my small one.

"So you're the flight attendant? You don't look like the normal flight attendants that I get." He was gawking at my chest. "Is that a tattoo?" He pointed.

I looked down and noticed that my hoodie had slid down, and my chest plate was peeking out. *Just fucking fabulous!*

"That would be none of your business, kind sir. Now, if you would please take your seat we can prepare for takeoff."

I adjusted my hoodie and smiled devilishly effectively giving him the brush-off. He sat in the cream-colored leather seat and stretched his long legs out in front of him.

"Hey." He called out, and I grudgingly walked back over to his seat.

"Yes." I smiled, but it didn't reach my eyes. He was already wearing down my almost non-existent patience.

Prison orange isn't your color Aubrey. I repeated this mantra on my way over.

"You never told me your name." He was attempting to play coy.

"Aubrey." I said flatly, wishing that I was anywhere but here.

"Pretty name, for an even prettier girl." He smirked.

I rolled my eyes and walked away.

I checked to make sure that the luggage was secure before giving Mark the go ahead to takeoff. On my way back, I made sure that Captain Celebrity was properly buckled. He made a smart-ass remark about how I should check. I ignored the urge to slap him and kept moving. *If he keeps this shit up, I won't feed him any of the pot roast I have cooking.* It was my mom's recipe, and it was good enough to make you want to sell your soul. Ten minutes later we were airborne. Once we reached altitude Mark came through the sound system and said that everyone was allowed to move about the cabin. I got up and asked if either of them wanted anything to drink. I told them that I would feed them in about an hour. I brought them each a bottle of water and went back to my seat. I was listening to music and getting lost in the land of fictional characters when the seat next to me shifted.

"Whatcha reading?" Jake asked, pulling an ear bud out.

"None of your business." I replied, not even bothering to look up.

I wasn't some groupie chick that he was going to walk all over. He put the ear bud to his ear, and I snatched it away.

"You're not going to share?" He cocked an eyebrow.

"It's an iPod not and usPod." I snapped. He ignored my attitude and smiled.

"If you could sum your life up in one song what would it be? Mine would be 'Turn the Page' by Metallica."

I looked at him confused and slightly annoyed. *Why the hell was he so interested in talking to me?*

"I hate to say it, but I think you need to change your pants." I looked at him curiously. "I think they're cranky pants." He started cracking up.

"Actually, not that it's any of your business, it probably has something to do with the fact that I've barely slept in three days.

Oh, and you're a rock god that likes to make fools out of girls like me. No thanks." I scoffed.

"Rock God? At least you admit it." He beamed. "Listen, we're going to have to learn to get along if we're going to be spending the next three months together. So how about a truce? I won't judge you if you agree not to judge me."

"I don't make promises that I know I won't be able to keep. We'll take it a minute at a time."

"Deal. So let's start over. I'm Jake Parker, and I'm not the womanizing asshole that the media portrays me as."

"I'm Aubrey Thompson. I *am* opinionated and downright uncensored. Fair warning." I shrugged.

"Nice to meet you uncensored, opinionated Aubrey. How old are you?"

"Twenty-three, almost twenty-four."

"I'm twenty-five, almost twenty-six."

"Well, almost twenty-six year old Jake I'd really like to get back to this." I held my e-reader up.

"I like you Aubrey. I can tell by your sarcastic undertones, rude comments and sheer lack of common decency that we're going to friends in no time. I can just tell."

"Whatever you say, Boss." I grumbled.

I turned my attention back to my book until the timer went off letting me know that the food was ready. I expertly prepared the dishes. They looked as if they came out of a five-star restaurant. I placed them down on the trays in front of the boys. Jake devoured it and moaned the whole time earning a secret laugh from me. Maybe he wouldn't be so awful after all.

He called to me over his shoulder. "If you cook like this all the time we're skipping the friend stage and getting married."

I take that back, we're going to kill each other. I sat down and curled into a ball. I lost the battle of the heavy lids.

Jake

"This tour is important to the label, and you're going to do it, whether you want to or not." Bruce Samuelson, an executive from the recording label was holding up the contract that I signed. His daddy sent him over here to do his bidding. I hated him and his fucking label.

I was supposed to be on a hiatus for a while. We just returned two days ago from a month long tour all across Europe. Now they go and pull this shit and decide that they need to use me as their cash cow again. I was tired and run down. I needed some R&R. At twenty-five, I was starting to get burnt out. I've always had issues with sleeping, but lately I'd be lucky to get an hour or two a night. I also haven't been able to write a song in almost a year. The rock star life wasn't all that it was cracked up to be. Sure, there is always an abundance of women willing to throw themselves at you, and you're pretty much guaranteed free things wherever you go, but it gets old quick. You never know when someone is being your friend for you, or for your rock star alter ego. I looked over the tour schedule. I hit the roof when I saw that we were set to leave tonight. That only left me with a few hours to get my shit together. I stormed out of the room and angrily yanked the luggage that I had just put away out of the closet. Dipshit left with a grin on his face.

I forced myself to call Brett, my bodyguard, and tell him that he needed to pack again. I felt horrible since we just got back. He hadn't seen his daughter in over a month, and now we were leaving again. I would make sure that he was able to come home sometimes in between shows, but it still sucked. The rest of the band seemed equally annoyed about hitting the road again so soon. At least life was slightly easier for them, they didn't have the persona or profile that I did. It made it impossible for me to go anywhere without being nagged.

"Hey, Jake. How's it going?" Brett asked.

"Hey man, apparently the record label decided that it wants to keep fucking me."

"Huh?" I laughed just imagining the confused look on his face.

"What I mean is Bruce just left. We're going on tour again." I bitched.

"Already?" He sounded just as surprised as I felt.

"Yeah, we're actually scheduled for takeoff today!" I said angrily.

"Alright. Let me just get some shit together, and I'll be by to pick you up."

"I'm really sorry, Brett. If you want some more timeoff, I can call Vin."

"Dude, it's fine. I mean yeah it sucks, but if you need me I'm there."

"Thanks Brett." I said sincerely.

"See you in a bit."

I hung up and finished packing, or as I called it 'throwing shit in a suitcase without folding it" and hoping I had underwear. I was lucky if it was clean. At least the label made arrangements for private air travel this time. It would mean that I would be safe from getting mauled at the airport like last time. I cringed remembering the incident. It was pre-Brett, and I was getting ready to fly out of Atlanta. I was walking toward my terminal when I was literally attacked by a group of four young women. They started tugging on me, and actually ripped a sleeve off my button up shirt. Airport security had to come and usher them away. It was right after that I decided I needed a bodyguard. I took my suitcases and left them by the door and waited for Brett to come collect me. When he knocked I tossed my bags out the door and locked up. I climbed into his truck and looked at my house as he backed out of the driveway. We made one final pit stop at the mecca of fast food, In-N-Out Burger. Brett pulled out into traffic and headed to the airfield.

The small commercial jet was waiting on the tarmac when we arrived. Brett pulled up and insisted that he check it out before letting me board. It made him feel important, so I let him have his fun. When he came back to give me the all clear he had a massive smirk on his face.

"Dude, wait until you see the hot little number on there!" He was grinning like the Cheshire cat.

"What are you talking about? Aren't all flight attendant's middle-aged, blonde women?"

"Not this one. She's feisty too, kneed me right in the balls."

I smiled, and it was actually genuine. I wondered if he was fucking with me. But, it was enough to peak my curiosity. I slowly walked towards the plane wondering if it was going to be a grandma, or something. It wouldn't be the first time. I really hoped that it wasn't some die-hard groupie either. As soon as I reached the top of the stairs I almost tripped and fell on my face when I got my first look at her. She was gorgeous! She looked like she walked straight off of a pin-up girl calendar. She had long, black hair with strands of hot pink. I appraised my way down her body. She had a slim waist and curvy hips. She was built like an hourglass. I noticed a couple of sexy facial piercings. She had an adorable little nose and big brown eyes. Then I saw a tattoo peeking out on her shoulder. I could tell that she had a chest piece. I was instantly hard. *Awesome...*

At first glance, it looked as if she was checking me out. Then her face changed. She looked disgusted. I introduced myself, but she wouldn't even give me the time of day. I knew that I never slept with her because I would have remembered. I've also been in a dry spell by choice for over a year. I tried making some small talk, but she wasn't interested. I let it go until she put her fucking pot roast in front of me. I had died and gone to food heaven, it was that good. It's been so long since I had anything that tasted remotely homemade, and certainly never from my mother. I practically proposed on the spot. I know, smooth move on my part. I looked back and saw her sleeping curled up in her seat. She looked peaceful. I noticed there were blankets set out, so I grabbed one and went over to cover her up. She genuinely was a beautiful girl, and I liked that she was sassy. I was a little discouraged that she obviously made her mind up that I was some kind of crazed sex fiend, I wasn't. I brushed some stray strands of hair out of her face using my fingertips. I wanted to get to know Aubrey and her buttons.

Aubrey

I woke up somewhere over the Midwest and mentally kicked myself. I sincerely hoped that I didn't piss anyone off, especially Mr. Rock God. I rubbed my eyes and staggered to my feet. I quickly walked over to Jake and Brett. Jake looked up from his book and smiled politely. Brett was snoring like a chainsaw.

"I'm so sorry." I apologized profusely.

"It's okay. You said that you were tired." He seemed unfeigned. "I figured I better let you catch up on your sleep now since we're going to be running around a lot."

"Can I get you anything? I brought some of my mom's chocolate cake." I offered.

"Do you have milk?" He grinned a megawatt grin, and I nodded.

I walked over to the tiny kitchenette and fixed him a slice of cake and a glass of milk. I set it up on the tray and handed him a fork.

"You're not having any?" He raised an eyebrow. I suddenly felt self-conscious. Was he taking a stab at my weight? *Sorry Mr.*

Parker, but I'm not one of your anorexic bimbos. I refused to divulge any emotion.

"Maybe later. I need to clean up and get ready for our landing. Let me know if you need anything else."

I cleaned up the few dishes and put them away. I went into the bathroom and quickly ran my fingers through my hair. Thankfully, I still looked somewhat decent. Not that I was trying to impress anyone. I headed to the cockpit talk to Mark for a minute. He said that we were scheduled to land in forty-five minutes and that a car would be there to take us to the hotel. He told me he was going to stay with some friends while we were in New York. Which, essentially meant that I was going to be on my own. *Great…*

We taxied into the runway a little before eleven. Jake whined that he was starving even though he just ate cake less than an hour ago. He said that we were going to have to stop for dinner before going to the hotel. Brett exited the plane first to make sure that it was safe. I went to grab my luggage, but saw that Jake already had it. I tried to get it back, and a bit of a struggle ensued. I lost. He stood there with a smug look on his face and insisted I go in front of him. I walked down the stairs and climbed into the waiting car. Jake slid in next to me, and we sped off into the night in search of food.

CHAPTER TWO

Better Dig Two

Jake held the door open as we walked into Margo's Bar and Grill. *I can't believe I got suckered into coming here! With him nonetheless!* I was getting the feeling this was a set up for me to hang out with him. The hostess ogled Jake in his black Henley that may as well have been a second skin. Though I strongly disliked him, even I could admit that he looked good enough to eat. I chastised myself, again.

"Right this way." The hostess purred.

Girls like her made me sick. He is still a human just like the rest of us. I was starting to get a better understanding of why he seemed so hostile in the media all the damn time. I would probably be locked up if I had to deal with this shit on a daily basis. She seated us right in the middle of the freaking restaurant. It was as if she wanted to put us on display, that or didn't want us to have any privacy. My guess was the latter. Brett sat a safe distance away at the bar and watched us with hawk eyes.

"Your waitress will be Carla. She'll be right over." She placed the menus on the table and strutted off making sure to add a little extra sway to her hips. Jake seemed oblivious.

As if on cue, a perky blonde with way too much perfume strolled over.

"How are you folks tonight?" She gushed enthusiastically downright ignoring me.

I rolled my eyes at her, but she wouldn't have noticed anyway since she was too busy eye-fucking Jake. At least he didn't feed into her. He was a total contradiction to what I was expecting.

"We're fine. We're actually ready to order." He said politely. She pulled out her little notebook. "I'll have the filet, done medium-rare and she'll have a salad."

I shot daggers at him. I looked at the server seething.

"Actually, I'll have a steak cooked medium, with extra mashed potatoes and a beer." She looked shocked, but turned and left to put our orders in. *Take that Parker!*

I glowered at Jake. It was going to be a long three months…

"Salads are for skinny bitches and people with health problems. I'm neither." I said sharply.

"You could have at least ordered a girly martini or something." He smirked.

I rolled my eyes and attempted to keep my temper in check. I sat on my hands like my mom used to make me do when I was little, so I wouldn't reach across the table and smack the smirk right off his handsome face. He seemed to be getting some perverse amusement out of the whole thing.

Better tell the gravedigger that he better dig two because we (mostly me) are going to strangle one another before the night is over.

"Seriously? Do I look like a girly martini kind of girl?" I cocked an eyebrow.

"Relax. The salad thing was just a test." He rubbed the back of his neck uncomfortably. "I kind of have a thing against girls with food issues. No offense. I think you have a fantastic body. I'm sorry that didn't come out how I wanted it to. Dammit! I'm just going to shut up now." He said getting flustered.

A small laugh escaped my lips. It was funny to see him get all worked up. We indulged in our dinners and engaged in some small talk. By the time, we were getting ready to leave my mood lightened slightly. He settled our bill, and we headed back to the car. I leaned my head against the cool glass of the window and felt Jake slide in next to me. Brett closed the door and climbed into the passenger seat. Apparently, we would be staying at the W Hotel. I watched as the lights of the city blurred by.

We slowed to a crawl, and I looked out the window. During dinner, Jake warned me that there was always a chance of paparazzi lurking in the shadows. Nothing could have prepared me for the sight when we pulled up. He swore so much that I'm positive it's still hovering somewhere in space. He claimed that the record company probably leaked his whereabouts. Brett said that we needed to be extra careful and to get to the door as quickly as possible. Ten seconds later we were thrust out of the car with lights flashing a mile a minute. The spots fogged my vision so badly that I tripped stepping up onto the curb. Jake quickly grabbed a hold of my waist to steady me. We walked double-time into the lobby.

Jake was clearly infuriated. "I can't believe that weasel threw me to the sharks like that!"

"Why would they do that?" I asked in utter disbelief trying get my wits back.

I mean sure you hear stories, but to be a part of it was something else.

"Free publicity. The same reason that the hotel's security doesn't do anything until we're inside." He spat looking directly at the hotel security guard, who quickly turned his head.

He pulled me towards the front desk to check in. The petite redhead behind the counter had a hard time forming a coherent sentence when she looked at Jake. She pressed a few buttons and handed him a key card. She kept a firm grasp on the card and looked admiringly at him.

"I'm off at one." She batted her eyelashes.

"Are you seriously offering yourself to me in front of my girlfriend? I mean no offense, but look at her and look at you." He scoffed.

I gasped.

I was going to sneak in his room and murder him in his sleep. He grabbed my hand, and I tried to pull away to no avail. His hand refused to leave mine.

"That's how rumors get started you know. Now let me go so I can check into my room." I said tersely, watching the cameras still flashing through the glass.

"Whatever, just wait until morning when pictures hit the press. I wouldn't be surprised if they're plastered everywhere in an hour."

"I'm going to kill you in your sleep." I mumbled under my breath.

"What was that?" He started laughing.

"Nothing." I backpedaled.

"It will be easy since we're sharing a room."

"What!?" I shrieked.

"I have the entire top floor. There's more than enough room." He shrugged.

"You have got to be kidding me!"

"Aubrey, I thought we were going to try and be friends. Why are you fighting the inevitable? I'm not that awful, I promise. I don't bite, unless you're into that kind of thing, then I'd gladly make an exception." He winked, and I slugged him in the stomach.

Damn, his stomach must be made of iron because it hurt my hand.

My dad was going to get a phone call, right after I showered. We made our way up to the room and waited in the hallway until Brett gave the go ahead. Jake told me about some of the things and people that Brett found in his hotel rooms throughout the years. They ranged from girls (and guys), young and old, to presents and death threats from angry boyfriends and husbands. I shuddered. The more he talked about celebrity life the more unpleasant it seemed.

He told me that he always loved music and writing songs, so it made up for the negative. He said when he stepped out on stage all of the crummy stuff dissipated and he was just Jake Parker, the kid from Arizona singing in the mirror. We walked into the suite, which was enormous but only had two bedrooms. I eyed him skeptically. I was ready to walk out the door when he said that Brett always slept in the living room while they were in New York. Just in case someone tried to break in. *Just lovely.*

I went into the room that he picked out for me and unpacked my toiletries. I headed into the bathroom to shower, and get ready for bed. When I got out I brushed my teeth and tossed my hair up on the top of my head. I dressed in a pair of black and pink plaid shorts and a hot pink tank top. I walked over to the end table and picked up my phone. I dialed my dad.

"Hi, honey." He answered sweetly.

"Don't you dare 'hi honey' me Timothy Thompson!" I chastised.

"Oh shit. You're really mad, aren't you?" He was clearly trying to hide his amusement, but was doing a shitty job of it.

I slid open the balcony door and stepped out to smoke.

"Mad. I'm not mad. I passed being mad about three hours ago. I'm pissed."

I lit up and took a long drag.

"Sorry pumpkin. How's it going other than that?"

"Mark is out with friends, so I'm all by myself in a penthouse with a rock god and his bodyguard. How does it sound like it's going?"

"Huh? Well, have a good time and be safe. I'll talk to you tomorrow."

I knew what he was trying to do, and it wasn't going to work. I hung up the phone and noticed that Jake was standing in the doorway. He was just wearing a pair of black athletic shorts that were slung low on his hips. *Damn, he's sinewy.* He was thoroughly ripped with every muscle clearly defined. Part of me wanted to take a microscope to him so that I could check out his tattoos. The other part of me wanted to wall-bang him, which was weird because I was a virgin with an aversion to touch. The more logical part said to stay where I was. So that is exactly what I did.

"Is this a bad time to ask you to come to our show tomorrow?" He asked amused.

"Seriously? Don't you know how to knock?" I rolled my eyes.

So what does the smart ass do? He knocks on the doorframe.

I walked back inside the room and sat on the edge of the bed. If my mother saw this scene, she would probably have a heart attack. I was actually talking to a guy, and I was wearing trashy sleepwear with no make-up and messy hair.

"Would you *please* come to my show tomorrow?" He pleaded.

"Since you asked so nicely... No." I goaded.

"Don't make me grovel." He walked into the room and sat on the bed next to me.

I could feel his body heat radiating off of him. He smelled so good too, like citrus and something musky. He put his hand on my shoulder, and I tried to pull away, but he had a firm grasp. I started to panic, but then I noticed that I didn't tense up, which shocked me even further. He started rubbing circles in my shoulder blades. It actually felt nice, and I let myself start to relax a little.

"Come on, Aubrey. Friends, remember?" I nodded still apprehensive. "So tell me about home."

"What do you want to know?" I asked.

"I don't know. Where are you from? What do you like to do? Who your friends are? I'll take whatever you're willing to offer up." He shrugged.

"I'm from Smithville, Ohio, born and bred. I like it there. It's home. Most of my friends went away for college and never came back. I don't blame them though. Small town living isn't for everyone. My best friend is Piper. If she knew that I was here with you right now, she'd be banging down my dad's door begging for him to fly her here."

He laughed.

"Maybe he should have sent Piper instead. At least she would have been happy to see me." He teased. "But in all seriousness, I'm glad it was you. You're refreshing. You don't have high expectations of me, so I can just be myself. I like it. Now, what do you like to do for fun?"

"I like to read. I listen to music. Yes, even yours. I especially love going for long drives with no destination. What about you?" I asked because I didn't honestly know too much about him at all.

"Same. It's been extremely hard to do a lot of those things the last couple years since I can't go anywhere without being hounded. I used to love road trips. You're going to laugh, but I'm a total sucker for bed and breakfasts'." I did laugh, but I actually felt sorry for him. I was feeling much more relaxed, thanks to his impromptu massage. "So about tomorrow… will you come?"

"I don't think I have a choice, do I?" I cocked an eyebrow.

"Then it's settled." He smiled and stood. "Night, Aubrey." He walked to the door and turned. "That chest piece is smokin' by the way."

I looked down and realized that he may have seen quite a few of my tattoos. Surprisingly, I actually didn't feel embarrassed which is highly unlike me. Something weird was going on… I might actually like Jake Parker. *Gasp!*

Jake

I left Aubrey's room, which was the room that I usually picked when we stayed here. I walked across the hall and into my room. I gave it to her since it had the better view. I past the bed and headed straight to the bathroom to jerk-off. I felt like a sixteen-year old boy again. All she had to do was laugh, and I was sporting wood. The way she smelled made me want to bottle it up so that I could keep it forever. She smelled sweet like honey and vanilla, and something else that I couldn't quite figure out yet. Whatever it was, it was delicious. I wanted it on my tongue. She was beautiful, even without make-up. I loved the fact that she had soft curves because I wasn't fond of super skinny girls. I always felt like I was going to break them. The ones that had the ribs showing through the skin were the worse. I avoided them all together.

The fact that she didn't seem self-conscious turned me on big time. I liked a girl that knew what she liked and took it. Aubrey seemed like that kind of girl, especially at dinner. Then my hands had a mind of their own and started touching her skin. It felt like silk under my fingers, and the *tattoos*… I saw a glimpse of the chest one earlier, but when I got to see it up close I knew that I was toast. I could tell that she put a lot of thought into it. It was extremely intricate, all blacks and grays. It was mostly flowers with a bit of a tribal design to it. It was sexy as hell. I loved tattoos on girls, but I didn't like when it looked like they just walked into a shop and said 'I want that.' I liked one-of-a-kind pieces. She had perfect tits too, a nice handful each. I cleaned up and jumped into bed. I was glad that I got her to agree to come tomorrow. It just might make it more bearable. My phone started buzzing on the end table. It was our bassist Blake Potter.

"Hey buddy, how was coach?" I teased.

"Shut up, asshole. Derek almost got pissed on by some tike and Kevin slept the whole time." He whined. "We just landed and should be there in an hour or so."

"About that…" I was going to get my ass kicked big time. "I sort of gave your room away."

Originally, Aubrey and Mark were supposed to have adjoining rooms on the floor below. When I found out Mark was staying with friends I didn't want her to be alone. *I wanted her close to me.* I told her that she was staying with me, and thankfully she didn't question it. The fact that she was across the hall was going to drive me crazy. *Calm the fuck down Parker!*

"You did what?" He sounded confused, but at least he wasn't angry.

"Listen, you'll understand tomorrow. Your reservations are under Harry Balls." I laughed. That was the new code name that we made up to put our reservations under in order to avoid stalkers.

"Yeah, fine. See you in the morning." I hung up and turned the TV on.

There on CNT (Celebrity News Tonight) was a picture of Aubrey and me plastered across the screen. I smiled. The hosts were speculating about who the mystery girl was. They thought that we looked perfect together. I agreed wholeheartedly. They wondered if she would be the one to tame bad-boy Jake Parker.

Unfortunately, in the beginning of my career I made a few missteps that have stuck with me. Nothing terrible, it was mostly just stupid twenty-one year old behavior, but all of it was available to the public and that's where my reputation comes from.

I thought that the two of us would make a great couple. Now, I just had to formulate a plan to convince her. That was going to be easier said than done. I never had to work so hard to get a girl before, but I knew that Aubrey was worth it. I shut the TV off and closed my eyes praying for sleep. I tossed and turned most of the night while sleep decided to evade me, yet again. I finally drifted off sometime after five in the morning. I was in the middle of a pleasant dream when I was startled awake. I felt someone jump into the bed, and hide under the covers. I was going to kill Blake!

"What the hell?" I yawned.

"There's someone in my bathroom. Brett told me to come in here." She said in a fierce rush.

It was Aubrey and something clearly freaked her out. I put my arm around her and pulled her close laying us both back on the bed. I was surprised when she went willingly. I also couldn't help but notice she fit perfectly in my arms. Unfortunately, our moment was short lived.

Blake and Derek burst into the room with mischievous grins.

"What the hell, douche bags!" I yelled at them.

I swear they acted like animals sometimes, well most of the time. But, they were like my brothers, so I dealt with them.

"Dude, don't blame us. You never take this room." Blake said with a smug look.

Aubrey looked at me with wide eyes.

"That doesn't mean that you just go around bursting into people's bathrooms like that." I scolded.

I held Aubrey tighter showing them that she was off limits. She leaned into me and turned so that her face was buried in my chest. I was praying that she didn't notice my raging hard-on. It was more than that though. There was just something about her that made me want all of her. Blake and Derek were the 'wham-bam-thank you- ma'am type.' Kevin was our rhythm guitarist and back up vocalist. He was much more mellow than these two. He's also had the same girlfriend for three years. Blake cocked an eyebrow at me, and I glared back.

"Now go wait in the living room before I break your faces, or have Brett do it for me." I chastised.

They laughed and turned closing the door behind them.

"Sorry about those two. They were raised by wolves."

Aubrey was still shaking. I rubbed her back soothingly until I felt her heart rate return to normal.

"Who are they?" She looked up at me and moved out of my arms. I almost laughed because I completely forgot that she wasn't like the other groupie girls that knew more about us than we did.

"That would be Blake, our bassist, and Derek, our drummer. Or as Brett refers to them, tweedle-dee and tweedle-dum."

"They scared the living shit out of me! One minute I'm sleeping soundly and the next minute I hear freaky-ass noises coming from the bathroom. I ran out of there and came right in here like Brett said. I'm assuming that he knew it was them because he wasn't actually running."

I'd have to thank Brett later for sending her in here because it made my day.

"I'm not complaining. You can wake me up like that anytime." I smiled.

She was so fucking cute first thing in the morning. She got all shy on me, and it was even sexier.

"I'm going to go get dressed." She scooted off the bed and hurried out of the room.

"I'll come get you in a few then." I called after her.

I watched as she walked out of the room. I looked at her legs and groaned. She had bows tattooed on her upper thigh right below her ass. *This girl is going to be the death of me.* My thoughts alone were going to send me to hell… I took an ice cold shower and dressed in a pair of jeans and a zip-up black hoodie. I spiked my jet black Mohawk and took one final look in the mirror. I chose to wear my black boots over sneakers since my options on the road were slim. It was days like today that I wished for anonymity. I wished that I could take Aubrey out somewhere nice and not be heckled by the media. I walked across the hallway to Aubrey's room and actually knocked on her door this time.

"Hey, it's me." I called.

"Come in." I turned the knob and opened the door.

She was dressed in a black and white plaid skirt with fishnets, a black shirt and a short leather jacket. She only had a little bit of make-up on. She looked like a fucking temptress. I was going to have to look into hiring another bodyguard, especially if she was going to dress like this for the next three months.

"Lookin' good." I managed to sound somewhat gentlemanly.

"You too." Her cheeks were turning pink. It was adorable.

"Aubrey, are you blushing?" I goaded.

"No." She said quickly and off pitch.

I walked over and put my hand on her shoulder. I realized I was making up any excuse that I could to touch her. I grabbed her hand and led her out to the living room.

"Morning, Brett." She whispered. She was still clearly embarrassed from what happened earlier, even though it wasn't her fault.

"Good morning, Miss Thompson." She rolled her eyes at him. I noticed she did that a lot.

"Guys, I'd like you to meet my girlfriend, Aubrey."

"I'm not your girlfriend, Jake." She scolded.

"That's what you say, but you will be. That's Blake and Derek, you kind of already met them, and that's Kevin." She nodded.

"Did you get your Google alert this morning?" Blake asked obnoxiously.

I gave him a look to *shut the fuck up,* but it was too late.

"Google alert?" Aubrey asked nervously and mumbled something that I couldn't make out.

I cringed because she was going to freak out. Aubrey wasn't the girl that was after fame or status. I pulled my phone from my pocket and reluctantly showed her the screen. She went pale as a ghost. Her bottom lip started to tremble, and I had a strong urge to kiss her. I probably would have tried, if the room wasn't full.

"It's okay. They do this shit all the time. It will be old news by this afternoon." I tried to reassure her. Though, it wasn't always true. Derek snorted. "Will you guys get the fuck out for like fifteen minutes? She's not used to this kind of thing, and you are not helping matters."

Since we joked around constantly, they knew by my tone that I was dead serious and not to fuck with me. The room cleared faster than when Blake had beer farts.

"They think I'm going to be the one to tame the famous Jake Parker." She scoffed.

"I don't need to be tamed." She huffed and turned to walk away from me. "Aubrey, please listen to me." She stopped and turned back slightly. "When I first got famous I was an ass. I'll be the first one to admit it. I was also a twenty-one year old idiot. By the time we made it really big I was already out of that phase. I don't go around screwing random girls. I don't really drink anymore. I certainly don't do drugs, and I like you alright. I like that you talk back to me. I like the way you look at me like I'm Jake Parker the person, not the rock star. So please don't shut me out, that's all everyone does. It's what they've done my whole life. I know I'm an ass, and I will fuck up, but I promise you that I'll make you happy. I know you're not ready to be my girlfriend, but that's what

I want. So just give me a fucking chance and stop making me chase you. I-" I was going to keep rambling until she said something, but instead she crashed her lips to mine. That kiss lit my world on fire.

Aubrey

Ahhhh! My brain was berating me for kissing him and his incredible lips. I pulled away when it was starting to get heavy. The sexual tension was still crackling between us. It had been two years since my last kiss, which was actually just a peck on the lips. His hand was rested on my cheek, refusing to pull away. I stepped back feeling slightly embarrassed by my brazen move. I wanted to say something, but it seemed that I was unable to formulate a coherent sentence. I smiled shyly and looked down at the floor. He put his finger under my chin and lifted my face. He pecked my lips lightly and told me that he needed to go talk to the guys about tonight. He left the room leaving me alone with Brett. My mind was racing.

"Aubrey," he said to get my attention. I looked at him and realized he just saw the whole thing go down. "I know it's not quite my place or anything, but he meant what he said to you. He's not who they make him out to be. In fact, he's one of the best people that I've ever met. I have a daughter, Kayley, and he flies me home between sets so that I can spend time with her. He didn't have the best home life growing up. His mom was a junkie, and he never knew his father so take it easy on him, okay?"

I nodded and went back to my room.

I pulled out my phone and called Piper. I stepped out onto the balcony and admired the view. I also delighted in the not so fresh city air. I lit up and listened to her shriek for the first five minutes when I told her where I was and who I was with. When she finally calmed down I went into the whole Jake Parker situation. Piper was life smart and always looked at the glass as being half-full. She knew my past and understood why I had the apprehension that I did.

"Bean, if it were up to me I'd rewrite history. I'd change everything that happened that night, but I can't. You can't go around thinking that every guy is like him. They're not."

"I'm not as nice as I used to be. I don't trust people or tell them my secrets. I know that I distance myself, but I only do it because I refuse to be used or hurt again. I can only depend on myself." I said firmly.

"Listen to yourself! You're difficult and stubborn, but if you give people the chance I promise that they'll see you're worth it. I love you, Bean. Just try, for me. A little bit at a time, and no I'm not just saying this because it's Jake Parker. I'm telling you this because it's time. Let it go and move on."

"And what happens when I finally decide to let him in, and he tells me that he doesn't feel the spark that I feel?"

"Then you Taser him and ask him again when he wakes up." She laughed.

"Oi! What am I going to do with you?"

"You love me, and you know it. I'm just telling you how it is. Now if you follow my advice and you'll be good to go." She said proudly.

"I'll talk to you soon. I love you Pipsqueak."

"You too, Bean. Call me if you need me."

I hung up feeling a little better. I decided that I was still going to keep him at arm's length until I could get a better grasp on the situation. Though, my hormones had other ideas. I've never felt such a strong connection to someone before and it scared me. Mark texted me saying that he would be staying with his friends until we were scheduled to leave tomorrow afternoon. Brett yelled through the door that room service arrived. My stomach growled at the thought of food. I walked into the living room and made a plate. I picked out some French toast and bacon and took a seat at the table. My phone went off a handful of times. Looks like some of my old friends are into celebrity gossip. I was stuffing a piece of bread in my mouth when I looked down and saw the name that popped up. It was a name that I haven't seen in two years. *Jeremy.*

I wanted to run to the bathroom and throw up. My hands were already turning clammy. I clicked on the screen and opened the message.

Bre-bre, saw you on the news this morning. Looks like you like banging rock-stars after all…

I got phantom pains as tears burned my eyes. Just as I was about to retreat to my room Jake walked back in with a huge smile on his face. It faltered the second he saw me about to burst into tears.

"Aubrey? Are you okay?" He asked concerned.

NO! My brain screamed. This was exactly what I was worried about when I saw his phone this morning. He was at my side in the blink of an eye. I didn't say anything. I couldn't trust myself to move a muscle. Normally, I was tough as nails, and I didn't let anything bother me. Jeremy was another story. Jake kneeled in front of me and put his hand under my chin to make me look at him. I flinched. He immediately pulled away and I saw worry etched on his face. A couple tears escaped. I couldn't do this. I needed to be alone. I got up and ran to my room locking the door behind me.

Jeremy Roberts was the reason I hated rock stars.

We met when I was a senior in high school. I was almost eighteen, and he was twenty. He played bass in a local band named

Gigawatts. He was the bad boy rocker, and I was the punk rock girl, we clicked. It ended *very* badly, and I swore off his kind forever.

CHAPTER THREE

Imperfect

Jake

As soon as I made it to their room they started ragging on me.

"Dude, she's so fucking hot!" Blake yelled. "I'm definitely not pissed at you for giving our room away. Though, I would have given it to us so that you could've hopped in the sack with her. That would have been the smart thing to do."

"She can sit on my face anytime." Derek chimed in.

"If either of you even look at her the wrong way again I'll castrate you. She's off limits!" I said seriously.

"Whoa, is Jake Parker actually serious about a girl?" Derek choked.

"I like her alright. She's different, and I don't need you assholes making her run for the hills by scaring her with your shenanigans."

"She seems nice, Jake. I hope it works out for you." Kevin said genuinely.

"Thanks Kev."

We were stoked about our show tonight at Terminal 22. It was sold out, and judging by our social media networks it was going to be an awesome crowd. I told them to get their asses in gear and not to be late for sound check. I hurried back to my room hoping to have some breakfast with Aubrey before sound check and pre-show stuff. I looked at her sitting at the table. At first I thought she looked content, but then I realized that she looked as if she was in pain. My automatic response was to hold her. I practically sprinted over to her. Her eyes were glassy with unshed tears. I wondered what could have happened in the fifteen minutes that I was gone. I couldn't even get her to look at me. Was she having an anxiety attack? I had no idea what to do in situations like this. As soon as I touched her beautiful face she flinched and ran away.

I asked Brett if he knew what happened. He said that he didn't have a clue, but mentioned that she was on her phone. I picked it up and saw that it was locked. If someone was going to start shit with her because of me, they were going to have to deal with me. I felt guilty for invading her privacy, but it seemed more imperative to find out what the fuck happened. I tried her birthday, a little piece of info that I finagled out of her last night at dinner. *Bingo.* I scrolled through her texts. They mostly consisted of people saying that they saw our picture on the Internet, no biggie. Others wanted to know what our relationship was. I wasn't surprised to see that she didn't respond to any of them. The most recent one was from a Jeremy.

Bre-bre, saw you on news this morning. Looks like you like banging rock-stars after all...

I was livid. Whoever this was must have been who upset her. Even I could tell that Aubrey wasn't that kind of girl. I wished that I could have reached through the phone and choked him. I decided that I needed to see if I could get her to talk to me. I needed to calm the fuck down first. I took a deep breath and focused on the task at hand. Once I had my composure back I slowly walked to her door and knocked.

"Aubrey, it's Jake. Can you open the door? I just want to make sure that you're okay." I pleaded softly.

I didn't get a response for a minute. I knocked again and was getting ready to break down the door when she finally came and unlocked the door. She went right back to the bed and buried her face in a pillow. I followed her over to the bed. She seemed so desolate. It was killing me.

"Aubrey, I'm going to sit down next to you." I moved very slowly. "Is it about the messages? I'm sorry. I didn't think about the effect it would have on you. I'm so used to it that it's normal. I'm so sorry." I felt like an inconsiderate asshole.

Her chest heaved up and down as she sobbed. I felt utterly helpless and was seriously starting to freak out until she reached for my hand. I precariously rubbed my thumb across her knuckles hoping that it was okay. I was relieved when she finally seemed to relax a little. I used my other hand to rub her back soothingly since she seemed to like that. I don't know how long we sat like that until she finally lifted her head to look at me. She looked like a beautiful hot mess. Her eyes were red and puffy, and her mascara had strewn all down her cheeks. I reached over to the end table and picked up a tissue to wipe her face. She looked solemnly at me. I needed to hold her. I wanted so badly to tell her that everything was going to be okay. I'd make sure everything was okay. The feelings that I already had for this girl were downright ludicrous. Something about her just grasped at me and pulled me in. It was like a vortex.

"Aubrey, I really need to hug you right now. Is that okay?" I asked her, feeling completely wretched.

She sat up slowly and opened her arms. I leaned in and wrapped my arms tightly around her and breathed her in. This had to do with more than just a couple of messages. There was obviously something else.

"What happened? I don't want to pry, but that was really scary and I need to know what to do in case that happens again."

"I can't," She choked and started getting upset again. "I don't want to taint you with it."

"How about I tell you my story and then you can decide if you want to tell me yours. I'm already tainted Aubrey."

"The wounds we have reveal us." She whispered.

"I was born to a teenage prostitute turned junkie. I spent my entire childhood rummaging dumpsters for scraps while my *mother*, who let's just call her by her name since she was never a mother. So, while *Crystal* spent our grocery money on cocaine and heroin, I had to figure out how to get by. My father was one of her many Johns. I have no idea who he could be, and I don't care either. When I was eleven she OD'd and the police found her body in a dumpster downtown. I was taken in by child protective services and put into foster care. That's where I met Ron through an outreach program. He ended up becoming my mentor. He was the one that got me into music. He saved me, and now I'm here."

I got emotional just talking about Ron and what he did for me. He was like my dad. I couldn't even imagine what fate would have had in store for me if he didn't come into my life.

"That sounds like it was harrowing. My story is nothing like that." She shook her head.

I knew she wasn't going to divulge anything. I decided to let it go until she was ready and felt less vulnerable. I moved so that she was next to me and leaned us both back until we were flat on the bed. I curled into her hoping to give us both a little solace. I counted her breaths and felt the rise and fall of her chest against mine. I was able to get a closer look at the tattoo across her shoulder blades since she took her jacket off. It was an array of birds and stars with a quote underneath: *It's always darkest before the dawn.* I absentmindedly traced my finger over it and wondered why she picked that particular quote. It was even more ironic that I had a similar quote around the same spot.

Our cuddling was interrupted when my stomach growled embarrassingly.

"Come on, it's lunch time and before you try and protest I know you barely ate. I saw your plate." I sat up and stood.

I took her hand and pulled her to her feet. The room service was no doubt cold and gross by now. I decided to chance it and take her out. I knew the perfect place where I was less likely to be recognized. Even if I were to be spotted no one would dare mess with the owner. I told her to grab her jacket. I went into the living room and asked Brett to make arrangements with the hotel to allow us leave out the back. They happily obliged and after Brett gave the all clear we headed out through the kitchen. We climbed into a regular taxi instead of the hire car to avoid any suspicion.

Brett gave the cabbie the address, and we headed into Harlem to Bee's Waffle House. A friend of mine, Big Mike introduced me to this place years ago when I was just starting out. I tried to stop in every time I was in the city. We walked in and were greeted by Mama Bee herself. It was a small, charming little place. There weren't any booths, instead there were several mismatched tables and chairs. The walls were painted sunshine yellow and plastered with pictures of her and her family. My picture was among them, which always earned a laugh. It was almost like eating in her kitchen.

"Look what the cat dragged in." She cooed wiping her hands on the front of her apron. A couple of patrons raised their heads but quickly looked away. She was a boisterous, fun loving woman with at heart of gold. She was short and rotund with short, dark hair and a smile that could light up a room.

"Mama Bee." I smiled brightly.

She pinched my cheek.

"Oh, you're getting scrawny, boy. Sit, I'll fetch ya'll some grub. Who's the beautiful lady?" She asked, looking at Aubrey.

"This Mama, is Aubrey Thompson. I'm trying to make her my *girlfriend,* but we're friends for now." I winked.

"Honey-child, when you gonna learn? You need to start the pursuit off nice and slow and let her figure it out on her own. Ain't no sense pushing, ya hear?" She raised her spatula.

"Yes ma'am." I said bashfully.

"Good. Now whatcha want to eat, Aubrey?" Mama beamed.

"I'll have whatever he's having."

I bit back a laugh. She had no idea what she was getting herself into. Mama Bee shrugged her shoulders and smiled. She started working away at the stove.

"I like her Jake." She yelled. *So do I Mama. So do I...*

Mama came over and placed our plates down in front of us. There were two pancakes, two pieces of French toast, two waffles, two eggs over easy, a large portion of corned beef hash, and two pieces of toast. She winked at Aubrey and plopped a container of syrup and a pitcher of orange juice on the table. She whistled on the way back to the kitchen. Starving, I dug in starting with the waffles because they were out of this world. I worked my way through the rest of the plate wiping up the last of it with a piece of toast. I was impressed that Aubrey was able to put a small dent into hers since it was a lot of food. I took out my wallet and pulled out five $100 bills. I left them under the plate since she always refused my money. I kissed her cheek.

"I'll see you next time I'm in town."

"Take care my sweet boy. Good meeting you Aubrey."

Aubrey nodded shyly.

"That was really sweet." Aubrey said once we were back in the cab.

"Mama Bee is an extraordinary woman. She's suffered a lot of loss and hardship, but you would never know. I'm going to tell you something, and it's not to boast. I just want you to get a better idea of who *I* am." Aubrey nodded. "Mama lives in this teeny, tiny house on Avenue B, it's the nicest one on the block. It's also a gathering point for her family and friends. Two years ago, Big Mike called and told me that it was going into foreclosure. Battlescars had just signed their first *really* solid deal, and I used a majority of my advance to pay off her mortgage, anonymously. She worked too fucking hard to lose her house. She only fell behind because she's always taking care of everybody else. Mama always puts herself last. If you go there to eat and you don't have any money, she feeds you anyway."

"I think that's amazing! That's exactly the kind of thing I would love to do if I had a ton of money." She said thoughtfully.

"I have a ton of money." I teased, and she pinched me. I was glad pre-meltdown Aubrey was back. "Just saying… Anyway, I have to get to sound check. I was kind of hoping that you would come along since you're coming to the show anyway. It will be painless, I promise."

"I guess." She shrugged.

I grinned excitedly. Brett told the cabbie to head over to Terminal 22. We pulled around to the stage door and hopped out. I took Aubrey's hand, and pulled her inside. I grabbed Brett's stage pass off his neck and gave it to Aubrey since the crew already knew him. He shook his head bemused. I introduced her to a couple of our roadies and some of the stage crew. I led her out onto stage, my home away from home. I stood on the X and grabbed the microphone.

I wanted Aubrey to see the real me, not the rock star. I started singing and dancing the Macarena. I was gyrating my hips and waving my hand around flamboyantly. I knew that I looked ridiculous, but when I looked at Aubrey laughing hysterically it only added fuel to my fire. When I finished I did an exceptionally theatrical bow and put the mic back in its stand. I walked over to her.

"Do you think Los Del Rios will pick me up if Battlescars ever kicks me out?"

"I think you should stick to your day job." She teased.

I put the back of my hand to my forehead feigning hurt. She leaned in and kissed my cheek. *Hell yeah!*

"If that's all it takes to get a little of your attention little lady, I reckon I'll be partaking in a lot more foolish activities."

"Oh, shut up. You're annoying me now." She rolled her eyes.

She's so hot when she does that.

Since we had a little bit of time to kill before the show started, I took her up to the rooftop to show her the view of the pier. We stared wordlessly out at the boats and the approaching sunset. I put my arm around her shoulder and pulled her closer to me. She turned and looked at me.

"Jake…" She stopped.

"What is it Aubrey? Just come out with it already, I know you want to." I pleaded.

"I'm scared. I want to try and let you in, but the last time I let someone in it ended *very* badly. For some reason you can touch me and I don't shy away. That has never happened with anyone that isn't my family, or someone I've known my whole life. It scares me, Jake." She whimpered. That sound fucking killed me.

"Aubrey, I don't know what happened. I won't hurt you, at least not intentionally and never physically. Is that what you're worried about?" She nodded. "We're going to take this one-day at a time, as friends. I'll earn your trust. You'll see." I vowed.

Aubrey

I was standing off to the side of the stage watching the opening act finish their set. I actually found myself looking forward to watching Battlescars play tonight. I always loved the aura of concerts. It was crazy to think that all these people came here to listen to Jake sing. He was turning out to have more depth than I originally gave him credit for. I thought back to this morning, and how compassionate he was during my episode and then his interaction with Mama Bee. He looked at her with fondness and respect. It was sweet. He was sweet. It was so easy to remember how he looked in the tabloids and the things they said about him. There was more than one side to Jake Parker and now I had a decision to make. Could I let him in?

He came and stood next to me with a huge grin on his face.

"I figured something out." He exclaimed.

"Oh yeah? Is it how to tie your shoes?" I looked down at his boots that had the laces tucked in. He looked at me dumbfounded and shook his head.

"What? No. I figured you out." He said proudly. I felt myself tense. *Did he know?* "You, my sweet Aubrey, are like a Tootsie Roll Pop. You've got to get through all the layers before you can get to the sweet inside."

Whew! If he only knew...

I wasn't ready to bare my scars just yet.

"Right." I said sarcastically.

"Anyway, we're up. How about a kiss for good luck?"

He leaned down and placed his cheek in front of my face. I leaned in. At the last second, that rat bastard turned his face. Just as my lips were going to touch his cheek I met his lips instead. He was clearly proud of himself. I secretly liked it, but I'd never disclose that little tidbit.

"Jake Parker!" I yelled. "You are in so much trouble!"

"Later, my sweet Aubrey." He winked.

He blew me a kiss and stepped onto the stage. The rest of the band followed closely behind giggling at our display. The roar of the crowd was deafening. Each member took their place, and prepared to start.

"How's everyone doing tonight?" Jake yelled into the mic. The crowd cheered in response. "What are we fucking sleepwalking out there? I said, HOW'S EVERYONE FUCKING DOING TONIGHT?" His voice reverberated through my bones. The response from the crowd was ear-splitting. "Then let's get this party started!"

Jake jumped in place and the entire stage illuminated. Blake started to play a mellow melody on his guitar. Jake looked completely in the zone. All the sudden Derek thrashed on his drum kit and pyrotechnics flew from around him. They broke into their hit song 'Ransom.' Jake looked over at me and winked. I watched as he moved lithely around the stage, the crowd was entirely enamored. Blake sang the occasional back-up line. I was in awe at how in sync they were with one another. It was almost like watching one person play. An hour and a half later they wrapped up their set and bid the crowd good night. A very sweaty, now shirtless Jake came off the stage. He lost his hoodie about half way through the set. I found myself slightly jealous that thousands of people got to see him like that. I wanted to slap myself.

"What did you think?" He hugged me tightly dripping sweat onto my forehead.

"I think you need a shower." I said, disgusted.

"If you're offering." He smirked. "Come on, we have a quick meet and greet. Then we'll head back to the hotel."

He tugged on my hand and led me to a room filled with fans, mostly women in extremely ill-fitting clothing. The rest of the band was already there waiting for Jake. They quickly went to sit at a table that was set up against the wall. He took a seat in a chair set up at the end and pulled me onto his lap. I went obligingly this time, mostly because I didn't think I had a choice. It was unexpected that I actually liked it. Brett came and stood next to Jake. He crossed his gargantuan arms and stood like a statue ready to spring at a moment's notice. Jake signed a couple autographs and had small talk with some of the fans. One girl asked for a picture. She looked like she was probably my age and was dressed exceptionally trashy. He reluctantly moved me off his lap and onto his chair. He stood next to the girl but didn't make any physical contact. She tried to wrap her arms around him. I saw Brett get ready to pounce, but Jake deftly stepped out her grasp.

"Sorry, sweetie. No touching." He said smoothly.

The girl shot daggers at me.

"She gets to touch you." She whined and pointed at me.

"Duh, that's because she's my girlfriend or haven't you watched CNT?"

Jake winked at me. I despised girls like her because they walked around as if they were entitled to whatever they wanted. They were like girl versions of Carter. They had no care for anyone else's feelings. Everyone is entitled to their personal space. Yes, even Jake Parker. I looked at the rest of the guys who, other than Kevin, clearly enjoyed the female fan attention. She stared at me repugnantly.

"What the hell is she wearing? It looks like something that came off my shoe?" I saw red. Someone needed to put her in her place. I stood up and stared her down.

"You know what bitch, why don't you go slip into something comfier? Like a coma! Get the fuck out of here before I help you into one!" I spat. Jake looked amused.

"Wow, swear much?" She mumbled.

"At least I sound like a *fucking* lady and not like a little boy just hitting puberty. Now go fly out of here on the broom you flew in on." I spat.

Brett took the girl by the arm and led her to the exit. Jake came back to me and kissed my hair.

"That was fucking epic!" He chuckled into my hair.

I smiled smugly and sat back on his lap. The rest of the meet and greet went off without a hitch. The hire car was waiting at the stage door. I clambered in and scooted over so that Jake could climb in. As soon as we started moving exhaustion hit me. I leaned my head on his shoulder and closed my eyes.

I woke up and realized that I had somehow ended up in my bed. I turned to look at the alarm clock. It was after three o'clock in the morning, and I really had to pee. I sat up and threw my legs off the side of the bed. I was startled when I saw Jake sitting in the chair across from the bed. I jumped. He looked somber. I stood again and held up a finger letting him know that I needed a minute. I ran into the bathroom and shut the door. I quickly did my business and splashed some cold water on my face. Since I was more awake I looked down and noticed that I was just in my ruffle panties and a tank top. Meaning that Jake had stripped me out of my clothes. I squashed the panic because he most likely did it so that I would be comfortable. I walked back into the bedroom and sat on the edge of the bed.

"Jake?" I whispered.

He looked anguished. He slowly pushed himself up from the chair and took a tentative step toward me. He placed his hand in mine and looked in my eyes.

"Aubrey." He whispered, there were tears glassing his eyes.

"Jake, what happened? Is everything okay?" I asked concerned.

"I'm sorry. I-." He sucked in a deep breath. "I just wanted to get you into bed. When I was taking your clothes off, something happened. Nothing inappropriate I swear. You had a total episode. You started thrashing and screaming. I was so scared. I can't fucking sleep. God, Aubrey, I'm so fucking sorry. I just wanted to do something nice for you. I didn't even do it to get a peek. I'm such an asshole!" He berated himself.

I squeezed his hand reassuringly.

"Jake, look at me." He hesitated but looked at me. "It's fine. I didn't even know that it happened. Sometimes I have these things called night terrors. They stem from something that happened. I've become so good at suppressing them that I usually don't even know they're happening. I'm sorry you had to see that. I really appreciate you putting me to bed. It was thoughtful." I smiled kindly hoping to ease his pain.

"Aubrey." My name sounded like a prayer.

I was going to do something that I had never done before.

"Jake, will you try something with me?" He looked surprised and hesitant.

"Not if it's going to hurt you." He said vehemently.

"I don't know how it will end, but I want to see if we can sleep in the same bed. I've never been able to do that before, and I want to try. I should be honest and say the last few boyfriends I have had have been lucky to get past the hand holding stage and get a kiss. You've already managed to do that, and you're not even my boyfriend. Even more strange is that I kissed you! Let's just try. Please." I gave him a puppy dog face that always made my dad cave.

I wanted him to hold me again. It felt so nice when we did it earlier, and I knew that he liked it too.

"Fine, but I'm sleeping in the chair if it gets to be too much." He warned.

I leaned back onto the bed and pulled him in next to me. He was clad in just a pair of blue and white plaid boxers. I felt his body heat rolling off of him. I moved onto my side and felt him hesitantly move closer to me. I closed the distance and curled into him.

"Night, Jake."

"Night, sweet Aubrey." He kissed my hair.

I closed my eyes and drifted into oblivion.

Jake

I woke up holding a soundly sleeping Aubrey. I was surprised how quickly I was able to fall asleep. She didn't have any more distressing dreams after I went to bed with her. I was still freaked the fuck out from earlier. I remember my mom having some fucked up dreams when she was strung out, but Aubrey was truly terrified. I stayed still and watched her peaceful, little face scrunch up. She opened her eyes and yawned. I felt her tense up momentarily. She relaxed as soon as she looked at me. She was so damn comfortable I never wanted to move.

"Morning." She croaked.

"Good morning, Bellissimo. We actually overslept, quite a bit. We're going to have to hurry so we can check out and get to the airport."

Knowing we had to get up I reluctantly moved away and stood. I stretched my arms over my head and shook my cheeks. She sat up on her elbows and stared at me. I saw her eyes widen in shock. I quickly realized that it was because Jake Junior was pitching a tent. *Embarrassing!* I shouldn't be embarrassed though; he was definitely a fine specimen if I do say so myself. Surely Aubrey knew by twenty-three that morning wood was totally normal, right? I quickly adjusted my boxers and excused myself to my room so that I could shower.

Once in the safety of my own room I quickly showered and got dressed. I decided on a pair of dark jeans, a white Henley and my boots. I spiked my hawk and tossed my stuff into the suitcase. I carried everything out to the living room. Brett was just coming back into the room with coffees. I said good morning and plopped down on the sofa to check my emails. We were going to be heading to Boston for our next show in two days. I looked up when I saw Aubrey walk into the room. She braided her hair into pigtails. *So fucking hot!* She had on a pair of high-waist trouser jeans with a gray, tight tank top and chucks. She was my high school fantasy, times a million. If I thought I was smitten before, I was officially captivated. In the span of a couple days, I was now in full on lust!

"You look so hot, I could totally jump for joy." I smiled gleefully.

"I'd jump with you, but my boobs are just way too big for that nonsense." She smiled.

I made the mistake of looking at her chest and was sporting full wood, again. I had gone from being pretty much asexual to being utterly enthralled.

"Hey, I wouldn't stop you if you wanted to just bounce along." I winked, and she smacked me in the chest. It was worth a shot.

She started rolling her suitcase toward the door. I quickly took it from her and put it next to mine. I handed her the coffee that Brett brought back and kissed her hair. She always smelled so fucking good. We headed down to the lobby. I looked out front and saw the waiting car. Of course, the paparazzi were circling like sharks waiting for the first drop of blood. I held my hand out to Aubrey. She looked at it at with apprehension but placed her dainty hand in mine. Brett pushed the door open. I sucked in a deep breath and stepped out into the feeding frenzy.

The cameras clicked away, and Aubrey handled it with grace. She smiled shyly, even though deep down I knew that she wanted to give them the middle finger. We kept going until we made it safely to the car. I knew that she didn't like the attention, but she handled it like a pro. *She could be my rock n' roll princess no problem.* I wanted that more than anything. Once the door was shut I put my hands on either side of her face, and kissed her. I pulled away and rubbed my thumb on her flushed cheek.

"Thank you." I said earnestly.

"For what?" She asked bewildered.

"I know this isn't what you signed up for, but I'm glad you're here. You make it bearable." I genuinely meant it.

Everything seemed better when she was around. She smiled sweetly and turned her attention out the window. She looked deep in thought about something. I pulled out my little notebook that I carried everywhere in case a lyric or something popped into my head. I started jotting down words, it felt fantastic to be able to put something meaningful on paper again. I haven't been inspired to write anything in such a long time. We headed through the streets of Manhattan until we reached the outskirts and made it to the airfield. Brett went to do his security check.

"Hey Aubrey, are you free tomorrow?" I asked.

"No, I'm fucking expensive." She laughed.

"I'm not buying what you're selling." I joked. "What I meant was, do you want to do something tomorrow? With me? Maybe we could go to the aquarium or something?"

"Maybe. I'll have to check with Mark and make sure we don't have another flight before you take off again."

I hadn't even thought of that. I didn't want her to leave... but how to take care of that problem?

"I'll be right back."

I opened the door and headed to the plane. Once on board I quickly got a dirty look from Brett. I ignored him and went into the cockpit to see Mark. He looked up at me in surprise.

"Hey Mark, right?" He nodded. "We haven't been formally introduced. I'm Jake Parker." I offered my hand, and we shook.

"Nice to meet you, Jake. What can I do for you?"

"Listen man, I have a dilemma. I'd prefer if you could have all other flights during your duration with me rearranged. Of course I would be willing to compensate you. I would like to have you at my disposal if needed." That sounded good enough.

"I'm sure we can work something out. Does this have something to do with Aubrey?" He raised an eyebrow. I shrugged not wanting to give too much away. "Jake, I love Aubrey like family. I talked to her last night before the show, and she said that she actually enjoyed spending time with you this weekend. I can honestly say that she hasn't said anything like that in a *long* time. She's also been through a lot in the last few of years, and she's extremely guarded because of it. She's stubborn and difficult, but if you give her a chance I promise she's worth it. I just want her to be happy. So Jake, if that's what you want I don't even care about the money and I'm sure her father feels the same way. We just want her to live again."

"Thanks Mark. I promise I'll be good to her." I was absolutely resolute in my response.

"You better be, or you'll have to answer to me." He smiled, clearly pleased with himself. He patted my shoulder, and I got up to leave.

I went back to the car to get Aubrey and tell her the news. I opened the door and held my hand out.

"My lady." I bowed.

She giggled, and it was the best sound in the fucking world.

We walked onto the plane. She stowed away our luggage and started getting ready for the flight. I wanted to stop her even though it was her job. It wasn't like I was incapable of getting a bottle of water. Besides, the flight to Boston was going to be a short one anyway. I sat in the comfy leather seat and stretched out. After a couple minutes of watching her fluttering around I was starting to get annoyed. Brett took a seat on the other side so that she could sit next to me. I'd thank him later.

"Aubrey, will you quit fussing over shit and come sit down already. I don't think we'll need anything during the flight. If we do, I'll get it. Just sit."

She stuck her tongue out but conceded. She sat in the seat next to me with a white box in her lap. She lifted the lid. It was filled with delicious looking pastries. There were cherry and cheese Danishes, apple turnovers, and cinnamon rolls. My stomach growled. I reached my hand over to take one, but she slapped it away.

"Mine." She growled adorably.

"Just one." I pleaded with puppy dog eyes. She held the box out. I ripped it out of her hands and smirked. "Can you get me a knife, sweetie?"

"If you want a knife why don't you check my back? That's where I've seen it last." She pouted crossing her arms in front of her chest.

"If you could find a way to turn snarky sarcasm into a paying job you would a very rich woman." I wasn't even joking. She would be in Forbes with Bill Gates.

"I know. Now, if you want to be able to sleep tonight and not worry if you're going to wake up tomorrow I suggest you hand over the pastries."

I picked out a cinnamon roll and an apple turnover and relinquished the box.

"Who's a good boy?" She cooed.

"Me. I am. Do I get a kiss?" I grinned.

She leaned in and lightly pecked my lips. Aubrey has unbelievably sensuous lips; picture Angelina Jolie meets Megan Fox. I ate my cinnamon bun in three bites and licked my fingers. Mark came over the intercom and said we were ready for takeoff and to make sure our seatbelts were secured. Aubrey's hands were filled with delicious confectionary treats so I reached over and clicked her belt. She rolled her eyes at me. She seductively stuck the last bite of cheese Danish into her mouth with her thumb. She made low moaning sounds and sucked her thumb teasingly. I was instantly hard. *That bitch plays dirty!* I scoffed in mock disgust. I huffed and turned my back to her. Pretty soon we were airborne. Once we got the all clear she got up and moved to where she sat the other day. Obviously she was planning on ignoring me. I let her be for a couple minutes before approaching her.

"What's the matter?" I prodded.

"I'm pretty sure it has something to do with you being a fucking asshole."

"I'm pretty sure it has something to do with you being strung to tightly. Relax."

"What do you know?" She spat.

Meow! She was in a feisty mood. I sat next to her and started rubbing her shoulders. I swear she was purring.

"Aubrey, has anyone ever tell you you're like a cat?" She shook her head no. "You are. You want affection when you want it and on your terms. The rest of the time you want to claw eyes out and draw blood."

"I do not!" She defended. "Okay. Maybe a little bit, but I have my reasons."

"That's better." I moved her head so that it was on my shoulder.

I pulled out my little notebook and started writing some more. She kept trying to peek over to see what I was working on. I turned so that she couldn't see. I was going to have to see if I could have the guys come up with some music to go with it. I felt bad because I pretty much zoned out for the rest of the flight trying to wrap the song up. When we landed in Boston, I hoped the media frenzy wouldn't be nearly as bad. Brett handed over the itinerary. I looked it over and saw a potential issue.

"Aubrey, can we repeat last night? The hotel where we're staying only has one bedroom suites."

"I guess." She shrugged.

"Good, then it's settled." I said smugly.

Another night snuggling in bed with Aubrey was just what the doctor ordered.

CHAPTER THREE

Blood, Sex, & Booze

Aubrey

We arrived at the Millennium Hotel without as much as one photographer lurking. It was a total three-sixty from New York. Jake checked us into our room without a hitch. Granted there was a man behind the counter, but still. Since it was pretty low-key, he told Brett to go out and have fun. Brett looked as if he wanted to argue, but Jake wasn't having it. It was just the two of us. I didn't want to tell him why I was such a bitch on the plane. It was childish and stupid. Luckily, he was easily placated and seemed to be over it already. I was actually kind of hurt the way he reacted to me putting myself out there, trying to be sexy. He completely ignored me and then accused me of being wound to tight. It didn't help that he made me feel things that I haven't felt before. I wasn't sure what to do about them, yet.

He rolled our luggage down the hallway and stuck the keycard in the door. He held the door open and gestured for me to go in. I walked into the room and looked around. We had a small little area with a couch and two chairs. Our balcony overlooked Quincy Market in downtown Boston. We had a king sized bed with a fluffy, white comforter. I walked over and flopped onto the bed.

Jake came and sat beside me. I looked at him and gave him a shy half-smile. He smiled back and it made my tummy do a somersault. I moved so that my head was resting on his leg. He rubbed my hair soothingly. He grabbed the remote and clicked the TV on. Since there wasn't anything good on, we decided to watch a movie. I moved so that we could get more comfortable. He wrapped his arm around me, and I snuggled on his shoulder. It was bizarre to be able to do this kind of thing. I honestly didn't think it could ever be possible for me again.

Around dinnertime Jake asked if I wanted to go out to dinner. I was still tired, so he ordered us room service instead. We decided on bacon cheddar burgers and onion rings. After dinner, I fetched my pajamas out of my suitcase and headed to shower. I locked the door and took a good, long look in the mirror. I was self-conscious of what I saw, and it wasn't my body. Afterwards, I brushed those thoughts aside and hopped in the shower. I brushed my teeth and put on a pair of flannel pajama pants and a long sleeve shirt on. When I went back into the room, Jake was on the phone with Derek. I curled up in bed and watched him talk. His voice was so sexy, I could listen to him talk all day long. He hung up and kissed the top of my head before going to shower.

While he was in the shower, I started thinking about how we might actually be compatible. We both had scars from our past. Maybe it could work? If only I wasn't such a chicken shit. I started feeling sleepy when Jake walked into the room. He just had a towel wrapped around his waist. He let it drop and I got a view of his glorious backside. *Holy hotness!* He slid into a pair of boxers and climbed into bed next to me. He wrapped his arm around me and placed his hand in mine.

"Sweet Dreams, Aubrey."

"You too, Jake."

Jake

I was glad that Aubrey had a good time on our un-official date yesterday. I took her to the New England Aquarium. Her favorite were the sea lions. We walked around by the wharf, and I only had to sign three autographs, which was a new record low. *Score!* I took her to Faneuil Hall. We window shopped, and I bought her a shirt that says, "I only date boys with tattoos." She picked the Hard Rock Café for lunch. I was recognized there, but they moved us to where it was more private so we wouldn't be disturbed. She smiled the entire time.

The past few days were the best that I had in years. Plus, I was getting the much-needed relaxation that I wanted. Everything was better when she was around. She admitted that she was pissed on how I reacted to her trying to be sexy. I told her she was the sexiest thing I've ever seen. She smacked me and called me a liar. So I kissed her.

I called Blake while Aubrey was in the bathroom getting ready for the show. I wanted to make sure everything was good for the show tonight. I was mid-sentence when Aubrey walked into the room, my breath hitched. I ended the call without another word. She looked phenomenal. Her hair was curled, and she had on a little more make-up than usual. She had on her new shirt, the one I bought her yesterday. She paired it with a black tutu, fishnets and a pair of knee high Doc's. I wiped the drool off my face and went to the dresser and picked up my lucky leather bracelet. I fastened it in place. I needed a distraction before I threw her on the bed and ravished her. We certainly weren't at that point yet. I wondered how she packed all that shit into that tiny suitcase. I was going to have to ask her for pointers. I usually just ended up throwing clothes out and buying new ones.

Aubrey

We arrived at the venue a couple hours early so Jake could do his sound check before the show. He said a lot of bands had their roadies do it, but he liked to do it himself. Today he sang 'Afflicted' by Age of Daze. His voice was so damn sinful. Brett was standing next to me keeping a close eye on things. He seemed to be in a better mood today too. Jake hopped off the stage and picked me up. He spun us around a couple times and kissed my nose.

"Are you excited about tonight?" He asked.

I grinned excitedly. I was actually really looking forward to watching another one of their shows. Just seeing Jake on stage was something to look forward to. It was entrancing. We headed backstage to join the rest of the guys. Jake ordered pizza and beer for everyone, and we ate in the dressing room while the opener was on. I couldn't really hear them, but from what I could hear they sounded good. I watched Jake bobbing his head along with the beat and smiled. When it was time for them to go on I walked to the side of the stage with him. I gave him a good luck kiss as he was taking the stage.

"Boston! ARE YOU GUYS READY TO ROCK?" He yelled. "We're going to start with a cover song tonight. This one goes out to my Bellissimo. You know who you are."

The thundering roar reverberated through the stadium.

"WELL COME ON!" Jake screamed and jumped three feet in the air.

It was completely enthralling.

The band broke into Hinder's 'Heaven Sent.' It was about an angel saving him from his hell. The more I listened to the lyrics, the more I wondered if he was singing it about me because I felt the same way about him. He was saving me from my own hell. I was amazed how much better I slept the last couple nights because he was there. I was still apprehensive, but it lessened with each day we spent together. It was going to be an uphill battle for sure, but with time who knows.

The Boston crowd was out of control. People were crowd surfing and moshing. Jake kept sneaking glances in my direction and winking. The guys had so much passion and enthusiasm tonight that it was insane. Battlescars finished out their set and killed it. They bid the crowd goodnight and exited the stage. After the show, we were going to an after party at a club downtown. Jake came off the stage dripping sweat and kissed me lightly. I looked into his blue eyes completely mesmerized at the intensity. I realized in that moment that if I had to leave Jake right now, I would be heartbroken. I was absolutely scared to death because the first time in a long time I felt vulnerable. My mentality for the past five years was, 'I'll keep you out and stay safe rather than taking a risk and winding up hurt.' With Jake, I was taking a huge risk.

I watched Jake change his shirt and put on a clean, white t-shirt. I wished that I could get close enough to look at all his tattoos. He took my hand and led me to the door. There was a limo waiting outside to take the band to the club. We all climbed in and drove across town.

"Dude, we fucking brought it tonight!" Derek yelled.

"Yeah we did." Blake said smugly.

Kevin just sat there with a smile.

"What did you think, Aubrey?" Jake asked me.

"I thought it was thoroughly entertaining. You guys did a really an amazing job." I said shyly.

Jake rubbed his thumb over my hand and smiled thoughtfully.

When we arrived at the club, the event security let us in through the VIP entrance. The place was jam-packed. It smelled like sweat and booze. Bodies were writhing all over and people kept bumping into us. Jake held me close to his side and headed towards the back. We spotted an empty booth near the corner and climbed in. I was happy when Kevin decided to sit with us. Brett stood next to the table to keep the crowd at bay. It didn't stop a couple hopefuls from trying to get to Jake.

Krewella's 'Alive' was pulsing through the speakers. I started talking to Kevin since I haven't had the chance before. He was really smart, but super shy. He had a girlfriend back in LA that was studying to be a doctor and said the after parties weren't his forte. Jake was in his own world. He seemed annoyed that I wasn't paying attention to him, but I ignored him. It was starting to get towards the end of the night, and the music had changed to a more hardcore beat. The crowd was starting to get obstreperous. Girls were losing their tops and dancing on tables. There were a couple fights going on and even more brewing. A majority of the patrons looked beyond drunk. I was glad to be safely tucked into a corner sipping on my beer.

Jake

I was getting extremely fucking pissed off at Kevin. I wanted to spend time with Aubrey, and he was totally monopolizing her. They were deep in conversation, and I was getting angrier by the minute. The one guy that I thought I wouldn't have to worry about was flirting with the one girl that I wanted. Besides, he has a fucking girlfriend that's going to be a doctor. *Aubrey's mine!* I was watching Blake and Derek out on the dance floor. They were having a ball. I took another long sip of my beer when I noticed a girl that kept checking me out. Maybe if I make Aubrey jealous she'll break. I stood up, and she barely even took notice.

Aubrey

I noticed a voluptuous redhead that kept looking over. She was checking out Jake. I ignored her and went back to talking to Kevin. After about a half an hour, Jake slid out from the booth and walked over to her. She whispered something to him. He laughed and nodded. She threw her arms around him and kissed him vehemently. I felt bile rise in my throat. He took a step back with red lipstick smeared all over his mouth. He smiled triumphantly. I couldn't watch anymore. I stood to leave. As soon as I took a step Jake walked back over and put his arm around me. I moved out of his grasp and pushed him away.

"Don't fucking touch me! Go chase your fame and fortune. I'm done!" I huffed.

"I'm not after fame and fortune. *I'm after you!"* He yelled.

"Really? Kissing some girl is a funny way of showing me that you care." I spat.

"Well, if you weren't fucking flirting with Kevin all night maybe I wouldn't have done it."

I lifted my hand and smacked his cheek. I focused on the dance floor trying to push past him. Nonpoint's 'Everybody Down' came on and transformed an already unruly bunch and made them fucking insane. They were jumping up and down and bouncing into one another. I just wanted to leave. I saw Blake making out with some skanky blonde girl. She was rubbing her hands up and down his chest when another guy came over. He grabbed Blake by the shirt and instigated a shoving match. The girl stood there screaming. A small group started to gather around them. Jake tensed up, but didn't make a move to help. He was too intent on watching me. Brett seemed to be hesitating whether to break it up or not, but I knew that he wouldn't leave Jake.

"That's my girlfriend, asshole." The guy yelled.

"Hey, she told me that she was single. Take that up with her, not me bro."

The guy cold-cocked Blake right in the face. A minute later, Derek walked out of the bathroom zipping up his pants. There was yet another random girl hanging on his arm. As soon as he saw what was happening he pushed her out of the way. He ran over and grabbed Blake. Jake officially called it a night.

"It's called blood, sex and booze. I swear it's a curse." Kevin whispered to me.

Everything that I felt for Jake earlier was out the window. We climbed into the limo. Blake held a napkin to his bloody nose. I sat as far away from Jake as the small space would allow. He looked distraught and kept staring at me. *Fuck him!* As soon as we were back at the hotel I sprinted to the elevator and hit the button before he could catch me. I grabbed my suitcase from our room and stormed out. I body-checked him on the way down the hallway. He tried to grab my arm, but I maneuvered out of his grasp. Brett said something to him, and he stopped. I went to the front desk and used the company credit card to get my own room. While I was waiting the elevator door opened. There stood Jake with red lipstick still staining his mouth. I turned and started walking away from him. I'd rather sleep on a park bench than be anywhere near him at this point.

"Stop. Aubrey, wait a minute!" He yelled.

"Fuck you, Jake Parker!" I screamed.

I walked out the front door of the hotel and made a left. He was running after me. I started walking down the street. I didn't care that it was two in the morning, or that I had no clue where I was. I knew he was right behind me, but I forged on anyway. I turned the corner and walked right into a large body. I fell right on my ass. I looked up and saw that it was Brett. He reached his hand out to help me to my feet. I crossed my legs and sat unmoving on the ground. I also didn't give a shit that I was acting like a five year old. Jake was not my boyfriend. I had no claim to him, and after tonight I didn't want one either. So what if he could touch me? Maybe I was over my aversion.

Jake kneeled down in front of me.

"Are you done?" He asked comically. My fury spiked.

"Get away from me!" I shrieked.

I stumbled to my feet and started back on my path.

Brett really looked as if he wanted to do something to block me. I glared at him. He shrugged and stepped out of my way. Jake continued following me. He started singing 'Brown Eyed Girl' at the top of his lungs. I wanted to laugh. I wanted to cry. I wanted to scream. I kept walking until we had gone at least a mile. Tonight sucked and I just wanted to go to bed. I stopped and turned around. Jake looked stupefied.

"Fine, you don't want to stop and talk to me? I'm going to talk anyway. You ignored me all night, Aubrey. You hurt my feelings, so I hurt yours. I know it wasn't the right thing to do, but you get under my skin!"

"Go fuck one of your groupies and leave me alone, Jake!"

"Come on, don't be like this. I don't want a groupie. I want *you.*"

"Too fucking bad!" I screamed.

"Hey, I told you that I could be an asshole sometimes. Tonight was a stellar example."

"Exactly. I don't want to deal with that kind of thing, Jake. I won't." I turned to look at him.

"*Maybe* if you would fucking let me in, I would be able to understand."

"Fuck you! I've known you for less than a week. I didn't deserve that, Jake. So what, I was talking to Kevin. Did you stop to think that maybe I would want to know the people in your band? I did it because they're important to you! Before tonight, I thought I liked you. If you could be like you were yesterday, I might even say that we could even have something. After tonight, you have about as much of a chance as a cold day in hell. I'm staying in my own room tonight." I stalked forward.

He stood there defeated.

"Everybody leaves. I guess I should expect the same from you." He called after me.

I stopped in my tracks. I turned and looked at him. It was his trump card, and he knew it. We both had huge trust issues. His stemmed from abandonment mine were from being hurt in the past.

"I'm still here, aren't I? I just don't want to be around you right now. I especially don't want to be in bed next to you. Can you blame me?"

"All because of a fucking kiss? Seriously Aubrey, it was just a kiss."

My anger flared. Fine, he said it was just a kiss. I overpowered my fear and grabbed Brett by the back of the neck. Before he could process what I was doing, I kissed him. I pulled away and smirked at Jake. He was steaming. *Good.* I ignored him and walked back into the hotel lobby to retrieve my bag. I hit the call button for the elevator and pushed the button for the third floor. When the doors opened I went to find my room. Once I was safely inside I felt a little relief. At least I gave him a taste of his own medicine. I grabbed my toothbrush and vigorously brushed my teeth. I changed into my pajamas and walked back into the room. I jumped out of my skin when I saw Jake was on the bed in his boxers.

"Get out!" I yelled.

"No. The way I see it is that we're even now."

"Jake, there is no even here." I seethed.

"I said I was sorry. Jesus, Aubrey, I'm fucking trying here. Why don't you learn to relax?"

"Oh I'm sorry, I didn't realize that you're an expert on my life and how I should live it. Please continue while I take notes." I spat.

I walked over to the balcony and opened the door. I stepped out and lit up. Jake grabbed one of my cigarettes and lit up too. I'd never seen him smoke before. I didn't do it all the time just when I was angry, scared, or frustrated. It helped take the edge off. Tonight I was all three. I stood there and glared at him. I tossed my smoke to the ground.

"Smoke your cigarette. I hope you choke." I pushed into him and walked back inside. I thought about locking him out there, but then he would most likely do something stupid and get himself hurt.

"Aubrey, will you stop already! I'm trying to understand. I wish I could take whatever pain you have away, but I can't do that if I don't know what the fucking problem is!"

"You should have tried to keep your tongue in your mouth. You're still wearing a lovely shade of slut." I sneered.

"Please Aubrey." He pleaded. "I actually sleep when I'm with you. Do you have any idea how long it's been since I've been able to sleep like that? I can't even remember."

I felt kind of bad, but I ignored him. He continued to stand there and stare at me.

"Since you're obviously not leaving you can sleep on the floor. If you put as much as a fingernail on my bed, you're going to be short an appendage in the morning. I'll make sure it's your favorite one too!"

He grimaced and took a pillow off the bed and went on the floor. I climbed into bed feeling dejected. I turned on my side and faced away from him. I wasn't going to let him know he was under my skin too. He said goodnight and I tuned him out.

Jake

I woke up feeling ridiculously stiff from sleeping on the fucking floor. I wanted nothing more than to climb into that damn bed and wrap myself around her like an octopus. I royally fucked up last night. It started out as a tit for tat and ended with me sleeping on the floor. Any other girl that I hung around with in the past wouldn't have bat an eyelash, even if I slept with another girl in front of them. It's happened. Aubrey looked like she wanted to string me up by my balls. Even worse was that she looked hurt. I wanted to kick my own ass for being a dick. Then she kissed Brett! What the fuck was that shit? If it were any other girl, I would have told her to fuck off. Instead, I actually found myself wanting to kick Brett's ass, which wouldn't have ended well for me. Aubrey and I had our first real fight. Now we had to make up. Since we didn't have sex, I needed to scheme up a ridiculously good plan. I wasn't used to pursuing girls, but I knew that I was going to have to grovel and beg for forgiveness. It usually involved something shiny.

I got dressed and tiptoed out of the room. I headed down to the lobby and assembled an array of items to try and redeem myself. Luckily, there was a gift shop attached to the lobby. I filled my arms and brought everything to the register to pay. I stopped at the front desk on my way up to put in a special room service order. I hit the button for the elevator and slowly entered the room.

Phew, Aubrey was still sleeping soundly. I started setting up the table. I arranged the three bouquets of flowers and was getting ready to futz with the rest of the stuff when I had another idea. I quickly slipped back out and went to bang on Blake's door. I had to knock for three minutes straight before he answered like an angry grizzly.

"What!" He barked.

"I need to borrow your guitar."

I shoved past him and grabbed it. I walked out of the room to resume my mission. I went back into our room and finished setting up. I pulled the cords to the song on my phone and memorized them lickety-split. I brushed my teeth and made sure there was no remnant of last night's lipstick.

Now the waiting game…

As soon as I noticed her start to stir I started strumming on the guitar. I broke into Kings of Leon's 'Use Somebody'. I put my fucking soul into that song. She sat up on her pillow and watched as I poured my heart out. She didn't even smile. I finished and put the guitar next to the chair. I picked up the flowers and took a tentative step toward the bed. She didn't look like she was going to kill me, so I proceeded on. When I finally made it to the bed, I put the flowers on the bedside table.

"I got these for you." I said shyly.

"Thanks." She mumbled.

"Aubrey, I'm sorry."

"I know. It still doesn't make what you did right. You did prove something to me though."

"What, that I'm an asshole who doesn't deserve you? I figured that out the moment I laid eyes on you. Doesn't mean that I haven't made it my life's mission to prove you wrong."

"No. You proved that you could be selfless. Last night I know how much you wanted to climb in to bed with me. Frankly, I'm still shocked you didn't, but you didn't because I didn't want you to." She gave me a half smile.

"Damn right I did. I just want you to be fucking happy Aubrey. I want to be the one that makes you happy. Why won't you just let me in already, dammit?" I grumbled.

"I'm just not there yet. After yesterday, it just reiterates the point that we need to get to know each other better. Especially, before we jump head first into something."

"But we're okay?" I asked.

"I guess." She shrugged.

"Can I still steal kisses?" I begged.

"Maybe sometimes." She shrugged again. *Dammit she was killing me!*

"Can I have one now? I'm fucking dying here. I need to kiss you more than I need my next breath."

She nodded sheepishly.

I didn't need any more confirmation. I laced her hand in mine and placed my other on the side of her face. I lowered my lips to hers until our lips melded together. I got brazen and prodded my tongue against her bottom lip to make her open. Our other kisses were all closed mouth, but not today. I needed more. I swiped my tongue against hers. I explored her mouth, relishing and savoring. She let out a low moan from the back of her throat. I literally thought that I was going to cream my fucking pants. It was the single, most sexy sound that I have ever heard. I had to move slightly so that she wouldn't see or feel how hard I was.

I pulled back and looked at my brown-eyed girl, the girl that stole my heart. The girl I lo-, really liked. I walked over and retrieved the stuffed bear that I bought at the gift shop. There was a knock at the door. I knew that it was either room service or an extremely angry Blake. My guess was room service. The little bastard down there better not have fucked up my order. I opened the door and moved so that he could push the cart into the room. I slipped him fifty bucks and pushed him out the door. I lifted the first lid to a fluffy cheese omelet with bacon. I lifted the second lid, bingo. I brought the tray over to Aubrey and sat it down. I grabbed a fork and started feeding her bites of breakfast. When she was done, I handed her the second plate. My heart was pounding out of my chest. It was a red box from Cartier. She lifted the lid and gasped.

"Before you start let me explain. The exceptionally charming lady in the gift shop explained what to get and why. There are three colors of gold, yellow for fidelity, white for friendship, and pink for… love. I'm falling hard Aubrey. The thought of you leaving killed me."

The ring was beautiful. It was a pink gold diamond-paved ring with a giant pink gem. It better be nice, since I dropped almost fifty grand on it. I also knew how much Aubrey loved pink, so I figured it was better than a diamond for now. The sun was shining through the window, and the facets were catching the light perfectly. Aubrey just stared at it like I gave her an alien.

"Do you like it?" I inquired.

"I love it, but I can't keep it. It's too much, too soon."

She closed the lid and handed it back to me. *Shot down!*

"Why is what's best for you always what's worse for me?" I mumbled.

"One day at a time." She told me. "It was really thoughtful. I just can't accept something like that. We're not even dating."

"That's your choice." I reminded her.

"I know. You go balls to the wall with everything you do, Jake. You're passionate, and I adore that about you. Please just have some patience." She leaned in and kissed my lips lightly.

She threw her legs over the side of the bed and walked into the bathroom. One step forward, two steps back.

Aubrey

Jake was in the shower when there was a knock at the door. I looked through the peephole and saw Blake standing there. I undid the chain lock and opened the door. His blonde hair was unruly, and he was in a wrinkled t-shirt and boxers. Blake could easily get a job as a model if his music career failed. He was tall and had a classic all-American look about him. He had perfect teeth and great bone structure. He breezed past me and picked up his guitar. He looked it over and threw it over his back.

"Morning." He rasped.

"Morning, Blake." I suppressed a laugh.

"Did you two make up?" He cocked an eyebrow.

"We're fine." I assured.

"Good, because I can't take him when he's a mopey bitch. He's never been so affected by a girl before. It's disturbing. He's normally all detached and whatever, but with you he'd chase you to Mars." He grimaced.

"I heard that, asshole." Jake yelled from the bathroom. He walked out with a towel wrapped around his waist. "She even made me sleep on the floor."

Blake started cracking up.

"We're all going to get some food downstairs. We wanted to see if you guys wanted to join."

Jake looked at me, and I shrugged.

"Yeah, okay. I have to go get some clothes from my room since there was a last minute change of plans last night." He glared at me.

"See you down there." He chuckled closing the door behind him.

I was already dressed in jeans and a hoodie. Jake grabbed my hand and tugged me out the door. He walked up to his room in nothing but a towel. We got a couple dirty looks from passerby's on the way. When we got into his room, I stayed in the living room part while he went to get dressed. He came out in a pair of jeans and a light blue thermal that made his eyes look even more radiant. We walked hand in hand down to the bistro off the lobby. The rest of the guys were already gathered at a booth. I scooted in next to Kevin. He gave me a nod leading me to believe he already knew what happened last night after we got back to the hotel. Jake sat on my other side and ordered us a couple coffees since we already ate.

"I heard you slept on the floor last night, Romeo." Derek teased.

Jake glared at Blake who shrugged mischievously. I looked at Derek who clearly found the entire thing hilarious. Derek wasn't as tall as Jake or Blake, but he was still good looking. He had green eyes and a short black hair. He had a lip ring on the right side, and his arms were covered in tattoos. He was every bit the bad boy rock star. He noticed me starting, and I quickly looked away.

"See something you like sweetheart? I can help you out if Mr. Celebrity isn't cutting it in the bedroom department." He winked.

"I wear heels bigger than your dick, so no thanks." I sneered trying to sound serious, than I broke into a laugh.

"Ouch. She's a keeper, Jake." Derek smiled.

"I'm working on it." Jake miffed.

I shrank into Jake's shoulder. He kissed my hair and smiled at me. I was feeling conflicted after the ring episode. Things were moving way too fast. We finished our coffee and headed back to our rooms to pack up. We needed to head to the next tour stop already. Brett loaded up the car, and we headed to the airfield. We were off to Albany for the next show. I decided since it was a few days before the next show that I would go home for a couple days. I needed a chance to work things out in my head. I wasn't going to tell Jake until we got there since I knew that he was going to flip. I went into the cockpit and told Mark my plans. He eyed me suspiciously. I knew he didn't want to, but he made the necessary arrangements. When we landed I handed Jake his suitcase. He looked at me skeptically. *Five, four, three…*

"Why don't you have your bag?" He asked, perplexed.

"I'm going home for a couple days? I need a break." I said, matter of fact-ly.

"Are you coming back?" He whispered. He looked crestfallen.

"Yeah." I shrugged. "I just need some space."

"Aubrey, please don't leave me. I can't take it." He pleaded.

"That's exactly why I need to go."

"My biggest fear right now is losing you. Don't make me face that fear, Aubrey. You have no idea how much you fucking mean to me!" He was getting emotional.

I kissed his cheek and walked into the bathroom before he could see me breaking into tears. I was so confused. Part of me wanted to get to know him and vice versa. The other part of me wanted to run away screaming. I heard Jake yelling at Brett to fuck off. He didn't want to leave. I made sure that my voice sounded strong before I yelled.

"Jake, just go!"

The noise stopped, and Mark came to knock on the door. He let me know that the coast was clear. I knew that he wanted to say something, but he kept his mouth shut. I shrank into my seat and closed my eyes. I woke up right before we touched down in Smithville. I headed straight to the tattoo shop to see Piper. She was finishing up a piece, so I took a seat and waited for her to finish. I explained everything that happened yesterday and then this morning.

"You need to see what everybody else sees in you Aubrey. We're on the outside looking in. We see a smart, beautiful girl. You can't just shut the door and run from the problems that caused your pain and insecurities. That is exactly what you've been doing for years. As much as you think otherwise; *you're* not broken, Aubrey. " She stood up and grabbed her bag. "Come on, we're going to Duke's."

I followed her to her car, and we headed off to Duke's, a local hole in the wall. We sat at the bar, and I ordered a Jack & Coke. I was silently processing what Piper had said when my phone rang. I went to hit the ignore button, but Piper picked it up.

"Hello." She said.

She listened for a minute before handing the phone to me. I put it to my ear.

"Aubrey, I need you to talk to Jake. He's being totally belligerent and won't listen to me. I've been trying to reel him in since we got here, but he just keeps asking for you." Brett begged.

"Fine. Put him on."

"Aubrey." Jake slurred.

"Are you drunk?" I already knew my answer.

"No, I'm buzzed. Actually, that's a lie. I've got a tab a mile long. I wanna sing you a song... I wrote you a song." He mumbled.

"Jake." I scolded. "Can't you see how unhealthy this is? I said that I needed a break. I told you that I was coming back. Instead you refuse to believe me, and you go out and get drunk. Stop giving Brett a hard time!" I yelled earning a dirty look from the bartender.

"I just feel like you pacified me to get away. I'll take whatever you throw at me, but you're not chasing me away. I'm here to stay baby, so bombs away."

"Jake, relax." I said soothingly.

"I can't shut my fucking brain down. I know that I'm not going to be able to sleep because I'm gonna be worried about you until you get back. I know it sounds crazy, but the only thing I'm crazy about is you."

"I'll see you in a couple days."

"I miss you. I'll never ask for anyone but you." He breathed.

I knew that he was referring to his groupie girls. I hung up the phone and mumbled *balls to the wall.* Piper and I finished our drinks, and I headed home to get some sleep. I tossed and turned most of the night. I found myself worrying about Jake, and his current condition. I knew that the chances of him being up were pretty good. I pulled my phone out and texted him.

Me: You up?

Jake: Is that a rhetorical question?

Me: I'll take that as a yes. You feel any better?

Jake: No. I can't fucking sleep. If I knew where I was going, I would have been on a plane and in bed with you hours ago.

Me: Don't you realize why that might scare me a little? I get it. I have feelings for you too. There was a point in time where someone else had some pretty extreme feelings for me and it left me broken. I'm not looking for a repeat performance.

Jake: I'd never hurt you Aubrey. I don't know what happened, and I know you'll tell me when you're ready. In the meantime just try and have a little faith in me. I'm going to be on my best behavior from here on out.

Me: We'll see. Goodnight Jake.

Jake: Goodnight, my sweet Aubrey. Wish you were here.

I found myself thinking *me too*. I finally managed to fall asleep. I woke up and had breakfast with my mom. I walked across the street to spend some time with Granny Jean.

"Why the long face, bran muffin?"

"I'm just trying to work some things out in my head." I told her, hoping that she would let it go.

"Spill the beans." She all but demanded.

"You know we're carting around Jake Parker." She nodded. "He's not at all who I thought he was, but I can't help that he's going to end up just like Jeremy. Granny, I can't deal with that again. We had a fight a couple days ago, and the next morning he gave me a ridiculously expensive ring to make up for it. I'm just so confused…" I put my head in my hands.

"Sounds to me like he genuinely likes you. I think you like him, too." She reached over and put her hand on my head. "Honey, you have to realize that if you keep yourself in this bubble you're never going to know, and you'll spend the rest of your life thinking 'what if' and I don't want to see that. I'm not saying to jump head first, but at least throw him a life raft."

"He is really balls to the wall." As if that would change her mind.

"Good. That's exactly the type of person you need in your life. Go start living and quit dragging the past around like a ball and chain. Let go." She got up from the chair and walked over to the china cabinet and pulled out the wedding photo of her and my Gramps. She placed it down in front of me. "George wasn't the easiest person to be with. He was a schemer, always trying to come up with the next best thing. He was also the most passionate man I ever met. I didn't fall in love with him right away either, but looking back I'm so glad that I did. Maybe Jake will be your Gramps."

It made sense when she put it that way. I carried around my scars like the plague and used them to push people away. I never took the opportunity to let anyone in. Maybe the fact that Jake could touch me wasn't a fluke thing. Maybe we were meant to cross paths. I decided that I had enough time at home. I called Mark and told him to meet me at the airport. I had a quick visit with my dad while I waited for him to show up. Before long we were airborne and on our way back to Albany. We grabbed a cab and made our way to the Lockwood Hotel. I went to reception and asked for Jake's room. The girl behind the counter scoffed at me. I didn't want Jake to know that I was there and if I called he would know. Instead, I called Kevin since we swapped numbers the other night. He told me that he was coming right down. Mark checked in and had already gone off to the hotel bar.

"Boy, are we glad to see you!" Blake yelled across the lobby.

I laughed when I saw that they all came down.

"He's been a miserable asshole since the other day." Derek chimed in. "Wait, was that just yesterday?" He rubbed his head.

"Come on." Kevin said walking up to the counter. "I need a key to room 501."

The girl reluctantly gave him the card.

"You better hope that she doesn't mention this, because if she does you're going to be out of a job." Blake told her. "She's Jake's inamorata."

She looked at me with pure disgust.

"She's just pissed because she auditioned for me last night and didn't get a call back." Derek said. "Isn't that right, sweet cheeks? She was pining for Jake, but he just whined all night about how much he missed his precious *Bellissimo.*"

I smiled slightly and headed over to the elevator. He wasn't expecting me for another two days, so I was hoping to surprise him. I walked down the hallway and stuck the key card into the door. I took a deep breath and pushed the handle down. Brett was standing there in full on defense mode until he saw me.

"Thank fuck!" He whisper yelled and threw his hands in the air. I laughed.

"Was he really that bad?" I teased.

"You have no idea. I was literally contemplating kidnapping." He joked.

I put my suitcase down and headed back to the bedroom and knocked.

"Go away!" He yelled.

I pushed down the handle, but it was locked. I knocked again.

"What!" He screamed opening the door. He was looking over my head. As soon as he looked down and saw me standing there he threw me over his shoulder and kicked the door shut. He gently tossed me onto the bed and crawled on top of me. I wrapped my arms around him. He crashed his lips to mine and kissed me at a frenzied pace. He pulled away and looked at me intently.

"God, I fucking missed you, baby."

"Don't hurt me again, Jake. If you do, it will be the last time."

"I won't. I promise. You're going to mistake me for a saint."

"I don't want a saint. I just want you to be Jake Parker."

"Baby steps." He whispered into my hair.

I nodded.

CHAPTER FIVE

A Step In The Right Direction

One Month Later...

Jake

I've spent the last month being Saint Jake. I've crossed my t's and dotted my i's. I haven't stepped as much as a toe out of line. Things with Aubrey were going pretty good. We were getting extremely close. She still refused to let me in, but I felt like she was at the point that she was ready. I formulated another master plan for the show tonight. I left her to get ready and checked in with Blake.

"Hello shithead." Blake answered.

"Hey turdface. Were you able to work something out with what I gave you?"

"Yeah, it's pretty good. Derek's working on putting the finishing touches on it now."

"Thanks, fucker. I owe you!"

"Yeah, you do. When did you turn into such a pansy-ass? Aubrey's it, huh?"

"I guess you could say that. She's just not like the other girls. You know that she doesn't expect shit from me. She doesn't care about the money or the fame. She likes me for me. And when I do something to piss her off, she slaps me and rolls her eyes. It's so fucking hot!"

"You're glutton for punishment, bro." He laughed.

"Whatever. You're just jealous." I teased.

"Maybe you're right. See you in a bit."

"Thanks again, Blake. I mean it."

"Jeez, do you have your period? Don't go getting all sentimental on me. We're best friends, it's what we're supposed to do. Now go get ready and I'll see you in an hour."

"Bye asshole."

I hung up and walked back into the room. Aubrey was in a black dress and a pair of black strappy shoes. She looked hot as hell. We headed off to do the sound check. I picked up the mic and started singing Justin Bieber's, 'Baby'. Everything sounded good, so we went to hang backstage until show time. I was suddenly nervous. Thankfully, the time flew by, and we were up. I kissed Aubrey and waltzed onto stage.

"BALTIMORE!!!" I yelled into the mic. "We're going to do something a little different here tonight. I wrote a new song, and I want to know what you guys think."

They went wild.

Kevin walked to the front of the stage and handed me over one of his guitars. I strapped it over my shoulder and started playing a couple cords. Derek started tapping on the drums. I started humming softly before looking at Aubrey. *Here goes nothing...*

"Please Aubrey... let me in, you shot me down, yet again,

It's chaos everywhere I go, I know, they won't leave us alone,

You're my little piece of heaven, the dream I never want to escape,

How I wish we could ride into the sunset, but I'll take what I can get,

I'll cross my T's and dot my I's until you see that you're the girl for me

All I really want is you... Aubrey

Let me in..."

I handed the guitar back to Kevin and smiled at Aubrey. Her eyes were glassy with unshed tears. *Score!*

"I know it wasn't great." I laughed. "Since my life is pretty much an open book I figured that I would share this with you. I know that there are a lot of discrepancies of whether or not love at first sight exists. I always thought that it was a crock of shit until I met this girl. Now, I'm a believer. I love you Aubrey, and I promise to spend every minute proving it to you."

The crowd was chanting her name. It was the first time that I actually wanted to rush a show. I wanted to get off stage and see if my hard work paid off. Her eyes were glued to me for the rest of the show. When we finished out the set, I practically sprinted off the stage. I grabbed her and threw her over my shoulder. I ran into an empty dressing room and sat her on the table. I crashed my lips to hers and practically devoured her. She kissed me back with equal passion. I pulled away and looked at her. I was completely enamored.

"Did you like your song?" She nodded shyly. "I meant every word, Aubrey."

"I know." She whispered.

Aubrey

There was nothing going on after the show tonight, so we all headed back to the hotel. Everyone said goodnight and headed to their respective rooms. Once Jake closed the door I tugged on his hand. I told him that I wanted to shower but that I needed to talk to him after. I grabbed my clothes and went into the bathroom. I gave myself a pep talk the entire time. It was time, and his song just reinforced it even more. I needed to let him in. He's been working so hard the last month to try and prove that he was good enough for me. If he only knew, I was the one that felt like I didn't measure up. I took my time getting dressed and walked into the bedroom. Jake said that he wanted to shower, too. I wondered how I should go about telling him. Do I just spit it out? Do I ease into it? I've never been close enough with anybody since *it* happened to have this discussion. I was nervously pacing the floor when he came back into the room in his boxers with a puzzled look on his face. I looked at him and decided to throw all my cards in.

"Jake, I'm going to talk to you about a couple things. I want you to promise that you won't judge me. Please." I begged. My biggest fear was rejection. I felt like damaged goods and was worried that once he knew what happened that he wouldn't want me anymore.

"Aubrey, I don't judge. I'm listening." He looked at me incredulously.

"I'm worried that you're going to be repulsed by me." I said sadly.

"Seriously, do you have any idea how sexy you are? I feel like a fucking teenager again. Every time you as much as smile I'm sporting a semi. When you roll your eyes, forget about it!" He lifted me so that I was sitting on his lap. "What's really going on, Aubrey? I know there's more to it. Help me understand." He pleaded.

I felt myself start to tear up. I lifted his hand to my chest and ran his fingertips over my tattoo. I knew that he could feel the raised lines under the ink. They were concealed so well you can barely notice them, unless I pointed it out. Something I've never done before. I was about to sever myself wide open for him.

"There's a reason for this tattoo. It was my first. I got it to cover something ugly. Can you feel them?"

"Are they scars?" His hand started trembling. His eyes were thick with emotion. I nodded and tried to hold it together.

"Yes, I have more. The others aren't nearly as bad. Some of them you can barely even make out anymore."

"How did you get them?" He inquired.

Here goes nothing…

"I was attacked by my ex-boyfriend. Je-." He quickly put his finger to my lip.

"I know his name, you don't need to say it." He whispered and pulled me closer.

"I was almost eighteen when it happened. My parents were away for the weekend, and he convinced me to stay at his apartment. I was a naive teenager, so of course I said yes. When I got there, he was strung out. Unbeknownst to me, he was on meth at the time. I didn't even know that he started taking it. I tried to leave, but he wouldn't let me. He snapped… He beat the hell out of me because I refused have sex with him. I was in and out of consciousness, but it was more brutal than sexual. It went on for over six hours until his roommate came home and called the cops. He went to jail for a measly two years. He claims that he doesn't even remember any of it, but I call bullshit. He's tried to contact me a couple times since, even though I have a restraining order. Hence, why I was so upset when I got that message in New York. Every time I see his name the pain comes to the surface. It's almost as if it's happening all over again."

I stood up and slid my pants down below my hips. I sucked in a shaky breath. I had to keep going if I was going to put it all out there.

"These stars are to cover up the x's that he carved into my skin. These were the deepest."

I pointed to the nautical stars that I had tattooed on each of my hipbones. I remembered the knife digging into my flesh before passing out. The scars were still somewhat visible but were less noticeable because of the tattoos. Jake looked distraught. He reached a tentative hand out.

"Can I touch you?" He stuttered.

I nodded. He reached his hand out slowly and ran it over the scars. I flinched involuntarily, and he pulled back. I grabbed his hand and put it back on my hip. We shared an intense stare between us. In that moment, there was no one else in the world. It was just Jake and I. He didn't go running for the hills either. He broke the stare and looked down at his hand.

"So you took something tragic and turned it into something beautiful. With the tattoos, I mean."

"I guess that's how I see it. I did it so that I could see beauty instead of pain. "

"That's really valiant. It helps me understand better. I want to know you Aubrey, all of you, not just the good. Thanks for sharing this with me. I know it's really difficult." He said sincerely.

"My Granny always says, 'women are like angels, when someone breaks our wings we continue to fly around on our broomsticks because we're flexible like that.' It doesn't define me. Except, ever since it happened I have a really difficult time around guys. Most people other than my family can't even touch me. I've always been sarcastic and kind of a hard ass, but after that I became frigid. Until you…"

I leaned forward so that we were nose to nose and kissed him. I kissed him the way that I've wanted to be kissed for the last four years. He pulled me closer and wrapped my legs around his waist. I wrapped my hands around the back of his neck as he ran one hand through my hair and wrapped the other around my waist. I kissed him until spots blurred my vision. I lightly bit down on his spider bite piercings and pulled away. We held onto each other. I felt safe.

"I'm ready to fall if you're the one I fall into." I whispered.

"Does that mean you'll finally agree to be my girlfriend?"

"I'll try."

He moved so that I was sitting on the bed and walked over to his backpack. He tossed a couple things over his shoulder until he pulled out a red box. He came back over to me and dropped to one knee. He opened the lid.

"Aubrey Thompson, will you please be my girlfriend?"

"Yes." I laughed.

"Thank God!" He kissed me and slid the ring onto my finger.

The tabloids were going to have a field day.

"I know we've talked a little bit, but you should know that I'm *really* inexperienced. I mean I did some things with Jeremy before the incident, but I've never…"

"It's okay. I get it. I haven't had sex in over a year. Waiting a little longer won't kill me. If, and when, you're ready we'll talk about it. There's no timeframe here."

"You haven't had sex in over a year?" I asked completely flabbergasted. It never came up before.

"Is that the only thing you took from what I just said?" He teased. "No, I haven't. I already told you that I'm not the man whore the press portrays me as. I even had a physical as soon as I got back from Europe. I'm completely clean. I mostly did it because I was overseas, and there's some weird shit over there. Anyway, enough

122

talk about negative shit. I wanna see the rest of your ink. Who did it? It's really good."

"Actually, Piper did. She's really artsy and started working at a shop as soon as she turned eighteen. She's really talented."

I got to work showing him my ink. I showed him the cute little owl on my ankle. I lifted my foot and showed him the one on my instep. *Hell on Heels.* I lifted up my tank top and showed him the one I had down my side of a cherry blossom stem. My last one was a quote across my ribcage.

Forget what hurt you, but never forget what it taught you.

"I don't know if I'll be able to get over what happened, or the scars I wear because of it, but maybe in time, who knows. My turn."

"We're going to rewrite the pages in our own words. Starting with one day at a time." He smiled.

Over the past month I've been keeping him at arm's length and I genuinely wanted to get a closer look at his tattoos. I pounced on him, and he laughed. I brazenly pushed Jake back on the bed. I finally took a chance to look over all his ink. Across his sternum said, "live free, die worthy." He had nautical stars too, one on either side on his shoulder blades. He had full sleeves on both arms filled with vintage artwork. They were extremely intricate and done in black and fade. Piper would die from excitement if she got to see them. I rolled him over and looked at his back. It looked like a gothic painting. He said it was a rendition of Hades. In gothic script, it read, *stuck between the burning light and the dusty shade.* It was exquisitely done and must have taken hours, upon hours. It reminded me of my own quote, *it's always darkest before the dawn.* He turned over and put his hand on my lower back rubbing the dermal piercings in my dimples.

"Do you have any more piercings?" He asked, cocking an eyebrow.

"I don't. Do you?" He turned bright red. "I'll take that as a yes."

Since I couldn't see them, I could only envision where they were…

They must have hurt!

"Maybe I'll show you one day, but right now I just want to snuggle."

He pulled me next to him so that we were nose to nose again. I was in bed with my *boyfriend* Jake Parker. It was surreal.

"Are you ready for Pittsburgh?" He asked.

"Yeah, I've been there before though. It's only about two hours from where I live."

"It is? The show isn't for five days. Do you want to go home? You can introduce your folks to your new boyfriend." He grinned.

"Are you sure you're ready for that? I mean we've officially been a couple for a half hour." I teased.

"Only if you want to. It would give me a chance to send Brett home for a couple days too."

"Okay. We'll go home and meet the folks." He kissed me lightly.

I kissed him back relishing in the feeling of truly being kissed. It was like Jake was waking a part of me that had been dormant. He was a live wire to my system. He pulled back and smiled contentedly. Jake was respectful and as much as he loved pushing my buttons, he was a gentleman. He opened doors and had manners that would make my mom proud. I ran my fingers through his hair. I knew that I would have to call my dad and tell him to be on his best behavior tomorrow when we arrived. He could be such a smart ass sometimes. I guess the apple doesn't fall too far from the tree. I turned and curled into Jake and closed my eyes.

The alarm went off at eight, and we were set to takeoff at eleven. Jake jumped in the shower, and I seized the opportunity to call my dad. I was not a morning person, so getting a call from me this early must have been a hoot.

"Morning, Aubrey Bean." He chuckled.

"Daddy!" I beamed. "I have some exciting news. I'm coming home for a couple days before the next show."

"Really? That's great. I miss that pretty mug of yours."

"I need to talk to you about something else too... I'm bringing someone with me."

"Okay?" He said skeptically.

"Jake Parker. Before you get started, you should know that I really like him. I already told him exactly what happened. He understands and would never push me to do something that I didn't want to. But, he can touch me without me having a meltdown. It's very bizarre. Please just try and be nice to him." I begged.

My mom and Granny already knew about the Jake situation, but I withheld the information from my dad. He was very overprotective since the *incident* happened.

"I'll see what I can do." He huffed.

"Thanks, Daddy. I'll see you in a little while then."

I called Mark and had him schedule a flight change so that we could just go straight back to Ohio. Jake called and booked Brett a ticket home. He was going to give it to him as a surprise when he came to check in this morning. It was really expensive, over three thousand dollars for a four-day drip, two of them travel days. Jake said that he wouldn't care if it were ten thousand dollars. He wanted Brett to see Kayley. I thought it was incredibly sweet.

I went to shower. I dressed in a pair of red skinny jeans and a white sweater. I tied my chucks and walked into the bedroom.

Jake was waiting for me right outside the door. He picked me up and tossed me over his shoulder. I repeatedly smacked his ass and told him to put me down to no avail. He walked out of our hotel room and went next door to Brett's room. He placed me on my feet. I looked up and saw an elderly couple walking down the hallway. They looked like they were about to have heart attacks. Jake knocked on the door, and Brett answered. He was already dressed in his signature suit.

"I'd like you to meet my girlfriend, Aubrey Thompson." He beamed proudly.

"About fucking time." Brett laughed and gave him a knock on the shoulder. I guess that was their caveman-ish way of saying "congratulations."

"Pack your shit dude." Jake yelled. He handed over the airline confirmation.

"You serious?" Brett beamed.

"Absolutely. Get going! You have a flight to catch." Jake patted him on the back.

Brett was clearly a devoted dad. It had to be hard for him being away as much as he was. I was lucky that my dad took over the business for his dad. It afforded him the luxury to be around while I was growing up. Since he was self-employed, he had a little more leeway. Some days during the summer he would take off just so we could go to do something fun like go to the beach or a zoo. Sometimes we would even take a plane and fly somewhere just to get lunch. I used to feel like I was a princess.

We didn't come from money. My grandfather, George Thompson, started the business from nothing. It thrived until the recession when companies started doing cutbacks. They still manage to stay afloat, but I know that it's more expensive to run the business too. He passed away in his sleep three years ago. I missed him terribly. Thankfully, Granny Jean was still full of piss and vinegar and would most likely make it to a hundred. We grabbed our luggage and headed to the airfield. Soon we were in the air and on our way to Smithville. I filled Jake in on the who's who. He was already familiar with names, and there weren't too many people, so he got it right away.

We touched down at home base. Mark lowered the stairs, and I knew that he was happy to be home for a few days too. I practically skipped down the stairs with Jake on my heels. My dad was standing there waiting for me. I jumped on him and hugged him tightly. I realized how much I missed him.

"Aubrey Bean." He cooed.

"Daddy! I'd like you to meet my boyfriend, Jake Parker."

Jake reached out his hand.

"Timothy Thompson, nice to meet you!" He said like a drill sergeant. I knew for a fact, he was squeezing Jakes hand way too tightly.

"You too, sir. Thanks for having me." Jake flexed his hand.

"Sure. A friend of Aubrey's is always welcome." He smiled. Then he leaned in to Jake. "If you hurt her, I'll break your fucking neck. You understand?"

I rolled my eyes.

"Understood." He swallowed audibly.

"Good. Your mom's waiting for you at home. She's making a ham and all the fixings. I'll see back there later."

I kissed my dad goodbye and led Jake over to my car. He was grinning from ear to ear about meeting my family. I knew it meant a lot to him since he didn't have any real family of his own. I just hoped that our trip wouldn't end in catastrophe.

CHAPTER SIX

Home Sweet Home

We loaded our luggage into my trunk and climbed in the car. I started the engine and watched Jake's eyes bugged out of his head.

"Baby, I think there's an animal under your hood or something." He teased.

"No, it's the muffler." I said feeling slightly embarrassed. "I'm working on getting something quieter."

"At least it's a stick. I think the fact that you can drive a manual is super hot."

Jake was looking around at everything as I drove the ten minutes until we arrived at the little ranch that I called home.

"Ready?" I asked.

"Definitely." He grinned.

I grabbed his hand, and we walked up the flower-lined walkway to the red door. I opened the door. My mom was in the kitchen working on dinner. Her entire face brightened when she looked at me, and then our entwined hands. I felt my cheeks flush. I knew that my parents were worried that I would end up alone, especially since it's been a good two years since I even went out on a date. I think Jake could have had a third eyeball, and they still would have been happy. She looked beautiful in a floral wrap dress and flats. Her light-brown hair was freshly styled. She smiled brightly waiting for an official introduction.

"Mom, this is Jake. Jake this is my mom, Caroline."

"Mrs. Thompson, it's a pleasure." Jake said kissing her hand.

"Nice to meet you, Jake. Aubrey, I'm finishing up supper and just realized that I don't have any marshmallows. Can you please go ask Granny?"

As soon as Jake turned my mom mouthed an *ohmigod.* I knew that my face turned bright red.

"Alright. Come on Jake."

I tugged him back out the door. We walked across the street. I opened Granny's door and called out a hello.

"In here, dammit." She yelled from the den.

"Jeez Granny, I have company."

"So?"

"Granny, this is my boyfriend Jake. Jake, meet Granny Jean."

"Good thing I have my library card, 'cause I'm checking you out." She catcalled.

"Nice to meet you, Mrs. Thompson." Jake laughed.

"Don't give me that Mrs. Thompson shit. Call me Granny Jean, or at least Jean. Damn Aubs he is mighty fine." She appraised him.

"Granny!" I scolded.

"What? Just keeping it real. Isn't that what you kids say nowadays?" She snubbed her smoke and stood up.

"Mom wants to know if you have marshmallows."

"What do I look like? A quickie mart? No, I don't. Grab my bag, we'll go to the store. I need smokes anyway."

I grabbed her purse and handed her the car keys. Jake was about to get his first real Granny experience. He climbed into the back of her ancient Cadillac. I told him to make sure that he put his seatbelt on. She started the engine and burned rubber pulling out into the road. We went to Main Street where all the shops were. Some guy was gawking at her at a red light, so she stuck her tongue out and gave him the middle finger. He quickly snapped his head back. I heard Jake chuckle. She mumbled something about him being an asshole and pulled into a parking spot. She climbed out and slammed the door behind her. Jake and I followed her into the store. I grabbed a bag of marshmallows and went to pay. There were a group of teenagers hanging out by the check out. I knew that they recognized Jake. I tugged his hand and pulled him with me. We had been in the press some lately, but I didn't want any unwanted attention. They were still speculating who I was, and they didn't have a name yet. Granny noticed the crowd.

"What are you little fuckers looking at? Ain't you ever seen a rock star before? Scram!" She yelled.

They took one last look and took off. Jake looked dumbfounded. I told him that this was what she was like *all* the time. We paid and practically ran back to the car. I was hoping that the news of Jake's presence in town wouldn't get spread around. It was very unlikely though. It was a small town after all. I just wanted a couple low-key days with him. I texted Piper and asked her if I could come into the shop after dinner. I didn't tell her that Jake was with me. She didn't even know that we were officially an item yet. She said of course. We headed back home, and I gave my mom the marshmallows. We collected our luggage, and I took Jake to my room.

I turned the knob. Thankfully, my mom must have cleaned after I left. It wasn't anything fancy, but I did have a window bench that I adored. It was filled with funky pillows I found over the years. It was my nook. My room had white wainscoting and trim. The top of the wall was painted hot pink. My furniture was white, and I had a queen size bed with pink sheets and a zebra comforter. It was girly with a funky edge. Mostly it was very me. Jake seemed to be taking it all in. He walked over and picked up the picture on my dresser. It was of Piper and me at the beach last year. Mitzy came over and started rubbing up against his ankles. I walked over and picked her up.

"Your room is cute." I shrugged. "What's the matter, baby?"

"Nothing." I lied.

"Then why do you look all pouty?"

He ran his thumb over my pouting bottom lip. I bit down. He groaned and moved his hand. He crashed his lips to mine and stalked forward until the backs of my knees hit the bed. He kissed me fervently, and I could feel him hard pushed up against my thigh. He felt *huge*. I wanted to reach out and touch him. I quickly decided that I wasn't ready to go where that would lead. Especially, not with my mom is the next room. He pulled back and bit my neck.

"Now what's the matter, baby?"

I never liked terms of endearment, but I actually liked when he called me baby.

"I'm just worried now that you've been spotted that word will get out." It was the truth by omission.

"Are you worried about anyone in particular, or just in general? I can call in another security guy I use sometimes if you want. I'm perfectly capable of handling myself, but if you're worried…"

"It will be fine, we'll just stay in. I wanted to take you to meet Piper at the shop in a bit. I'll just tell her that I had a change of plans."

"We can still go. If it gets out of hand, then we'll leave. Deal?"

"Fine." I gave in because I really wanted to see her.

My mom yelled and said that dinner was ready. We all sat down at the table. She made ham, macaroni and cheese, candied yams with marshmallows and homemade biscuits. We didn't say Grace or any kind of blessing. Instead, my dad spoke.

"Let's have a moment of silence for all those idiots on their way to the gym to ride stationary bikes while we're here feasting on a delicious meal and getting plump."

"Screw the people riding stationary bikes, the joggers are the freaky ones. They're always the ones finding the bodies. Coincidence, I think not." Jake chimed in and my dad beamed.

Jake's sense of humor fit in with ours perfectly.

I laughed, mostly because they were both true. Jake filled his plate and dug in. My parents kept looking at me and smiling. It was embarrassing, but I could tell that they were happy. I laughed again because if most kids brought home a guy that looked like Jake they would probably have an aneurism. Jake didn't look scary, or weird, it's just the stigma that he had attached to him. *The same one I accused him of.*

"Jake, where are you from?" My mom asked.

"I was born in Arizona. I lived there until I was twenty, then I moved to LA."

"Your parents must be so proud of you. You're very accomplished for being twenty-five." She boasted.

"Actually, my mom passed away when I was eleven, and my dad isn't in the picture. It's okay, you didn't know." He quickly reassured, seeming unfazed.

"What are you kids planning on doing for the next couple of days?" My dad asked.

"Probably just hanging around here." I shrugged. "We're going to see Piper after dinner though."

"Tell her we said hello." They said at the same time.

We finished up dinner, and Jake demanded that we get to clean up since she cooked. I eyeballed him, but he dragged me to the kitchen. He washed while I dried. He kept splashing me with water, so I grabbed the hose and squeezed the nozzle soaking his shirt. After we cleaned up the mess, he changed his shirt, and we headed to TruInk. I warned him that Piper was somewhat of a super fan. He laughed, but he had no idea. I parked in the nearest available parking space, and we walked inside. I said hi to Josh, the owner, and went back to Piper's room. She was flipping through a magazine when she looked up and saw me, and then Jake.

"Holy fucking shit!" She screeched. "You brought Jake fucking Parker to my shop!!!!" She stood and jumped up and down. She threw her arms around me and squeezed.

"Jake meet Piper. Piper, meet my *boyfriend*, Jake."

"Did you just say boyfriend? You did, didn't you? Holy crap! You're dating Jake Parker!"

I looked at Jake, who was clearly embarrassed by Piper's outburst. I just smiled and mouthed *I told you so*. He kissed my hair and smiled.

"Are you done?" I teased.

"Sorry. It's nice to meet you Jake. I'm a huge fan. Your voice is like sin."

"Um, thanks." He looked uncomfortable.

"So what brings you guys here? Are you visiting? Aren't you guys on tour?"

"We are, but we had a few days before the next show in Pittsburgh. Since we were so close, it seemed silly not to come see where Aubrey's from." Jake shrugged.

"Awesome! I'd love to see you guys some time."

"Why don't you come to the show in Pittsburgh? I can get you a stage pass." He suggested. It made me happy that he was doing something nice for someone that I loved like a sister.

"Seriously? I would love to!"

"I'll take care of it. It's on Friday night."

"Yay!" She squeaked.

We hung out in the shop for a little while before leaving to go back to the house. We were on our way to the car when I heard my name being called. I halted and looked around to see where it was coming from.

"Aubrey?" I heard again, this time it was Jake. "Do you know who that is?" He put his arm around my shoulder and pointed. I tensed. Before we could get to the car, Jeremy was walking over. I felt myself start to shake. Jake looked menacing.

"Bre-bre." Jeremy sneered. "Were you even going to say hi?"

Seeing him brought all the horror I went through to the surface. It was like watching it happen again in slow motion. The cutting, the screaming, the pain. I felt myself gasping for air, just like I did when he choked me until I was unconscious. I felt my vision start to blur. Jake quickly moved me so that I was leaning up against the car. He looked torn. He took a step away from me toward Jeremy and glared at him.

"Jake Parker, the guy who's trying to bag my sloppy seconds."
Jeremy taunted.

Jake raised his fist and punched him square in the face.

"Jake Parker, the guy that's going to fucking kill you if you come near my girlfriend again." He roared.

The whole thing was a blur. I watched as Jeremy fell to the ground. Jake helped me in the passenger side. He climbed into the driver's side and threw the car in reverse. He sped back towards my parent's house. When we reached my parents road, he pulled off to the shoulder. He leaned his head against the steering wheel and sucked in a deep breath. He turned to look at me.

"Baby, are you okay?" He whispered.

He hesitantly reached his hand over to touch my face, but stopped right before he made contact. He looked in my eyes for reassurance that it was okay. I closed my eyes and gave a slight nod. He touched my cheek with his fingertips. I found consolation in his touch. Tears slowly trickled down my face. I unbuckled my seatbelt, and he helped me climb into his lap. I wrapped my arms around his neck and sobbed. My whole body hurt. I felt like I was going to shatter. I knew that I couldn't go home like this and managed to choke out Granny's name. He moved the seat back so he could drive without moving me. He parked in her driveway and effortlessly carried me to the door. He opened the door and walked in. Granny was sitting at the table on the phone. She hung up as soon as she saw me. Once I knew it was okay I went into self-preservation mode, or as I referred to it "robot mode".

"What happened?" She demanded.

I looked at Jake and pleaded for him not to tell her. He ignored me.

"We had a run in with Jeremy at the tattoo parlor. I punched him in the face. I'm pretty sure the cops will be here soon." He whisper shouted, clearly pissed off.

"That needle-dick bastard." She pushed out the chair and walked over to the curio. "I'm gonna kill him!"

She opened the drawer and pulled out her .380 pistol. Jake sat me in the chair and went to perform damage control. He told her that it wouldn't do me any good if she went to prison. She said she would be dead soon anyway. He managed to coax the gun from her. He slid the safety back on and put it back in the drawer. Granny huffed and went to light up a smoke. She put it in my mouth, and I took a long drag. Jake walked over to her hutch and poured a shot of Jameson. He tipped his head back and swallowed. He poured another one and brought it to my lips. I felt the warm liquid burn down my throat. It did little to soothe the ache burning inside me. He sat the glass on the table and lifted me up so I could sit on his lap. I leaned on his shoulder and breathed in.

Jake

Aubrey was still catatonic. I watched as the minutes ticked by like days. Being helpless has to be the worst fucking feeling in the world. I was trying to do anything that I could think of to make her come around. I was singing softly in her ear and rubbing lazy circles on her back and shoulders. Then I switched humming and saying little things hoping to try and make her feel better. I leaned in and kissed her forehead and used my fingertips to brush her hair out of her face. Granny Jean retreated to the den after the gun incident. She said that she couldn't stand to watch Aubrey like this again. I could only imagine how hard it must have been to watch her in pain after what that fucker did to her. After an hour, I finally thought that Aubrey was starting to come around. She tilted her head to look at me. I thought my heart was going to jump out of my chest.

I wanted to go back and kill him with my bare hands. What kind of sick and twisted asshole does something like that? There's no way he didn't know what he was doing, he knew damn well. Aubrey's scars were much more than on the skin, they ran deep. I experienced a little bit when she had that night terror, but this was something entirely different. It was like a storm brewing inside her. Her eyes told me much more than her words ever could. There was nowhere for her to hide, so she hid in herself. I only hoped that I was doing something to offer her solace. Her bottom lip was trembling.

"Jake. Sleep. Home" She stuttered.

"Yeah baby, I'll take you home." I kissed the top of her head and scooped her up.

I called a goodbye to Granny and told her to behave. I walked past her car and crossed the street. Looks like that pussy didn't call the cops after all. Thankfully it looked like her parents had gone to bed for the night. I walked into her room and closed the door. I flicked on the light and placed her on the bed. I told her that I was going to take her shoes off. I knelt down on the floor and took her foot in my hand. I untied each shoe and gently pulled them off. I placed them next to the bed. She started struggling to take her shirt off. I put my hands in hers so that she was doing it, but I was able to help her from getting frustrated. She stood in front of me in just her bra and a tiny thong. It was easily the sexiest sight that I've ever seen, but I wasn't even slightly turned on. Instead, I felt like I was going to have a breakdown. I hastily unzipped my suitcase. I pulled out a long sleeved thermal shirt and pulled it over her head. She dropped her bra to the floor. I helped her put her arms in the sleeves and pulled her to me. Watching her look so hurt and broken tore my heart right out of my chest. I wanted to take her pain, all of it. I started to cry. I quickly pulled myself together because I needed to be strong for her.

I hastily took my jeans off and slid us both into bed. I pulled her as close to me as I could. I ran my fingers through her hair and started humming until I felt her breathing even out. I knew she was sleeping. I sat up for hours just watching her sleep. I didn't want to risk falling asleep if she was going to have a bad dream. A little after three in the morning she rolled over and opened her eyes. She looked up at me.

"Jake?" She whispered.

"Yeah, baby? I'm right here." I assured her.

"I was so scared that you were going to leave me. I'm sorry. I'll try not to do that anymore…" She cried. *What the hell?*

"Stop. Aubrey, I'm not going anywhere. I couldn't leave even if I wanted to because you're it for me. I love you. I'm here for as long as you'll have me. I'm hoping that forever works for you. I know it seems really fast, but I know how I feel. But, it's never going to change no matter what."

I know that I already said it on stage in front of thousands of people, but I never said it directly to her. I wished there was something that I could do to reassure her that I was here, and I wasn't going anywhere.

"You love me?" She asked incredulously as if it was questionable. I'd tattoo it to my forehead if that gave her the assurance that she wanted.

"More than I've ever loved anything. I don't know what it is about you, but it's like you're the sun in my universe. You came into my life and set my world on fire." I kissed her nose. "I knew that you were something special as soon as I saw you. You looked at me like I was gum on your shoe and I knew you weren't like the others. You make me feel alive. It's like my life has been empty for so long, and you fill it. I'm not upset with you baby. I'm upset because it literally kills me to see you like this. You're so strong Aubrey, and seeing you broken, it breaks me. I'm here. I'm not going anywhere. I love you so fucking much baby."

"I love you too." She whispered.

It was barely audible.

"What?" I wanted her to repeat it. I needed her to repeat it.

She looked at me. Her brown eyes burned with intensity.

"I love you Jake Parker. I don't know how to explain it either. You make me feel whole."

"Ditto, baby. Now get some sleep. I have to run out in the morning. Record label stuff. If I'm not here in the morning when you get up, I promise you that I'm coming back." I kissed her lightly.

She leaned her head on my chest right over my heart and closed her eyes. I managed to fall asleep with the girl I loved. I woke up a couple hours later and quietly slid out of bed. I picked my jeans up off the floor and pulled them on. I grabbed a zip up hoodie from my bag and my shoes. I tip toed into the hallway.

Aubrey's dad was sitting on the couch drinking a cup of coffee. I pulled my sweatshirt on and walked to sit next to him so that I could put my shoes on.

"Morning." He said.

"Morning. Hey Tim, can you do me a favor?" I asked nervously.

"Depends what it is." He said speculatively.

"I don't want to upset you, but I think that you deserve to know. I need to go down to the police station. We had a bit of a run in with Jeremy last night. Aubrey's fine now, but I was kind of hoping that maybe my public profile might sway them to keep a better eye on their parolee's." I sneered. I still wanted to find Jeremy and give him a taste of his own medicine. Luckily, Ron taught me that two wrongs don't make a right because I would love to make this right.

"He didn't get near her? I'll kill him." His neck muscles were bulging.

Tim was bad-ass kind of scary. He looked like a guy that could rearrange your face if he wanted to.

"I was right there. I punched him in the face if it makes you feel any better. It didn't make me feel an ounce better. She was pretty catatonic for most of the night. We went to your mom's because she didn't want you to see her like that. I'm going to talk to my security guy when we get to Pittsburgh. I want to see about bringing on another guard to be with her when I can't."

"That son of a bitch. Let's go."

He was up off the couch and had his keys in hand. I followed him out to his pick-up truck. It gave me another idea. We sped out the driveway and arrived at the police station five minutes later. An extremely, angry Timothy went right up to the empty front desk and started slamming his hand down on the bell.

"Morgan! Get your goddamn ass out here right now!" He yelled.

A heavy set, balding man in a uniform came out from an office in the back.

"What?" He yelled.

"What? I'll tell you what! Last night while my daughter was out with her boyfriend, she was accosted by Jeremy Roberts! That's what!" Tim bellowed.

The guy paled a little.

"Oh. He's not supposed to be within 100 feet of her." He stated matter of fact-ly.

"No shit, Sherlock. You need to do a better job tracking that animal." He roared.

I held my hand up.

"Sorry. Sheriff, this is Aubrey's boyfriend Jake Parker. Jake, Sheriff Morgan." Tim gestured.

"As in the lead singer of Battlescars Jake Parker?"

"The very same." I said slightly annoyed.

Hopefully, it would get me my leverage.

"My daughter Megan has posters of you covering every square inch of her room."

"I'll sign something for you. I'll take a picture. Whatever you want, but I want something in return. I want you to make sure that asshole doesn't get near her again. He's a monster. I grew up around people like him, and he's not going to go away. She's been through enough already."

"I'll see what I can do." He said.

I got right in his face.

"You see Sheriff, that's not going to work for me. I want your word. I love this girl, and if something happens to her I won't be held responsible for my actions. Got it?" I seethed.

He gulped and nodded. *That's right motherfucker I can be a bad-ass too.* Tim looked at me with wide eyes. Shit, I had just said the L word in front of her dad. At least he didn't look angry. He promised to have an officer trail him while we were in town. Tim and I left and climbed into the truck.

"Tim, about what I said in there. I want you to know that even though it's happened extremely fast I love your daughter, a lot. I know you probably think it's crazy and kind of whirlwind, but I know what I feel."

"I know, I could tell. Dads have spidy-senses. If you hurt her, I'll hunt you to the end of the earth. If I knew that I could get away with it, I would take Jeremy out of the picture. Permanently."

"She told me everything that happened *that* night. I want to help put her back together. He's obviously still pining for her. While we were in New York, he sent her a disturbing message. He's a loose cannon, so we're just going to have to do our own security."

"I'm actually happy that the two of you found each other, Jake. She hasn't let herself get close to a guy since that piece of shit. It's been painful for her mother and me to watch, especially knowing that there wasn't a damn thing we could do. Right after it happened, if anyone would try and touch her, even just to change a band-aid, she would scream bloody murder. She's much stronger now, but deep down it's always going to be there."

"I know. I understand exactly what I'm getting with Aubrey. I'll do whatever I need to make her happy, which brings me to the other thing I want to do... I want to buy her a car."

"You what?" He looked at me incredulously.

"I want to buy her a car. Actually, a Mini Cooper, I think that she would like one of those. Her car has seen better days, and I don't want her driving something that doesn't have airbags."

I knew her car probably had airbags, but it was the most justifiable reason I could think of at the time.

"I don't know. I mean it's really generous of you and all, but it makes me a little uncomfortable."

"Tim, I don't want to sound conceited, but I made enough money to buy it last night while I was sleeping." *I only slept for four hours.* "I'm going to buy it for her with or without your permission. Please, let's just go do it."

He reluctantly relented and drove a half hour away to the nearest Mini dealer. They were just opening when I walked in. I told the sales guy exactly what I wanted. They had it in stock and were washing it and filling it with gas. I put the car in her name and paid for it. I wanted to laugh when he handed the receipt because it wasn't much more than her ring. I'd keep that little tidbit to myself because chances are that would make good ole Tim really uncomfortable knowing his daughter was wearing a rock that cost more than his pickup truck. When they pulled it around, the sales guy handed me the keys. I grinned at Tim, who rolled his eyes. *Must be genetic.*

I followed him out of the dealership and back to Smithville. We pulled in the driveway at a little after nine. Chances are that Aubrey was still sleeping. I felt so giddy that I wanted to go jump on her and wake her up. It felt so nice to be able to do something nice for her after last night, especially since she had no idea and would never in a million years be able to guess. I headed inside and said good morning to Caroline who was at the stove making breakfast. I walked to Aubrey's room and climbed back into bed. The little dip made her wake up. She turned over and wrapped her arms around me.

"Morning, beautiful. It's time to get up." I said excitedly. "I got you a present."

She shook her head no and squeezed me tighter.

"I don't want to move." She whined sleepily.

"Don't you want your present?" I cooed.

"You're my present."

"That's sweet, but it's something else."

I threw the covers off of her, and she pinched my rib. She stumbled out of bed and walked into the bathroom. Ten minutes later she came out looking much more awake. She slipped on a pair of leggings, but left my shirt on. I needed to keep Jake Junior under control because she looked smokin'. I took her hand and led her to the living room. Tim was grinning, pretending to read his paper. Ha! And he acted like he didn't want to go along with my plan.

"Morning, princess." He said.

"Morning, Daddy."

I opened the door and led her outside. We had strategically placed Tim's truck to block her new car from view. I put my hands over her eyes so that it would be a surprise. When it was in clear view, I pulled them away.

"What's that?" She gasped.

"It's your new car." I said proudly.

I picked out a cherry red Mini Cooper convertible. It had navigation, premium sound and black leather seats. It screamed Aubrey.

"You're funny. What is it, nine in the morning? There's no way." She turned and started going back inside.

"Aubrey, I'm serious. I had your dad take me this morning. A Mini just seemed very you. Do you like it?" I asked, holding out the keys.

"You're serious?" She cocked an eyebrow.

"As a heart attack."

She eyed me suspiciously. I waited for a solid minute before a smile broke across her face. She jumped and wrapped her legs around me.

"It's too much. You know that, right? But, I love it. Thank you!" She squealed.

"Nothing's too good for you, baby. I'd buy you a fucking Porsche if that's what you wanted because *I love you.*"

"I love you, too." She grazed her perfect lips along mine.

Pretty soon we were making out on the hood of her new car in broad daylight.

"Will you kids get a room already? It's like watching pornography in 3-D." Granny Jean yelled from across the road. "Nice wheels kiddo!" She winked.

"I know." Aubrey yelled.

It was almost like she repressed everything that happened last night. I still felt myself on high alert waiting for the other shoe to drop. As much as I liked Aubrey's family I wanted to get the hell out of here. I wanted to get her somewhere that Jeremy couldn't reach her.

CHAPTER SEVEN

Claws & Daggers

Aubrey

"I cannot believe we're here!" Piper squealed. "Jake Parker is literally like the best boyfriend ever!"

"Eh, he's alright." I teased.

We were sitting backstage at the show in Pittsburgh. Since it was only a two-hour drive, I convinced Jake to let us drive, especially since I got a new car. I pouted and said who knew when I would be back to drive it again. He gave in without a fight. *He could be such a pushover.* I still couldn't believe that he bought me a damn car. Piper was jumping up and down as soon as we pulled up. She professed her undying love and faux proposed to Jake saying she would be a way better girlfriend. He laughed, and said he was, "a one girl kinda guy."

I didn't want to rehash what happened the other night with Jeremy. But, just having Jake there made it easier to get through. It was horrible seeing *him* again though. He still freaked me the fuck out. I pushed *him* out of my mind and focused on hanging out with my best-friend and my boyfriend. We were going to a place called Randy's after the show to get some food with the rest of the guys.

Someone from the stage crew came to tell Jake that it was time to go on. He led us over to a little section that he had set up with two chairs for us to watch the show. He leaned in and kissed me before taking the stage. Piper looked at the whole thing in awe.

"PITTSBURGH!!! How's everyone fucking doing tonight? Are we ready to rock?"

A loud sea of "*hell yeah*" followed.

"Then LET'S GO!"

The band started playing, and the whole place turned electrifying. It was intoxicating to watch. Jake pretty much demanded stage presence with his ostentatious Mohawk and his virtuoso moves. Blake nailed his killer guitar riff on their song 'Hurricane.' Piper beamed the entire time. Even I could admit that it was pretty neat being backstage. When the show was over Jake sprinted off the stage and right over to us.

"What did you think?" He asked Piper.

"You guys are even more spectacular live. It was phantasmagorical!" She said completely in awe.

"Thanks." He beamed. He leaned down and kissed me long and hard. "I'm going to change my shirt quick. Don't move."

"You are seriously the luckiest bitch on the planet." Piper said. "You told him about what happened with Jeremy, right?"

She was another one that was really protective after what happened.

"I told him everything. He understands, Piper. He didn't exactly have a picket fence childhood. We're good for each other." I shrugged.

"I'm happy for you Bean." She hugged me.

"Hey! Can I get in on that?" Blake asked.

I rolled my eyes. "Piper, meet Blake."

"Piper, I'd like to lay some pipe for you." Derek yelled coming up behind Blake.

"Jeez, what are you guys animals? Where are your manners? She's a fucking lady. Treat her like one." Kevin scolded.

"I'm Kevin. Don't mind them."

I really liked Kevin. I adored all the guys, but Kevin was more like me. He didn't take any shit, but he didn't go looking for it either. Jake came back over, and we headed to Randy's. We walked in and ordered a bunch of food and a couple pitchers of beer. The place was your typical bar. It had a couple of pool tables and a karaoke booth.

"Who wants to play pool? I call Piper." Blake grinned.

She got up and happily obliged. I watched as they set up the pool table. Blake was totally checking out her ass the entire time. Derek decided to go and play with them too. Every time one of them missed a shot, they had to take a whiskey shot. They came back after two games and ate some appetizers. Kevin just sat quietly, and people watched the entire time.

"Dude, our friendship is bad for my liver." Derek said to Blake.

"No, it's not. You just suck at pool." Blake teased.

"I do not." He yelled. "Okay, you're right. I do." He laughed.

"Hey Piper, I'm no weatherman, but you can be expecting about six inches tonight." Derek teased.

"Wow, how original of you. Did you come up with that all by yourself?" She said sardonically.

"Ouch. Blake, I think we've met our match."

Blake took a long sip from his beer and nodded. He was totally into her, I could tell. They decided they wanted to sing karaoke. Blake went first. He sang 'Talk Dirty To Me' by Poison. Derek went up next. He was horrible and should definitely stick to the drums. At the end of the night, we said goodbye to the guys and told them that we would see them at the next stop. Jake said that he would drive back since it was late and he never slept. I climbed into the backseat and snuggled with Piper.

Jake

Two weeks had gone by since Pittsburgh. We were backstage after our show in New Orleans. There was a pretty sizable crowd gathered for our VIP meet and greet. I always hated these things. I felt like I had a bulls-eye on my head. We were waiting for Kevin to come back from the bathroom before heading to the table. A slew of girls came over and got pretty close. They were each looking to become a "groupie" for the night. I guess that you could say they were a good-looking bunch. Honestly nothing got me going anymore, except Aubrey. Nothing. Blake and Derek felt otherwise.

"Well hello, you look like a bad decision. Come with me." Derek said to a dark haired girl. She grinned excitedly and took his arm. Aubrey looked utterly repulsed.

"You need to share him sometimes, Aubrey." Blake teased.

"I will not share him with a bunch of skanky girls that have daddy issues. My thoughts on that alone would be enough to give you nightmares." She shook her head as if she was trying to shake the thought out of her head.

I chuckled and leaned down to kiss her. When Kevin was back, we were escorted over to the table. It was mayhem here tonight. Two fans even tried to trip Aubrey while we were making our way through the crowd. Luckily I had her hand, so she didn't fall. These girls were a whole new breed of crazy tonight. Aubrey was looking *seriously* pissed off. She looked at me and glared.

"What's the matter baby? Are you mad at me?" I suppressed a smile.

"I'm not mad at you. I'm mad at the situation you created." She pouted.

"The situation I created? I do nothing except show up and do my job. As a matter of fact, whenever I'm up on stage and I look out at the crowd you're everywhere. It's not my fault that your boyfriend also happens to be an extremely desirable rock star." I joked. "All I want to do right now is go back to our room and snuggle *you*."

I rubbed her shoulders until the first gaggle was escorted over. I knew how much she hated coming to these things because the girls were vicious to her. By vicious, I mean they were flat out nasty, horrible, brutal, monstrous and cruel to her. I felt guilty because she didn't have to be here, but I hated these things too and she made them tolerable. I also hated having to be away from her. I cringed when I saw the first girl come up to the table. It was Veronica. She was a bleach blonde groupie that had been pining after me for as long as I've been famous. She was also a witch. I thanked all that was holy that I never slept with her because lord knows she tried to deliver herself on a silver platter more than once.

"Hey boys." She purred.

She looked at Aubrey with venom in her eyes. I shuddered.

"Veronica." Blake said irritated.

Derek was too busy making out with his companion for the night to notice that she was even there. Kevin ignored her, so she came over and stood in front of me. She was appraising Aubrey as if she was competition.

"Are you a hipster or a hooker? I can't tell the difference." She spat.

Oh shit, this is going to get ugly!

"I'm neither, but you call that classy? The proper length of a skirt is two inches below your cellulite." Aubrey spat back.

"I can't believe that you're with someone that looks like her, Jake. She's just bleh! You could do so much better, like me." She pushed her tits together. I was getting ready to open my mouth when Aubrey glanced at me. I nodded for her to say whatever she wanted.

"You don't like me... that's a shame, I'll pencil in some time to cry later. Right now I'm busy enjoying life." Aubrey grabbed my hair and crashed her lips to mine. I liked jealous Aubrey. She pulled back with a smug look on her face. "Granny always says if someone hates you for no reason then you give that motherfucker a reason." She smirked.

"You're so pretty when you're mad." I teased.

"If I'm pretty when I'm mad, than I'm about to get fucking gorgeous!" She turned back to face Veronica.

"I'd take my anger out on your face, but I think genetics already did a pretty good job."

"Word on the street is that you're just a homely simpleton after Jake for his money."

I had to laugh at that one because that wasn't even close to the truth.

"Awe, you're spreading rumors about me? At least you found something to spread other than your legs."

Veronica huffed. I nodded to Brett who had her removed. I apologized to Aubrey and promised that I would make it up to her later. She was still seething when the next gaggle came over. At least they were a little tamer. They were also smart enough not to try anything and risk being tossed out. I signed CD after CD until they called a wrap. We clambered into the limo and headed back to the hotel. Derek still had his groupie in tow.

"Aubrey, those were some good comebacks tonight." Blake said.

"If you're looking for my comeback go wipe it off your mom's face." Derek said.

"My favorite position is called WOW. It's where I flip your mom over." Blake retorted.

"That's fucking hilarious!" Derek laughed.

"Boys are disgusting." Aubrey grumbled throwing her hands in the air.

~~~~~~

I kept my promise last night to make up for Veronica and ordered Aubrey the biggest brownie sundae that the hotel had to offer. She moaned the entire time, which led to me having to excuse myself to the bathroom for the "shits." This morning we were meeting everyone in the lobby for breakfast. Surprisingly, we got there first. Aubrey and I ordered waffles and bacon. Brett ordered eggs and sausage. Kevin came down next. He was always so laid back and easy going. Aubrey called him the Valium for the group. He said good morning to everyone and ordered his tofu scramble. Blake was next. He stumbled into the booth half awake. He ordered a coffee and put his head on the table. Derek was last. He showed up with a huge grin on his face. He was most likely up all night doing horrible things to corrupt the girl that he brought back to his room.

"Good night?" Blake mumbled to Derek.

"She told me she wanted a magical night with a rock star. So I fucked her and disappeared." Derek said.

Blake laughed, and Kevin scoffed.

"You found it offensive, I found it funny. That's why I'm happier than you." Derek said to Kevin.

"Acting like a dick won't make yours any bigger." Kevin said.

"I'm sorry my sense of humor offended you." Derek laughed.

"Alright, it's too early for all these insults." I reprimanded.

We spent the rest of the morning with a more friendly banter. We headed back to our rooms to gather our luggage. The whole band was flying with us to the next show in Biloxi, Mississippi. Aubrey warned them to be on their best behavior or she would make sure that the emergency exit accidentally opened. I was so crazy in love with her. I was looking forward to when the tour was over. I was hoping that we could have some downtime in LA to kick back and relax. Maybe I could take her to Arizona to meet Ron. I missed him a lot, and he wasn't getting any younger. He's been the only father figure that I've had in my life, and he's been an incredible one. He's the one that showed me how to be a man. I watched as Aubrey packed up her bag. She looked over and smiled at me.

I want to marry this girl. Period.

CHAPTER EIGHT

Alive & Out of Control

One Month Later…

Aubrey

The last month with Jake as my boyfriend has been beyond incredible. We were at the halfway point through the tour schedule. The tour has been sold out, and the shows have been amazing. Except for the meet and greets. I hate those. Today is Valentine's Day, and we just arrived in Houston. The show isn't until tomorrow, and I had huge plans for tonight. I was nervous as fuck, too. It felt awkward having a boyfriend for Valentine's Day. I haven't had one in so long that it's weird having one at all, but Jake was literally perfect. I don't think that I could have conjured up a better guy if I tried. He's always so kind and considerate. He does little things that most guys wouldn't even think of. For instance, if he goes to buy a soda he buys me a candy bar just because he knows it will make me smile. After all, chocolate is the way to a girl's heart.

He was beyond proud to show me off to everyone once we made it official. Even when I wasn't looking my best he was always saying, "That's my girlfriend!" We both got the stomach virus in Michigan and made it three disgusting days without killing each other. He's even said some pretty brazen stuff in his interviews lately. He mentioned the "M" word on more than one occasion. Once the picture of my ring hit the press the allegations of a secret engagement were flying. My mom, of course, is over the moon with excitement. My dad and Jake have some male bonding thing going on. They talk like a couple girls every time I call. They said being men they have to stick together.

Jake was finishing checking us in at the Granduca Hotel. The clerk handed him the key card, and we headed up to our suite. I was suddenly really anxious. What if I did something wrong? I've been having Piper coach me for the past two weeks ever since I made the decision. Each step was a step closer to losing my v-card. I was ready. I was *beyond* ready. Frankly, I think if I had to wait any longer that I was going to spontaneously combust.

He put the key card into the door and pushed down the handle. I sucked in a deep breath. As soon as we were over the threshold Jake went to put the luggage down. He looked especially yummy today, and I was fresh out of willpower. He had on a pair of low-rise, faded, ripped jeans and a tight, white t-shirt that showcased his broad upper shoulders. I looked at him and bit my lip. I wore a wrap dress for this reason. I waited for him to turn his back before I deftly undid the tie. I knew that he'd seen me scantily clad before, but we've never been completely naked in front of each other. I let the dress pool at my feet but left my wedges on. I had on a red lace bra and panty set. He turned and looked at me with an open mouth.

"Happy Valentine's Day." I beamed.

"Yes, it is. You look ravishing."

I blushed as he took a step toward me. He was looking at me with total admiration making me feel sexy and comfortable. He loved me despite my scars, inside and out.

"I'm ready. I know that you said we could talk about it, but I don't want to talk… I want to do!" I purred.

"Are you sure?" He choked.

"I'm positive. I didn't want you to know because I just want it to happen naturally."

I reached up my fingers and tugged them through his hair pulling his face down to mine. I pushed him back towards the bedroom. He longingly looked at me with complete adoration making my pulse speed up. He slowly unhooked my bra and slid it down my arms. He reached a hand out and rubbed his thumb over my already sensitive nipple. I gasped. He lowered his head and took the other one in his mouth, sucking gently. I tossed my head back and relished in the feeling of him touching me. I was tugging at his shirt trying to get it over his head, but he refused to pull away. I grabbed a handful of hair until he pulled away with a pop.

He smirked at me happily. I was already soaked, and he barely did anything yet.

I tossed his shirt on the floor and masterly undid his belt. I slowly undid the zipper to his jeans and pushed them down his long legs. Jake Junior was bobbing in my face. I stuck my tongue out and swiped it against the thick head, he moaned loudly. I seductively looked up at him as I took him into my mouth. I ran my tongue underneath and felt the piercings. There were four of them, a Jacob's ladder. He pulled me away and eased me back onto the bed. I pouted, but then I saw the fire in his eyes. He turned to his side so that we were opposite each other. I took him back in my mouth as he lowered his face. I wrapped my hand around the base of his thick cock and started pumping. He swiped his tongue across my aching clit, and I cried out at the sensation of it.

"You have no idea how long I've been wanting to do this for." He moaned.

I wanted to be embarrassed, but I was too enamored by him to feel even slightly awkward. Blood was pounding in my eardrums as I took the length of him further in my mouth. He lowered his head and started slowly running his tongue back and forth. I was right there, when he pulled away. He lay back on the bed and pulled me on top of him. I kissed him hard and possessive tasting myself on his tongue. He was gently rubbing me with his hand. He added a finger and gently rocked in and out, then added another. I felt like I was going to explode when he abruptly pulled out.

"I wanna feel it Aubrey. I *need* to feel it. Do you want me to wear a condom?" He stammered.

I shook my head no. "I started the pill a month ago, and they said that I was good to go. I didn't want anything between us."

I looked at Jake Junior and worried if it would even fit.

"I want you on top, baby. I want this way too badly. I don't trust myself not to go hard and fast. Take my hands and move how you want. It's going to hurt, I'm sorry." He said in a rush.

He looked pained, and it just made me want him more.

I lined him up and slowly lowered myself down. My heartbeat echoed thunderously behind my ribcage. I felt as his swollen head slide in. It felt so good. I lowered myself a little more until I knew it was the breaking point. I squeezed his hands and slid the rest of the way down until he filled me completely. It hurt, but it wasn't anything unbearable.

"Let your body get acclimated before you start moving. Go real slow." He whispered through gritted teeth.

I lifted up slightly and moved back and forth a couple times. It was exactly where I needed the pressure. I felt my release coming like a freight train. Jake moved his hands and teased my nipples.

"Look at me Aubrey. I want to see your face when you come."

I looked down at him filling me. It was infuriatingly sexy. The next moment I was boneless and floating. My muscles were pulsing hard around him, holding him in a vice-like grip. I couldn't hold myself up anymore, so I leaned onto his chest. He moved so that he was on top. He moved in and out slowly, kissing my lips, my face, my neck.

"Aubrey, you feel like Heaven. I could forget the whole fucking world at this moment and never look back."

He started picking up the pace a little, and I felt him start to thicken. *It hurt so good.* I felt the pressure of another orgasm start to brim at the surface. I could feel the piercings each time that he would move in or out. I felt his thick cock start throbbing, filling me. Spots blurred my vision. I dug my nails into his shoulder blades and cried out his name.

He leaned down and kissed me. "I love you Aubrey."

"I love you too."

I had sex for the first time, and it was wonderful, magnificent, sensational...

Jake

I was lying next to Aubrey brushing the hair out of her face. I can't believe that we just had sex for the first time. I swear it was the single best moment of my life. I couldn't believe that I was her first. I was beyond humbled she trusted me that much. She let her inhibitions fly, and it was so damn sexy. Just thinking about her gliding up and down my cock was making me painfully hard. It was too soon to go again. She was probably going to need to take a couple days off to recover. I started thinking of anything that I could, in an effort to distract myself. My thoughts turned to the show tomorrow. It was our biggest venue yet, and it was outdoors. I pulled her close and cradled her in my arms.

I was so comfortable when my stomach growled. Shit! I realized that we completely missed lunch. I asked Aubrey if she wanted to go out since it was Valentine's Day. She said that she just wanted to eat in, and I was more than okay with that. I picked up the phone and ordered room service. I ordered us a romantic feast consisting of a plate of nachos, steak fajitas and a banana split. I collected my shirt from the bed and pulled it over her head hoping that it would help, it didn't. It actually made it worse. She smiled brightly. *I wanna marry this girl.* I found myself thinking that a lot lately, at least a half dozen times a day.

Now that I knew what it was like to have something other than meaningless sex I was ruined. It was probably all I was going to want all day long. I wasn't kidding when I said that I could forget the entire world when I was inside her. It was as if my body was transported to another realm. When our food arrived we curled up on the couch and watched American Horror Story re-runs. I continuously asked if she was feeling okay. I knew I was bigger than average, and I was genuinely worried that I hurt her. Maybe I should have taken my piercings out the first time. I berated myself over and over. Aubrey could tell because she sat up and looked at me angrily.

"I'm fine, will you stop chastising yourself. I know that's exactly what you're doing. I'm not made of glass!"

"Sorry." I said looking at the floor.

"I knew exactly what to expect. Other than the piercings, those were just an added bonus." She paused as if she were remembering. They hurt like fuck when I got them, but now that I knew they brought her pleasure it made the pain totally worth it. "I knew that I would feel sore after, but it's a good sore. So cut the shit, Parker!"

"Yes ma'am." I kissed her hair and pulled her closer.

We spent the rest of the night relaxing before going to bed. I pulled her close to me and managed to drift off. The next day when we woke up we had to scramble to get to the venue. It was an all day thing, and we were doing three different sets throughout the day. I showered and spiked my hair. I needed to look every bit the rock star today. I grabbed a pair of shorts since it was abnormally warm today, and threw on my sneakers. I picked out the shirt that she bought me in St. Louis that said, 'I wrote you a song, it's called go fuck yourself.' Aubrey came out in a pair of black shorts and a tight gray t-shirt with her chucks. Her hair was in fucking pigtails! She winked devilishly at me. *That bitch!* I grabbed her and tossed her over my shoulder not trusting my restraint to be alone with her.

Brett was waiting for us to meet the rest of the guys in the lobby. A small crowd had assembled around them. I waved to everyone, but kept walking and climbed into the car. We arrived at the venue and went to the tent that had been set up for the musicians. I was whispering to Aubrey when my arch nemesis, Ian Voss, came over. She was aware of our ongoing feud and scoffed when she saw him. He was a shit stain.

"Jake Parker." He looked at me, then Aubrey. "You must be Jake's new girlfriend. I'm Ian Voss, lead singer of Blood to Bleed. I'm sure you've heard of us. We're much bigger than your boyfriends shit band." He said condescendingly.

"Nope. Sorry, can't say I have." She spat. "But I'm sure you've heard the phrase getting into her pants? I think you took it too literally."

I looked to see what she was talking about. He was in skinny jeans. I smiled and suppressed a laugh.

"How about I give you something for that smart mouth?" He put his hand on his junk and took a step toward her. Brett was on high alert, but just stood at the ready.

"Sorry, but my mom says never to put small things in my mouth." She shot back.

I fucking love this girl!

"Ouch. Well, if you get tired of hanging with the bottom feeders come find me."

Aubrey looked enraged. She smacked him in the face.

"Did you see that? She just slapped me." He cried.

"I didn't slap you. I gave you a high five, and you missed." She grabbed my hand and pulled me away.

"That was epic and so fucking hot!" I cooed.

I pulled her into an empty room and kissed her passionately. She lowered her hand and grabbed onto my hard cock. I moaned loudly from her touch. I was never much into exhibitionism, but with Aubrey it didn't matter where I was. I knew that she was still sore from last night, but I had to have her. I moved her shorts over and rubbed her gently waiting for her to tell me to stop. Instead of telling me to stop she unzipped me so that I sprang free. She moved back to sit on the edge of the table. She wrapped her long, sexy legs around my waist and pulled me until I was pressed up against her hot, wet heat. I slowly sank balls deep into her tight pussy. She wrapped her arms around my neck and pulled me down to kiss her. I thrust in and out carefully trying not to hurt her anymore than she already was. I swallowed her moan and felt her convulse around me. I loved the little sound she made when she was done. My balls instantly tightened, and I spilled myself into her with a raspy moan. I stayed where I was for another minute before pulling out. I never wanted to leave.

She smiled shyly.

"I can't believe we just did that." She giggled.

"Stop being so damn sexy and it won't happen. Though I don't think it's possible." I kissed her. "I love you, baby."

"I love you too."

I helped her up and made sure that we both looked presentable. I laced our fingers together, and we walked back into the main part of the tent. Brett was standing outside the door with a smirk on his face. He kept his mouth shut and followed me around until it was time to get ready for our set. Blake and Derek had picked up their groupies for the day, and Kevin was sitting on a stool tuning his guitar. I kissed Aubrey and walked out onto the stage.

The crowd started chanting as soon as we were in view. "Ransom, Ransom, Ransom."

"Houston! How the fuck are we today? It's hotter than Satan's nutsack out here today!" I yelled into the mic.

They cheered back, and Blake broke into the beginning cords of Ransom. I jumped around enthusiastically. It probably had something to do with the quickie that Aubrey just gave me. I might have to consider asking her to make that a preshow ritual. I was beyond pumped. Four songs in the extreme heat started to get to me, and I felt myself starting to wan. I put the mic back into the stand and exited the stage. I was proud of our set. I grabbed Aubrey's hand and led her back to the room that had finally been set up in the tent for the band. I was beyond thankful for the cool air the fans were giving off. I grabbed a bottle of water from the ice bed and pulled Aubrey on my lap. I wasn't fond of either of the groupies that Blake and Derek picked up.

We hung out with the guys in the tent until we got called for the next set. When we exited the tent, I noticed that it was already starting to get dark out. The atmosphere had changed; it was electric. I kissed Aubrey and told her that I loved her. She grinned happily and slapped my ass as I took the stage. We broke into our first song. It was hard to see anything with the lights glaring in my eyes. The lighting in this place was shit. I was literally being "blinded by the light." I still made sure to put in 110%, just like every show. I finished the set and tossed my sweaty towel out into the crowd. Thankfully we only had one set left.

When I walked off stage I looked for Aubrey, but she wasn't standing where I left her. I asked Brett where she went, and he said that she went to go get some food. I started berating him for letting her go alone, but I knew his first priority was my protection, especially at a venue like this. I refused to leave until she came back because I didn't want to get separated and worry about her trying to find me. Five more minutes passed, and I was starting to freak out. I grabbed the guys and asked them to please go and look for her. Without a second thought, they all went and started looking. Ten minutes later I had Brett get event security involved. They put out a BOLO, but they said there wasn't really anything else that they could do.

I was done sitting around. I demanded that someone from security stay here while I went out looking myself. I left specific instructions that if she came back they were to call me that instant. I checked all the food places and bathrooms. I came up empty. I was coming out of the last set of bathrooms and saw that Brett was on the phone yelling. He pulled me into a football tuck and moved me as quickly as he could. I tried to fight him. I wanted to know what the fuck was going on. We didn't stop until we reached the parking lot.

There was Aubrey's lifeless body sprawled out on the concrete.

My heart stopped, and I felt my knees give out. Brett caught me and said that the police were on their way. EMT's were already there working on her, but she wasn't fucking moving. I kept trying to pull away from him. Aubrey needed me. He finally let me go, and I went and kneeled next to her. I rubbed my hand over her head. It was wet. I lifted it and saw it was covered in blood.

"Pulse is normal. So is BP." One of the EMT's called. He looked at me. "Do you know her?"

"She's my girlfriend. Her name is Aubrey." I choked out.

"She should be fine. We need to get her transported to the hospital so that she can be looked over by a doctor. You can ride with us if you want."

I nodded. Brett looked unhappy, but said he would meet us there. I wasn't leaving her, no matter what. They loaded the stretcher into the ambulance and slammed the door shut. The siren sounded and off we went. I took her hand in mine.

"Aubrey, can you hear me? You're going to be okay, baby." I whispered.

It took us fifteen minutes to get to the hospital. As soon as we walked in through the emergency entrance I was spotted. It looked like a fifteen-year old girl with a broken arm. She started screaming, and I wished that I thought to bring a hoodie. A nurse came rushing over to the girl to see what the problem was. I saw recognition flash across her face. She instantly ran over and ushered us to a room. A doctor came in and immediately started working on assessing Aubrey. My stomach was in my throat as I watched helplessly. They said that they needed to take her for some scans and that I could wait here until they came back. As soon as she was out of the room I dropped my head into my hands and cried. I cried like I've never cried in my life. I felt a hand on my shoulder and looked up to see Brett and the guys. Kevin kneeled in front of me and pulled me into a very unmanly hug.

Brett said that police were on the scene and questioning concertgoers, but so far no one saw anything. There's no reason that she would have ended up in a fucking parking lot. She went for food. We weren't fighting so she wouldn't have been trying to get away from me. Blake and Derek pulled over some chairs and asked me if I needed anything. The only thing that I needed was for Aubrey to be okay. We waited for over an hour and a half before a doctor finally came in. He said that she had a bad concussion, and there was swelling to the brain, but it didn't appear that anything was broken. He said that they needed to put her into a medically induced coma until the swelling went down to prevent further damage. They were admitting her into the ICU for observation. As soon as the doctor left some bitchy woman came in looking for insurance information. I didn't know where Aubrey's wallet was, but I knew she had insurance. I told the lady that, and she looked at me like I was an asshole. I told her that she could put my credit card on file, which earned a good laugh. *What the fuck!*

"Listen lady, I know you think I look like a scumbag, I'm not. I promise you I have enough money to add an entire wing to this hospital. Take the credit card and put it on file." I pushed the credit card back to her.

The nurse from earlier came over and told the woman that I could afford whatever treatment necessary. She scoffed and finally took my card. She handed it back to me, and I went to go find the ICU. I set up a bedside vigil and pulled my phone out to call her parents. Tim answered on the first ring.

"Hey kid, how's it going in Texas?" He chirped.

"Tim, Aubrey's been in some kind of accident. No one knows what happened. I was on stage and she went to go get food. Security found her in the parking lot unconscious. We're at the hospital now." I said in a rush.

"Is she going to be okay?" He stuttered.

"I think so. They had to put her in an induced coma because of a concussion. Other than that, they said she seems to be fine." I faltered.

"Fuck." He cried.

"Can you get here?" I asked.

"What kind of moronic question is that? Of course I can, I own my own airline. We're leaving now."

I hung up the phone and took her small hand in mine. I hated that they felt cold. The nurse said that it was because of the IV fluid, but I still didn't like it. Her face was covered in dried blood and dirt. I stood and went to the sink. I ran a couple of towels under warm water and rubbed in a little soap. I gently cleaned her face off and threw the towels in the garbage. I sat back down in the chair and told the guys to go back to the hotel. I just wanted to be alone right now. Brett was standing outside the door keeping watch.

I watched her chest rise up and down until exhaustion kicked in. I put my head on the bed and closed my eyes. I was startled awake when I felt a hand on my shoulder. Aubrey's hand was still in mine. I lifted my head to see Tim, Caroline and Granny Jean standing in the room. I rubbed my free hand over my face refusing to let go of Aubrey for a second.

"Hey, sweetheart." Caroline said kissing my head. "Any news?"

"Nothing's changed since I called." I rubbed my tired eyes.

I stood up so that Caroline could take my seat and sat next to Aubrey on the bed. Tim looked near tears. It was tearing me apart. Granny Jean kissed Aubrey's head and grabbed me by the arm yanking me back to my feet.

"You, up!" She demanded. "We're going to get some fresh air, and I need a smoke."

I wanted to protest, but there was no protesting against her. I already knew that. She hooked her arm in mine and walked out the door. Brett followed closely behind as we walked out the front doors of the hospital. We stood off to the side as Granny sifted through her bag and produced her Lucky Strikes. She lit up and blew out a plume of smoke.

"Relax, will ya. She's going to be fine. You're going to go prematurely gray if you keep this shit up." She scolded. "Listen Jake, you kids are young, and you have your entire lives ahead of you. It was obviously an accident. They happen, and there's nothing you can do about it. We all have dues to pay in this life. The only thing that you can do is try not to fuck up your make-up in the trenches. Look at me." She motioned to herself with her cigarette. "I'm old. I know things. When George died all I got was a bad liver and a broken heart. I still look good because I don't worry about shit that I have no control over." She teased.

The way she put it made sense. As much as I hated to admit it, she was right. We all had dues to pay. Except, I would gladly take both mine, and Aubrey's.

"I know." I acknowledged.

"Now we're going to go back in there and get you something eat. Then you're going to pull your big boy pants up and act like a man. My granddaughter needs her strapping boyfriend to be strong and not act like a pussy."

She snubbed out her cigarette and took my hand. I looked at her and wanted to smile. If there was such a thing as a walking contradiction it was Granny Jean. We headed to the cafeteria. I picked out an assortment of things that didn't need to be refrigerated. I didn't want to have to leave her again. I grabbed a couple bags of pretzels, some fruit and an armful of bottled water. I was anxious to get back to Aubrey. I paid and started back to ICU. I asked Brett to call and get Aubrey's family put up at the hotel across the street. Granny told him to make sure that she got a room with a balcony so she could smoke. When we got back, I could tell there was still no change in her condition. I grabbed another chair for Granny Jean and sat across from Tim and Caroline. My heart was breaking for them. I looked at Tim.

"I asked Brett to make arrangements at the hotel across the street for you guys. If you need anything just let me know."

"Thanks Jake." Tim nodded.

"Do you happen to have Aubrey's insurance information? I don't know what happened to her wallet. When we checked in I gave them my credit card to keep on file, but if you have it on hand we can get that beast of a woman off my back."

"I'll call and get it." Caroline said picking up her purse.

"I'll go change the payment information." Tim started to stand up.

"You will not." I argued. "Listen, I don't care if I have to pay for the entire thing. I was just mentioning it, in case you have the information handy. You should know by now that money means nothing to me. Aubrey means *everything* to me. Sure I have enough of it, but I want to take care of her. You've done an amazing job of that for the last twenty-three years, it's my turn."

Tim just looked at me in shock.

"Sorry, I didn't mean to snap at you like that. I just want her to wake up." I apologized and rubbed my face with my hands.

"I know, son." He walked over and clapped my shoulder.

I decided that even though I didn't want to leave I needed to. I needed to calm down. The longer I sat here the harder it was getting. I knew as long as they were here that Aubrey wouldn't be alone. I told them that I would be right back and grabbed Brett. We headed back to the hotel so I could shower and change. We drove in total silence. As soon as he pulled into the entrance I practically sprinted to our room and jumped in the shower. I dug a hat out of my bag not wanting to waste ten minutes perfecting my hair. I grabbed a small bag of Aubrey's and put some things in it that she might want when she got up. I tossed the pink floral bag over my shoulder like a champ and headed out the door. Brett was laughing, and I told him to shut the fuck up.

We were back at the hospital in less than an hour. I walked back into the room, and they all looked exhausted. I told them to go get something to eat and get settled at the hotel. I promised that I would call if there were any changes in Aubrey's condition. After they left I had Brett call the label and tell them to reschedule the next two weeks of tour dates. There was no way in hell that I was leaving Texas without Aubrey.

The days were blurring together. The next day there was no change. The day after, no change. On the third day of Aubrey being in a coma, she finally started coming around. Her eyelids were fluttering, and she was starting to mumble a little. I kept a watchful eye on her for any clue that she was going to wake up. The minutes ticked by like hours. The hours seemed like days. Until at 5:42, I felt her squeeze my hand. I was out of my chair so fast it fell backwards with a crash. Brett peeked into the room to make sure everything was okay. Tim and Caroline had just left to get something to eat, and Granny mostly stayed at the hotel. It was just me, myself and I. Her beautiful brown eyes opened and peered into mine. I could sense her anxiety.

"Baby, it's okay. You're okay." I cooed moving close to her.

I hit the button and called for the nurse. She came breezing in a couple moments later with the doctor in tow. I refused to let go of Aubrey's hand. The doctor checked her pupils and started asking her basic questions. She didn't really remember what happened.

"I remember going to get something to snack on because I wasn't feeling well from the heat. Someone grabbed me from behind and pulled me away. I tried to struggle, but it was too crowded. They hit me in the head and I remember them taking my ring. That's all I remember." She was getting frustrated. I shook my head at the doctor to let him know that it was enough questioning for now.

I looked down at her left hand and saw that the ring I gave her was missing. I must really be losing it. *How the hell did I miss that?* I made a mental note to send out Brett to get a replacement. There had to be a Cartier in Houston, right? I was just relieved that she was awake and talking. The doctor said that it was okay for her to have something light to eat, but she really needed to rest. I called Brett in and gave him orders to get Aubrey food and a replacement ring. I put my hand on the side of her face and lightly kissed her lips. They were dry, but I didn't care.

"You gave us all quite the scare, baby. Your mom and dad are here. So is Granny Jean. I'll call and let them know you're awake."

She held a hand up.

"Just come hold me for a minute. I missed you." She whispered.

"I missed you too. So much."

She scooted over so that I could climb into bed next to her. She leaned over and put her head on my shoulder and her arm around my stomach.

"I dreamed about you." I raised an eyebrow. "Actually, I dreamed that we had a baby. I never thought that I wanted kids. But, after seeing you with our baby I want at least three." She teased. My heart swelled. A baby with Aubrey would be amazing. I bet she would look fantastic pregnant.

"A baby, huh? I'll give you a football team if you want. I just want you to be happy." I leaned down and kissed the top of her head.

"I know. You make me happy." She smiled.

"You're going to need to give a statement to police. It can wait until after you eat and see your parents."

Brett came back a little while later with some food and a small red bag. I took the red bag and set it aside. I pulled everything out and set it up on the tray table. He got lemonade, soup and grilled cheese. I fed her bites of the broccoli cheddar soup. When she finished, I called Tim to let them know that she was up. They were on their way, but Granny Jean beat them over. Brett was going to let the police know she was awake. Granny stormed into the room.

"Bran muffin, you look like hell."

"Thanks so much, Granny." Aubrey said rolling her eyes.

"Glad to see you're back to your smart-ass self. I was worried when you hit your head that you'd become a regular." She teased.

I laughed. Tim and Caroline breezed into the room a couple minutes later. I got up to move off the bed, but Aubrey dug her nails into my leg. I looked quizzically at her. She shrugged and gave me a half smile. They came over and hugged her tightly. She assured them that she was fine, just a little achy. They visited until the cops showed up. They found her wallet in a garbage can and brought the contents from it. They were keeping the actual wallet hoping to pull a print and get a match. They questioned her about what happened and informed us that there were no surveillance cameras for them to cross check. Then they asked about the missing ring in question. I told them since it made the press that anyone could have known about it, and how much it cost. They asked about the price, and I told them it was just under fifty thousand. The cop looked at me dumbstruck. I didn't tell them that I just bought a replica. I could only imagine the look they would have given me then. I explained to them that I was in love and that *nothing* was too good for my girl. They left and told us that they would be in touch.

Aubrey wanted to shower, so I called for the nurse again. She said it was fine, but for her to be careful because she was going to be weak. I helped her out of bed and over to the bathroom. I untied the hospital gown and looked at the bruise that took up most of her side. She must have gotten it when she fell. I helped her into the shower and washed her hair for her. When she was done, I wrapped her in a towel and carried her back to the bed. I fished out a clean pair of underwear from the bag that I brought. She cocked an eyebrow at me, and it was my turn to shrug. I pulled out her hairbrush too. I helped her get into a fresh hospital gown and brushed her hair. She looked tired, so I told her to sleep. As I was watching her, I had an idea. Once she was sleeping I went into the hallway to talk to Brett. I asked the doctor when the discharge would be. He said as long as she was feeling up to it that she could go home tomorrow. I had Brett make all the necessary arrangements and went back to lay with Aubrey.

Aubrey

I opened my eyes and felt my head throbbing. Jake was still sleeping next to me, which was a first since he was always awake before me. If I didn't know better, I would have sworn he was a supernatural or something since he barely slept and yet still had more energy than anyone I knew. I wanted to get out of here and sleep in a normal bed that didn't smell like disinfectant. I tried to move so I could to get up to go to the bathroom, but Jake opened his eyes. He insisted on helping me, and I reluctantly let him, knowing fighting was futile.

My parents came with breakfast sandwiches and to say goodbye. They were going home today since I was being released.

My mom kissed my cheek. My dad hugged me tightly and told Jake to take care of me. Jake went back into my bag and pulled out a pair of sweat pants and a hoodie for me to change into. I pulled my hair up in a hair elastic and piled it on the top of my head. He insisted on helping me get dressed. I may as well have been an invalid as far as he was concerned. He even tied my shoes. The nurse came in and went over the discharge instructions. Then she wished us a great trip. *Trip?* I looked at Jake.

"We're going to LA for some R&R." He looked at me intently. "Everything is already in the car. We just have to get to the airport." he grinned. "You'll get to see how your better half lives."

I climbed into the wheelchair for the mandatory ride. Once we were out the doors he helped me up, and we climbed into the waiting SUV. There were a couple paparazzi waiting to snap a picture, but overall we got away unscathed. We went directly to the airport and boarded the plane. We arrived in LA at three in the afternoon. Brett said that it was business as usual, and he wasn't taking any risks. He walked off the plane and checked the car and the surrounding area. Once he came back with the all clear we exited the plane. We drove to Jake's house in California traffic. I decided that if I lived here I wouldn't leave the house, unless I could walk.

We pulled up to a house on the ocean. Brett punched in a series of numbers into a keypad, and the gate swung open. Jake was grinning like the Cheshire cat. He climbed out and held his hand out. Jake told Brett to go home. He said could come back tomorrow, but not before he called. He fished his keys out of his pocket and unlocked the door pushing it open. He walked over to the wall and quickly shut off the alarm. The house smelled like the beach. As soon as the bags were inside he locked the door and reset the alarm. There were no walls on the inside, and the entire back of the house was glass. It was painted in varying shades of light blues and greens. It was filled with high-end electronics. There was a spiral staircase off in the corner. I looked at it in awe. Ever since I was little I always wanted a spiral staircase. I used to beg my dad to build me one. It was impossible since we lived in a single story ranch. He said it led up to his room. He took my hand and led me over.

I took the stairs up to Jake's room. The entire room was painted in ocean blue and white. His furniture was made of driftwood. He had a king sized bed in the middle of the room facing the ocean. I walked over to the sliding door that led to a balcony. He unlocked it and slid the door open. There were two turquoise chairs and an umbrella strategically placed on the white plank boards. I felt the warm breeze off the ocean across my face. I breathed in the salty air. I walked over to his bed and flopped down. It was comfortable and smelled like him. He came and sat on the bed next to me. I was already feeling much better.

"What do you think?" He asked.

"I think I never want to leave." I told him.

"I was kind of hoping that you would say that." He kissed me gently.

He leaned over and grabbed the remote to switch on the TV. He ordered us some Chinese take-out and told me we would have to go food shopping tomorrow. He also said that we could go to the beach and the hot tub. I sulked and told him I wanted to go in the hot tub now. I won. After dinner, we were in the hot tub soaking away. I slipped across and straddled his lap. I brushed my lips against his. He tried to protest, but I wasn't having it.

"I missed you." I pouted my bottom lip.

"Aubrey, you were just in a coma for three days."

"Exactly, which means I was without this for three whole days." I grabbed his crotch and massaged gently. "I'm feeling slighted." I pouted.

"Baby, my restraint isn't that good. Come on." He pleaded, but I persisted.

I slipped out of my bottoms and pushed his down. I slowly slid down onto him. He leaned his head back, and I bit his neck gently. We made love by the stars, and I relished in every moment of it. Later when we were in bed, I remembered something and mildly freaked out.

"Jake, you're going to be so mad at me." I cried.

He looked slightly freaked out. "What's the matter baby?"

"I haven't been taking my pill, and we just had sex."

He let out a deep breath. "Yeah, so?"

"So, I could get pregnant." As if it wasn't blatantly obvious.

"You said in your dream that we had a baby. It'll just happen sooner if that's the case." He shrugged like it was no big deal.

"You're not even upset? I wouldn't want you to feel trapped." Gah, how could I have been so stupid.

"It would throw my other plans off a little… but I would still be happy about it. And woman please, I'm hoping you'll trap me so I can have you forever. Fuck it," He reached over to the nightstand and pulled something out. "I had this whole smooth thing planned, but I don't want to wait anymore. I got you replacement."

He pulled out a red Cartier box and dropped to one knee. He opened the lid and nestled in the cream colored velvet was an exact replica of the ring that was stolen.

"Aubrey Jean Thompson, you are and will always be my better half. You're my smart-ass, eye-rolling partner in crime. The day I met you, was the day I learned what it was like to breathe. You make everything in my world better, and I want nothing more than to spend my life being lost in you. I wish I could give you everything, but for now I hope this ring is enough. Will you marry me?"

I looked down at Jake and was completely overcome with emotion. Here he was, pouring his heart out proposing and I was blubbering like an idiot. I threw my arms around him and knocked him on his ass.

"Yes!" I shrieked. "Yes, Jake Parker. I will marry you."

"Thank God! I love you, baby."

"I love you too."

He slid the ring on my finger, and we had round two.

CHAPTER NINE

Partner In Crime

I woke up the next morning with the sun shining through the windows. I looked down at my hand where my engagement ring was and smiled happily. I heard music coming from downstairs and went to go find Jake. I got out of bed and padded down the spiral staircase. The music was blaring. It was Lit's 'Partner in Crime.' *How fitting...* Jake was sitting at the dining room table on his laptop. He didn't notice me, so I snuck around and yelled, "Boo!" He jumped, and I laughed. He put his arm out and kissed my ring.

"Good morning, my beautiful fiancée."

"Hey handsome."

"Do you like dragons?"

"Random question, but yeah I guess they're cute. Why?"

"'Cause I'm gonna be dragging my balls across your face later. Get it?" He laughed.

I smacked him in the shoulder.

"That's foul Jake Parker." I scolded playfully.

"You love me anyway."

"I love you with all my heart." I feigned dramatically.

"I love every bone in your body, especially mine." He winked.

"Yeah, well I want an Australian kiss. It's like a French kiss, but down under." I smirked.

"Nice!" He hooted.

"Someone woke up on the perverted side of the bed today." I teased.

"It's just that we're engaged now and all that baby talk last night. Its got me excited. I've been up most of the morning doing research."

"Jake, I just said it was a possibility, not that we're going to start actively trying."

"What if I want to start actively trying? Are you ready? 'Cause baby I was born ready." He smirked.

"Oh great, I've created a monster! Let me just think about it, okay? I haven't actually thought about anything other than the overall possibility."

He stood up and kissed my nose. He looked content and so fucking hot. I decided to go shower so we could go food shopping because if I stood there any longer we weren't going to get anything done today. I dressed in jeans and a pink t-shirt that said, "Don't cry, it's only rock & roll." Jake was standing at the island in the kitchen making a list. I loved his kitchen here and couldn't wait to cook in it. He had all sleek, black cabinets with stainless steel appliances and pale, granite countertops. The walls were painted a bright green and he had these really neat vintage lights hanging from the ceiling. I looked at the list that he was compiling.

Milk

Bread

Juice

Prenatal Vitamins

Heaven help me! I cocked an eyebrow, and he got all red. He grabbed my hand and led me to the garage. We headed to a black Range Rover. I noticed that there was a motorcycle next to it. He never mentioned a bike before. He told me it was a must living here, especially with the traffic. We got in the car and headed to the store. We called my parents on the way. My mom was ecstatic, and it turned out Jake had already asked my dad, so he knew it was coming.

"Did you tell her what I said when you asked me?" My dad asked.

"I haven't had a chance yet." He laughed.

"Well princess when he came to me and asked for your hand I asked him what was wrong with the rest of you!"

I started cracking up. That line was very much my dad.

Next, we called Granny Jean. The first thing she asked is if I was knocked up. Jake said not yet, but hung up with the promise of making her a great-grandma sooner rather than later. We went into the store and loaded the cart with all sorts of stuff, including the damn vitamins. He protested on the way here that if I were indeed pregnant from last night it would be particularly beneficial for me to be getting folic acid. I argued that the chances were slim, but gave in to appease him. I found myself doing that a lot lately, which was very unlike my normal personality. We paid and headed to the car. The paparazzi were there snapping pictures. Jake wrapped his arm around me and threw them a bone.

"I would like to introduce you to my *fiancée*, Aubrey." He beamed proudly.

He opened up the car door and helped me inside. It was going to be a media circus once word spread. He called his publicist and told her to put out a press release. I listened while he was on the phone.

"No, I want you to say, 'Imagine finding someone who understood even the dustiest corners in your fucked up soul. That's Aubrey.'" He looked at me and smiled. "I don't care, that's what I want it to say." He hung up the phone. "I just want to go somewhere really high, and scream I love you at the top of my lungs." He grinned excitedly.

I giggled like a stupid schoolgirl. What was happening to me? We got back to the house and started putting groceries away. I was reaching up to put something in the pantry. He came up behind me and wrapped his arms around me.

"My magic watch tells me you're not wearing any panties." He ran his fingers across the hem of my pants. "Oh you are. I must be running fifteen minutes too fast."

He tossed me over his shoulder and carried me upstairs. He placed me down gently on the bed and leaned in to kiss me.

"I wanna get lost in you." He whispered.

We spent the entire afternoon 'getting lost'. When it was close to dinnertime, I decided to cook something. Chances are we'll end up ravishing each other, and it will get burned, but it's the thought that counts. I was sprinkling the mozzarella cheese over the ziti to put it in the oven when my phone rang. It was Piper.

Shit, I forgot to call her!

"Hey Pipsqueak." I said putting dinner in the oven.

"Don't Pipsqueak me. Holy crap, you're freaking engaged!"

"I know. I'm sorry I didn't call. We've been, um, busy… Yeah, busy."

"Busy my ass. The only thing you've been busy at is screwing each other's brains out."

"Maybe." I teased.

"I'm happy for you Bean. After everything that fuckwad did to you, it's about time that you found happiness. It doesn't hurt that it's with Jake Parker either. On an off subject did you hear Jeremy moved to LA?"

"No." I gasped.

"Your dad didn't say anything? I'm pretty sure even Jake knows."

I felt my heart rate start to speed up.

"Let me call you back." I clicked off without saying goodbye. I went to go find Jake. He was sitting out on the patio on his laptop. He was scrolling through all the news surrounding our engagement. He looked up, and I glared angrily at him.

"What's the matter baby?" He asked suspiciously.

"Don't baby me. You've been talking to my dad about Jeremy? He moved to LA!" I yelled.

"Yeah? I've been trying to keep a closer eye on things with him. I know he's in LA. He's on the other side, and my address isn't listed." He defended.

"And you didn't think I was privy to this information?" I roared.

"Baby, it brings up bad memories. So, to answer your question, no." He said calmly.

I was so angry he kept something like that from me. I stormed off. Obviously, they saw Jeremy as more of a threat than I originally thought. I grabbed his keys from the bowl on the counter and headed to the garage. I started the car and threw it into reverse and hit the button for the gate. I drove it like I stole it. I didn't have a clue where I was going, and I didn't care either. I drove around aimlessly until I came to an overlook. I pulled in and got out to sit on the hood of the car. I pulled my knees to my chest and watched as the sun was starting to set. The lights of the city illuminated the sky. I heard a loud noise off in the distance. It grew closer and closer. A black bike pulled next to the Range Rover. I knew it was Jake.

"I have GPS tracking on all my vehicles." He smirked.

"That's nice. I don't want to see you right now." I snapped.

"Come on, don't be like this." He pleaded.

"Like what? It should have been my choice to say whether or not I wanted to know." I yelled.

I looked at him and knew that I was going to have a hard time keeping my resolve. He had on a black motorcycle jacket, and his full-face helmet was resting on the top of his head. He looked hot as hell. I huffed and jumped off the hood so I could turn away from him. I was still seething. I hated being treated like a victim. I was a survivor and life goes on. He came up behind me and ran his tongue across my neck. I shivered.

"I love you. I just wanted to protect you. That's what husbands do."

"You're not my husband yet and if you keep acting like this you won't be."

He gently bit his way along my shoulder blade. I was melting into a puddle.

"Come on baby, let's go home." He whispered, running his nose along my ear.

"Fine." I threw my hands up in the air in exasperation.

He mumbled something like 'that was easier than I thought' and climbed back on the bike. I got into the car and followed him home since I had no clue where I was. I was actually kind of glad he found me. I probably would have ended up in Mexico trying to get back. I pulled in through the gate and parked in the garage. The house smelled like burned food. *The ziti!* I ran into the kitchen and pulled our blackened dinner out of the oven.

"Cereal it is." He smirked pulling a box of Lucky Charms from the cabinet.

He pulled out two bowls and poured the cereal and milk. He handed me a spoon, and I ate. The marshmallow goodness reminded me of being a little kid. I felt my mood lighten slightly. After dinner, Jake pulled out a guitar and took my hand. He led me out to the patio and started a small fire in the fire pit. He started singing Rod Stewart's 'Reason to Believe.' I laughed remembering the conversation we had in Virginia after he was scrolling through my iPod.

"You like Rod Stewart?" Jake looked at me like I was crazy.

"Sure, what's not to like? My mom always listened to him while I was growing up. It reminds me of happy times." I confessed.

"It just seems weird to go from bands like Battlescars and Three Days Grace to Rod Stewart and James Taylor."

"What can I say, I have eclectic taste." I teased grabbing my iPod back.

He sinfully crooned out the lyrics. It was weird how much I liked them better live than on their records. I asked him once why he never played an instrument on stage. He said he didn't think he was good enough. He also liked to have the freedom to move across the stage and playing made that more difficult. He broke into another song. I watched him skillfully move his fingers along the guitar neck. I decided he was forgiven. Especially, after he broke out the supplies to make s'mores.

The next day he was on the phone arguing with the record label. It turns out that they added one last stop on the tour, which ended here in LA. They were thrown onto another large venue with Blood to Bleed, and Jake didn't want to play with Ian again. He was furious. I knew they didn't like each other, but his reaction seemed a little over the top. It had something to do with when Jake was starting out. Ian screwed him over and tried to set Jake up for failure. It obviously didn't work since they sold out every show and were pretty much a staple for any rock and roll fan. I didn't care for Ian either, but it was mostly because he was an arrogant asshole. Jake threw his phone against the wall. It fell to the ground with a crash.

"Sorry." He said pulling me into a hug.

"What the hell was that about?" I inquired.

"Just the stupid shit that they always pull. Every fucking time!"

He needed to calm down. I pushed him up against the wall he just threw his phone at and dropped to my knees. I undid his zipper and went to town. I took as much of him as I could in my mouth while he was running his hands through my hair. When he was finished, I stood and smirked at him. He grabbed me by the waist and spun me, so I was standing where he just was.

"How about that Australian kiss?" He grinned.

He pushed me against the wall and hitched my leg over his shoulder. He moved my panties to the side and dropped his face between my legs. He bit, licked and swirled until I was writhing. He moved so that I slid down onto him. *Fuck his happy place, I was in paradise.* He continued to thrust into me until I cried out again. My legs felt like jelly, and I was completely spent.

"I should get angry more often." He smirked. I playfully smacked his chest.

The next day we got up and headed straight out. We were going to do some volunteer work at a local soup kitchen that Jake helped out at when he was home. We climbed into his truck and headed downtown. I watched as the ocean view disappeared and the city came into view. We pulled into what would be considered a 'shady section' of town. We walked through a back door and into a kitchen. Jake grabbed two aprons from a hook and handed me one. He took my hand and led me further in. The place looked like any other commercial kitchen that I've seen. There were people all over preparing food, while others getting them into serving dishes.

"Rosie!" Jake called.

"I'm over here you knuckle head." She yelled.

I noticed a woman who looked to be in her mid-sixties. She was short and stout with curly, gray hair and glasses. She came over and embraced Jake happily. I was going to have to tease him about having a thing for older women later. First Mama Bee, and now Rosie.

"How you doing, baby boy?"

"I'm doing great, Rosie. How's everything been around here since I've been gone?"

"We're hanging in there. Thanks to you."

Jake blushed.

"It was nothing Rosie. I told you that already." He rubbed his hand across the back of his neck uncomfortably.

"I hardly call one hundred-thousand dollars, nothing." She pressed.

"Can we stop talking about this? It makes me uncomfortable."

"Sure thing, sweetie. Is this Aubrey?" She turned her attention to me. Jake nodded.

"It's nice to meet you, Rosie." I offered her my hand.

"Pleasure to meet you, Aubrey. You make sure he stays in line, ya hear?" I giggled. "Now go get to work."

"Yes, ma'am." Jake said.

He led me out to where the food was being served. There was a line out the door already. Jake greeted each person that came through the door with a smile. He even took pictures and signed some shirts. He was a completely different Jake here. He was humble, but I already knew that Jake had a soft side. I've seen it first hand when he helped me through my panic attacks. We helped serve and wash dishes for most of the morning into the afternoon. At two o'clock Jake told Rosie we had to leave because he had a visit scheduled at a local children's hospital across town. We hung up our aprons and said our goodbyes.

It was a shame that none of his good deeds ever made the news.

A little while later we pulled up to a state of the art hospital. Jake parked out front and came to open my door with a grin on his face. I could tell that he was excited to bring me here. We walked through the revolving door into a brightly colored reception area. There were murals painted by some of the patients lining the walls. Jake signed us in and led me down a hallway to where the recreation room was. The kids were already in there waiting for him to arrive. As soon as he walked in the room they got so excited to see him. I looked around at their smiling faces. I couldn't help but feel a little sad since they were all here for a reason, they were sick. Jack squeezed my hand reassuringly as we made our way further into the room. A little girl ran over to him and hugged his leg.

"Princess Penelope." He cooed.

He dropped to his knees so that he was eye level with her and pulled her into a hug. She was so frail and tiny. I don't think that she could have been older than four. She had a pink bandana around her head. My heart broke. She was so little to be going through what I could only imagine was some form of cancer or other childhood illness. She had the most adorable round face and large, green eyes.

"Jakey!" She wrapped her arms around his neck.

He stood up with her and kissed her cheek.

"Aubrey, I'd like you to meet Princess Penelope."

I did a curtsey, and she giggled. Her laugh was magical.

"It's very nice to meet you Princess Penelope."

"Aubrey's going to be my Queen soon." Jake told her. "We're going to get married."

"Can I come?" She squeaked.

"If the doctors and your mommy and daddy say it's okay, then you can absolutely come." He kissed her cheek again and placed her down.

She clapped her hands excitedly and ran over to who I assumed was her mom. She looked over at Jake with tears in her eyes and mouthed *thank you.*

He walked up to a little boy with brown hair and freckles next.

"Hey, Daniel. How's my buddy doing?"

"Good." He said shyly.

"Have you been playing the Wii lately."

"Yeah, and Rock Band. I want to be just like you when I grow up." He grinned.

"Keep practicing, and you will be." He patted the little boys head.

We went over to the TV where Jake played Rock Band with Daniel. After they were done we had a tea party with Penelope. Jake said he needed to make a couple more stops before we left because some of the kids were too sick to come down to the recreation room. He was so kind and patient with all of them. He made each one of them seem like they were the most special person in the world. Seeing him like this eased my fears of possibly being pregnant. He was going to make a great dad someday, and I was lucky he was going to be my husband. On the way home, I complimented him on all his philanthropic work. He shrugged and said it was nothing.

"When I was a kid before my mom died, I would have starved if it weren't for soup kitchens. They help a lot of people. The kids are special though. They just deserve a chance to be kids, I love going there and seeing them smile. I like thinking that maybe, just maybe

I had something to do with it. Penelope is my little doll baby, I freaking love that kid!"

"It's noble Jake. You shouldn't be embarrassed about it, you should be proud."

"Alright, enough talking about me. It'll go to my head." He teased.

He quickly changed the subject to food and demanded that we stop at In-N-Out burger on the way home. I agreed and had my first In-N-Out experience. Yes, they are all they're cracked up to be, and more…

We spent the rest of our time in LA relaxing and hanging around the beach. We didn't have any more fights either. We were both sad tonight was our last night here before heading back on tour to finish up the West Coast shows. I was going to miss our little bubble. I made us shrimp scampi for dinner, and we ate on his patio by the ocean.

Everything was perfect… Almost too perfect.

CHAPTER TEN

Love Drunk

Tonight we were in Omaha. I was laughing at Jake spraying his newly dyed Mohawk. Since I decided it was time to dye my hair he demanded that I add some pink tips to his, so we could match. I laughed because I thought he was kidding, he wasn't. So in front of me stood my bad-ass rock star with pink tips in his black Mohawk.

"What do you think?" He asked.

"It suits you." I teased.

"I thought so." He grinned and leaned down to kiss me.

We walked into the hallway and Brett broke into a fit of laughter. Jake slapped his shoulder. We went to the guys' room at the end of the hall. I was looking forward to their reaction the most. Jake knocked on the door. Kevin opened the door with wide eyes but didn't say anything. Blake and Derek were sitting on the couch. When they looked over at us, Blake was instantly on the ground clutching his stomach with uncontrollable laughter.

"Oh my God, what did you do?" Derek laughed.

"Is it that bad?" Jake looked at me.

I smiled and shook my head no.

"Do I need to start buying you tampons?" Blake asked, picking himself off the ground.

"Shut the fuck up, asshole." Jake tossed a pillow at him.

They kept laughing as we made our way down the hallway. Jake grabbed my hand and pulled me into the elevator. He pushed me up against the wall and kissed me. The boys whistled behind us. He pulled away and smirked. I patted his back reassuringly. We made it to the venue in plenty of time. He sang Adele's 'One and Only' during sound check. We hung around and they teased Jake relentlessly until it was time for them to go on. I gave him his preshow kiss and shoved him onto the stage. It was the first time that he was performing since the news of our engagement broke. Blake stepped up to his mic.

"What do you think of this tool's new hairdo?" He yelled.

The crowd cheered in response.

"Sorry ladies, it looks like Jake Parker is officially off the market. I, on the other hand, am still, without a doubt single."

Some guy in the front told him to shut up. Blake flung a guitar pick at him and hit him right between the eyes.

"See, I have great aim, just ask your girlfriend." Blake winked at the girl standing next to him who turned all love struck.

I chuckled.

Derek started drumming, and the place went wild. The lights started going, and Jake screamed into the mic.

"Omaha, let's do this!"

He jumped and moved lithely around the stage. I loved watching him perform and was actually going to miss it when the tour ended. Earlier we had been discussing where we wanted to live after we got married. We mutually decided that we would split our time between LA and Ohio. He wanted to buy some property and build a house near my parents. He figured that we would probably end up being there full time if we had kids. He said he would still need to come to LA to record so we would keep his place for getaways.

I still couldn't believe we were planning a freaking wedding. I didn't want anything crazy, or even big. My mom was having a hard time with the fact that I wanted to get married in a black dress, but I told her white just wasn't my color. We were looking to do it pretty soon after the tour ended. Only a little over a month away! At first it seemed like it was really fast, but Jake pointed out that we were meant to be together. Neither of us saw the sense in dragging out the inevitable. He finished out the set and tossed his sweaty towel out to some girl that would most likely sleep with it on her pillow. He walked off the stage and picked me up. I wrapped my legs around his waist and kissed him. Sweaty Jake was something I'd grown to love.

"That was a great show!" I praised.

"Thanks baby."

They had a meet and greet scheduled backstage for some contest winners and then they had an interview set up with a local radio station. I walked with him back to the room filled with adoring fans. He took a couple pictures and signed CD's and t-shirts. When the room cleared out, they assembled on a ratty couch and got ready for their interview. I stood back with Brett. Jake wanted me with him, but I told him this was about him and the band.

"Hey guys. I'm Ryan from WRU." A tall, thin guy with dark hair and tattoos came over and introduced himself to the band.

"Jake, Derek, Kevin, and I'm Blake."

"I know who you all are." He laughed. "I have some questions for you guys if you want to get started." He took a seat and reached into his bag. He pulled out a notebook and set up a recorder.

"Question one comes from Terry. Are you guys currently working on a new album?"

"We're not currently in the studio, but Jake has some pretty fresh stuff that we've been working with. Hopefully we will be able to get into the studio after the tour is over." Kevin answered.

"Next, you guys had to reschedule quite a few tour dates due to personal reasons. Care to elaborate?"

"My fiancée was in an accident and needed time to recover. It wouldn't have been fair to the fans for me to perform under those circumstances. I definitely wouldn't have been at my best. As much as I'm married to the music for better or worse, Aubrey is my top priority." Jake said.

"Glad to see she's better." Ryan said looking at me. Jake growled. "Alright here's the doozy. Word just broke that you guys will be one of the headlining acts at this year's Radioactive Tour alongside Blood to Bleed. The industry is no stranger to the longstanding feud between Jake and Ian. It's also rumored that Blood to Bleed just acquired a new bassist that could rival Blake. Any comment?"

"Ian's a shit stain. My skill is unparalleled. Yes, I know that's conceited, but it's the truth." Blake said smugly.

"Ian reminds me of something a cow would shit out." Derek chimed.

"Listen, I don't want to go around kicking a dead horse here. Yes, Ian Voss and I don't get along. He tried to sabotage my career from the beginning and failed. Yet he refuses to give up. Battlescars has its own following of fucking kick-ass fans. We'll go to Radioactive, we'll kick ass. Then I plan on getting married and getting into the studio. The end. Ian has no place in my life other than acting like a flea."

"Are wedding plans in the works?"

"Nice try. They are, but I won't be disclosing anything until after it takes place. It will be a low key event, just family and close friends."

"Thanks for your time tonight guys. I really appreciate it and good luck Jake. She's a knock out."

"Look at her like that again and I'll knock you out." He smirked.

He walked over to me and put his arm around my shoulder.

"Let's go." He led me over toward the door.

We climbed into the waiting car and headed back to the hotel.

Jake

We got back to the hotel and as much as I wanted to get wrapped up in the sheets with Aubrey something about the interview was bothering me. I told her I wanted to talk to the guys about something and that I would be back in a bit. She smiled and went to go take a bath. Brett and I headed to their room. I knocked and walked in. It was a pretty low-key night for them. At least there weren't any groupies philandering around. I told them that I needed to talk to them. We raided the mini bar for some beer and sat around the living room of their suite.

"I love you guys like you were my brothers, and I'm going to tell you something in absolute confidence. If one word of this gets breathed outside this room, I will personally fucking kill you, with my bare hands."

They looked at me to proceed.

"Tonight at the interview the guy mentioned something about Blood to Bleed having a new bassist. I looked it up on my phone on the way back, and it's someone that Aubrey knows. It's not a good thing either. See, when she was a teenager she dated a bassist, and it's this guy Jeremy. He has some sort of sick obsession with her. Here's the thing… almost all of her tattoos are to cover up scars. Scars that he gave her."

"You're fucking with us right? Are we on an episode of Punk'd?" Blake asked, looking around for a hidden camera or something.

"You are just kidding right?" Derek asked.

"I wish I was. He attacked her pretty bad man. She's got *a lot* of scars. He took a hunting knife to her and pretty much carved her up like a piece of meat. He actually carved his name into her chest. She's had some surgery to reduce the scarring, but it didn't go away completely. That's why she got the tattoos to cover them up."

"That's sick!" Derek yelled, kicking over the coffee table.

Kevin looked like he was going to be sick. I knew he really liked Aubrey and they'd grown close over the past couple months. He thought she was good for me.

"I don't want her to find out if we can help it. He has some vendetta against her, and I want to protect her as best I can. It's going to be a problem since she's at every show, and now we have to play with them. I need to try and find a way to get her to stay home from the show that day. I need you guys to help me come up with a plan. She's not going to be easy to placate." I cringed.

"We'll figure it out bro." Blake said. "I can't promise that one of my guitar strings won't end up wrapped around his neck, but we'll make sure Aubrey's safe."

"Fuck a guitar string! I'm gonna stab that asshole in the eye with a drum stick."

"Kill with kindness." Kevin laughed. All of us looked at him like he'd grown another head. "Just sayin'."

I retreated back to my room and packed up for our next gig. I couldn't shake this feeling of dread hanging in the balance. I looked at a sleeping Aubrey and tried my best to get some sleep too. Brett was going to start carrying his gun again. He always brought it along just in case, but the instance never came where we felt threatened. Now knowing that Jeremy was out lurking we needed to take extra precautions. There were instances that we could end up in the same town for an overlapping period of time. I was still awake when Aubrey woke up the next morning. She eyed me skeptically. I admitted that I had a rough night because of the interview and couldn't sleep. She berated me and told me I should have woken her up. I just pulled her close to me and breathed her in. It didn't do anything to settle my nerves. I knew I was going to have to tell Tim, but I needed to make sure Aubrey wasn't anywhere within earshot when it happened.

We showered and headed to the plane. We were due to play in Denver in two days. I was looking through my phone when a reminder popped up that it was Aubrey's birthday next week. *Shit!* I needed to think of something memorable. I wanted to make it special for her. I started racking my brain for ideas. We touched down in Denver and checked into a Bed & Breakfast that I picked out. It was off the beaten path, and we would be able to maintain some privacy there. We pulled up to the mini mansion and were greeted by the owner, Ruth. She showed us to our room and left. It was a nice place. Our room was painted red and was exceedingly Victorian-esque.

"A bed and breakfast." Aubrey teased.

"What can I say? I told you, I'm a sucker. It's even better now that you're here to share it with me." I kissed her.

She started crying. *What did I say?*

"Baby, are you okay?"

"I'm fine." She laughed.

"Why are you crying?"

"I don't know. I'm just feeling emotional today, that's all."

"You're going to be excited tomorrow when you see who we're playing with." I grinned.

She was going to freak out and go total fan girl on me.

Aubrey

We arrived at the Red Rocks Amphitheater and were hanging around back stage. Jake had finished his sound check. I was surprised to find out that they were actually the opener tonight. We were walking when I stopped dead in my tracks.

OHMYGOD!!!!!! My pulse started hammering.

"That's Brian Fallon! From Gaslight!" I screeched.

"Yeah. You want to meet him?" He cocked an eyebrow.

I beamed and nodded my head. He took me by the arm and led me over. Jake tapped him on the shoulder. He turned around.

"Hey Bri."

"Jake, how's it going man? I hear congratulations are in order."

"Definitely. This is my fiancée, Aubrey. Aubrey, meet Brian Fallon."

I was completely star-struck.

"It's nice to meet you." He smiled.

"You too. I'm a *huge* fan!" I chimed.

He laughed at me. "I'm glad to hear it. It was nice meeting you Aubrey. Good seeing you Jake."

"Why don't you get all fan girl with me?" Jake teased.

"Shut up." I teased and pinched him in the rib.

"Ouch." He laughed.

All the sudden I started feeling really icky. I didn't want Jake to worry, so I didn't say anything. It was most likely from being on the road for too long and the lack of sleep that went along with it. I still wasn't completely recovered from the incident either. I watched as he rocked the stage. I begged him to stay so that we could watch Gaslight play. He smiled and pulled up a chair so we could sit and watch. I absolutely loved them, and they were so much better live… if that were even possible. They opened with 'Handwritten', and I sang along. Okay, I sang along to the entire set. They were utterly electrifying. I was completely captivated. I felt mildly embarrassed that I was more excited about seeing them than my future husband. At least Jake was a good sport about it.

When they finished the set Brian handed me a guitar-pick, and I nearly fainted.

Jake carted me to the car, and we headed back to the B&B. I pretty much violated him on the way there. Once we were inside our room I all out assaulted him. He didn't mind. If anything he was right there along with me. Until, I started feeling icky again. I pulled away and ran to the bathroom. Jake was on my heels and held my hair back as I threw up. I was groaning.

"I hope you didn't pick up another bug. Kevin said he wasn't feeling great either."

He ran a washcloth under some cold water and held it to my forehead. I stood up and brushed my teeth. Jake called down and ordered some crackers, chamomile tea and ginger ale. He helped me get into my pajamas and put me to bed. He fed me crackers, but my stomach was still feeling unsettled. I spent most of the night puking, so did Kevin and Blake. I was feeling miserable. Jake had to have them reschedule the next two shows. By the time I was feeling better, he got it. Thankfully, it was just throwing up and not the shits. Thank goodness for hotel suites with two bathrooms. I felt bad because he was woozy and we still had a flight to catch. I helped him into the car. Brett closed the door and poured hand sanitizer into his hands. Brett and Derek were the only ones that remained unscathed.

We touched down in Seattle and decided to stay in and rest. I was still tired from being sick, and Jake was still sick. We got into our pajamas and rented some movies. I was playing nursemaid to Jake who looked miserable. I felt horrible knowing that he was going to have to perform tomorrow. It was a big show too, and there was going to be a lot of press there. I made sure that we both got to bed at a decent time with no hanky-panky.

The next morning I was thankful that I felt much better. I showered and got all decked out for the big event. I dressed in black leather pants, a slinky silver top and black stilettos. Jake whistled approvingly when I walked into the bedroom. He still wasn't feeling great, but since they couldn't afford to reschedule without fucking up the rest of the tour dates he was doing business as usual. He pulled me onto his lap and kissed the top of my head.

"I want to run an errand while you're doing sound check. I won't be long."

"Where are you off to?" He cocked an eyebrow.

"It's a surprise." I said coyly.

I kissed him and climbed off his lap. I headed to the door feeling naked not having my other half. For almost three months straight, we've barely been apart. Most people would have killed each other. Not that there weren't times I felt the urge to choke him, but I felt naked without him. I walked out the door and headed to Lulu's Bridal Boutique.

I had been doing dress research and Lulu's designs were unique. I decided since we were already here I would check her out. I walked down the street until I came across a pink and black damask awning reading Lola's Bridal Boutique. I opened the door and went inside. The store was small and decorated very Parisian chic. There were lots of blacks and whites with pops of pinks and turquoise throughout.

"Hi. How can I help you today?" A girl asked.

She couldn't have been much older than me. She had bleach blonde hair with red and black streaks. She was beautiful and eclectically dressed in designer threads that she probably made herself.

"I actually wanted to look at some of your dresses." I told her.

"I'm Lulu." She walked from behind the counter and offered her hand.

"Aubrey." I smiled. "I'm actually really interested in one of your black dresses."

I pulled out my phone and showed her the picture I saw online. She looked at it and grinned. She walked over to the wall and pulled off a black garment bag.

"One of my personal favorites. It's probably because it was my first bridal design. This is just a sample. We can alter yours to exactly how you want. We can change colors and ribbons to whatever you want. When's the big day?"

"April first." We both laughed.

We picked that day on purpose so we could play pranks every year on our anniversary. It would also be an easy date to remember. She produced the black dress from the garment bag. It had a lace corset bodice and a satin mermaid style bottom with a lace overlay. It was simple yet elegant. I wanted to try it on to make sure it didn't make my hips look too big. Lulu showed me into the dressing room and helped me lace up the corset back. I turned to look in the mirror. I absolutely loved it, and I could totally see myself getting married in this dress. *It was the one!*

"Could I order one and have it ready in time?"

"Absolutely. Let me just take down some measurements." She pulled out a measuring tape, a pad and a pen. "What's your fiancé like?"

"He's amazing. I'm sure all your brides say that, but he's really great. Funny enough, I actually hated him when we met. Then he finally convinced me to date him. A month later he proposed and here we are a month later getting ready to get married."

"Wow, you guys didn't waste any time." She joked.
"Wait…Aubrey. Aubrey? As in the one that's engaged to Jake Parker?"

"Um, yeah." I said shyly.

"You are one lucky girl. That boy is delicious!" She sighed. "All finished. I just need to take some information where to send it."

I filled out the contact information and thanked her. I walked outside and grabbed a cab to head to the venue. When we arrived the cabbie looked at me like I was crazy when I told him to pull around back. Event security stopped him from going any further. I pulled out my backstage pass, and they still said that I couldn't go through. I was going to argue, but instead I pulled out my phone and called Jake.

"Hey, I'm here and they won't let me come back." He hung up on me.

The security guard eyed me skeptically. Two minutes later Jake was strutting across the parking lot with Brett in tow. He looked enraged.

"You're lucky I don't get your fucking ass fired. She showed you her pass, and she told you that she was with *me!* I get it. I'm all about being secure too, but come on! Bullshit! Total bullshit! Now you better fucking apologize and hope I don't see you again." He yelled.

"Sorry ma'am." I nodded and took Jake's hand to pull him away before he went on another rant. "Sorry." I said to Jake.

"Why are you sorry? That asshole should be the sorry one." He opened the door and led me into his dressing room. "Did you get your errands done?"

"I did. How are you feeling?" I asked.

"I'm better that you're here. I missed you." He pulled me as close as he could.

"I missed you too. It's weird, right?" I laughed.

"Very. I literally felt like I was missing something. You know when you leave the house and realize you forgot your wallet or your keys? That's how I felt."

He rubbed his nose along my hair. "Me too."

I walked over and climbed into his lap and curled up into a ball. He rubbed my shoulder blades soothingly. It was the times when I was away from him that I knew we were meant to be together. I couldn't imagine life without Jake. He helped me. He helped me heal. He makes me want to be a better person. He gives me strength when I don't have any. He makes me feel complete. *I should write that into my vows.*

Derek came to tell him it was time to go on stage. I reluctantly climbed off his lap and watched him take the stage. After the show, it was more of the usual. They did an interview and signed some autographs. I started not feeling well again. I brushed it off. I grabbed a bottle of water and sat down. I saw Jake look at me concerned. I smiled and waved. I hoped he wouldn't pick up on anything. As soon as he finished up we headed back to the hotel. He ordered some snacks, but I still wasn't feeling much like eating.

"Baby, you feel okay?" He asked concerned.

"I don't know. I was feeling better, but now I'm not. One minute I feel like I'm on top of the world and the next I just want to climb into bed and sleep for days. I feel like a basket case."

"Maybe we should get you checked out by a doctor tomorrow. Just to make sure there's not something more serious going on." He said worriedly.

"We'll see."

I tried to brush the symptoms off and even managed to eat a couple Buffalo wings. That seemed to appease him. I brushed my teeth climbed into bed. I passed right out. The next morning I woke up starving since I didn't eat much the day before. I picked up the phone and ordered room service before I even got out of bed. Jake was sitting on the couch laughing at me when I walked in.

"What? I'm hungry."

"You ordered two of everything. Do you have any idea how much that's going to cost me?" He teased.

"You can afford it. You have lots of money." I stuck my tongue out and grabbed my cell phone to call my mom. I stepped onto the balcony and lit up. I told her that I ordered my dress. She was elated. We talked a little more about the wedding and how we were all getting over being sick. One minute I was talking and felt fine, the next my stomach turned, and I groaned.

"That's it! You're eating breakfast and then we're going to find a doctor."

"Fine." I grumbled.

Breakfast came and I scarfed down two giant plates of French toast and bacon. After we ate and showered we set out to find a doctor. We walked into the office and filled out the necessary paperwork. A nurse came out and handed me a cup to pee in. I brought it back to the receptionist. I picked up a magazine and waited to be called back. When they called me back, another nurse took some blood and said the doctor would be right in. A young doctor, probably in his mid-thirties, came in. He was tall, dark hair, dark eyes.

"I'm Doctor Chang." He offered his hand to both of us.

"I'm Aubrey, and this is my fiancé, Jake."

"Doc, everything in here is in confidence right? There are privacy laws and such."

"Of course. We never disclose any patient information."

"Please make sure your staff is aware of that. If something gets leaked to the press I will own you, and your practice." Jake said tersely. The doctor nodded. *Wow, Mr. Protective much?*

"What brings you in today, Aubrey?"

"We're all just getting over the stomach flu, and since I'm still feeling sick nervous nelly over there demanded I see a doctor."

"Let's take a look."

He checked my throat, my ears, my mouth, my glands, and my heart. He had me lay flat and pushed around on my stomach. He grabbed the chart and took a look. He said he would be right back. He came back into the room wheeling a machine with a paper in hand.

"I think we might just have an answer." He lifted my shirt up and squeezed some cold gel on my stomach. He glided the probe across my skin.

CHAPTER ELEVEN

Great Expectations

My heart was in my throat as I looked at the machine. I knew what they were usually used for. I watched the screen as he started hitting buttons. I had no clue what I was looking at, but it looked like a bean.

"You have kidney stones." He pointed to the screen.

"Kidney stones?" I choked.

"They can be caused by dehydration along with other factors, but they're right there." He pointed to the bean. "They generally pass on their own, but I will warn you that when they do they are extremely painful. If it persists you should see another doctor right away."

We thanked him and I got cleaned up. I looked over at Jake who was moping.

"What's the matter?"

"More like what's not the matter. First, you're sick, and it's going to hurt you. Second, I thought as soon as he wheeled that thing in that he was going to tell us we were pregnant."

This was clearly bothering him. Seeing Jake like this made me wish that it were true too. For whatever reason I felt ready. I was really nervous about what I was going to say next.

"Why don't you take me home and try and knock me up." I cocked an eyebrow.

"Seriously." He grinned.

I nodded. In that moment, something just clicked, and all was right with the world again. We were out of that office like the place was on fire. Jake had me in the back of the car and told the driver to book. As soon as we were back to the hotel we headed straight to the bedroom.

Jake

I would never admit to Aubrey how disappointed I was when they said it was kidney stones. Don't get me wrong, I was miserable when the doctor said that they would cause her pain, but I seriously wished that she were pregnant instead. Growing up like I did and coming from a fucked up broken home made me want to have kids. I wanted to give them everything I didn't have. Aubrey would make a fantastic mom too. It was nice to see her coming out of her shell more lately. I liked to think that I had something to do with it. Every day I tried to do something to show her how much I loved and cherished her no matter how small or trivial. She looks at me like there's nobody else in the world and that's all I could ever hope for. I'm seriously the luckiest guy in the fucking world that she agreed to marry me. I never in a bazillion years thought this existed for someone like me.

Our last few tour dates were coming to an end. We would just have the Radioactive show left, and then it was off to Arizona for the wedding. We decided to get married at Ron's ranch since he was in a wheelchair now and wasn't up for travelling. I felt like it was important to involve him especially because he was the closest thing I had to family. He was beyond thrilled about Aubrey. He couldn't wait to finally meet her. We were flying everyone in to stay there a couple days before the ceremony to have a meet and greet. It was plenty big enough to house everyone. The ranch was a little extreme for what he needed but I wanted to make sure that he could get around in his old age. After what he did for me, the least I could do was buy him a crazy, big house and make sure that he was set for life.

I'm sure a shrink would have a field day with me.

Tomorrow was Aubrey's twenty-fourth birthday, and I had grandiose plans in the works. I watched as she slept peacefully beside me. She always looks like an angel when she's sleeping. *I can't believe I get to do this for the rest of my life.* I felt bad because she had a bit of a rough day with the kidney stones passing. I was hoping she would be better tomorrow. I thought about rescheduling the first event, but I thought it was something she would really enjoy so as long as she was feeling up to it we'd still go.

I woke her up at a little after ten. I wished her a happy birthday and gave her breakfast in bed. She seemed to be in a great mood and was feeling much better today. After breakfast, I told her to get ready and to dress comfortably. She came back in the room fifteen minutes later wearing jeans and a hoodie, with a grin on her face. To me she looked like the most beautiful girl in the world no matter what she was wearing. I led her down to the car with Brett following closely behind. He was on high alert with all the activities I had planned for today. She was shocked when we arrived at our first destination.

"I know you've been up in one of these plenty of times, but I don't think you've ever jumped out."

She clapped her hands and grinned excitedly. We watched a video, and they gave us a quick lesson before we were strapped in our harnesses. We ushered over to the plane. I was cracking up because Brett was jumping too, and he looked hilarious in his tight harness. Once we reached altitude they opened the hatch. I kissed Aubrey before our tandem jumpers grabbed us and jumped out the door. At first I was scared to death, but it was so freeing and the view was spectacular. Brett screamed like a girl the entire time.

Once we were on the ground Aubrey ran over and tackled me to the ground.

"That was so much fun!" She squealed.

I smiled because her happiness was contagious. I told her there was more, and we left to go on our next adventure. We headed off to start the scavenger hunt that would lead us to her main present. I worked really hard all this week setting everything up. I had the guys out most of the night helping me finish setting it up so that she wouldn't get suspicious. I handed her a basket that held a clue. It would help her find the first place on the list.

"Let's see, it's got something to do with chocolate." She beamed.

I nodded. *My little chocoholic.*

We pulled up to the main street in Polk, Oregon and climbed out of the SUV. Brett was following closely behind as Aubrey followed the trail of cupcakes drawn in chalk up the sidewalk to Cora's Confections. I opened the door, and we walked in. In the front of the store was a table set up with an assortment of cupcakes. There was an edible note attached that said *Eat Me.* She sat and happily ate her cupcakes feeding me the occasional bite. Aubrey was a sucker for anything sweet, especially chocolate. Cora boxed up the rest of the cupcakes and wished Aubrey a happy birthday. She put them in a pink bag and handed her a brown lunch bag with a note attached. Aubrey opened the envelope and pulled out the note. It said *Feed Me* and there were directions attached.

They led us to a little pond that was full of swans and ducks. The bag was filled with breadcrumbs. There was a purpose for this one other than her entertainment.

"Did you know swans mate for life?" I told her.

She nodded sheepishly making me laugh. It was funny how little things like that seemed to embarrass her. We fed them for a little while, and when she was out of breadcrumbs I told her to go check under the bench nearby. There was another note that read *Mark Me!* along with another set of directions. I didn't want her to overdo it by walking, so I told her to hop on. I gave her a piggyback ride to our next stop. It led us to a tattoo shop. This was more for me than her. She eyed me skeptically and I shook my head not giving anything away. I walked inside and said hi to the owner, Paul. He was a friend of Blake's from high school and already had the sketch ready to go.

I sat in the tattoo chair and let him get to work. Aubrey watched as the needle bit into my neck. Forty-five minutes later he was done. I turned to let her get a good look. *Aubrey* was tattooed in elegant script across the left side directly below my ear. She looked shocked, but kissed me and told me that she loved it. She knew that I put everything I had into everything that I did. She called it 'balls to the wall.' It was one of the things I loved most about her. She accepted all of me. She surprised me by climbing into the chair after Paul wrapped my tattoo. She whispered something in his ear, and he nodded. He changed gloves and needles and took her left hand. She got a *J* tattooed on the inside of her ring finger. I shook my head and laughed. She never did what I expected her to.

"Tit for *tat* baby. You got me, so I got you." She grinned.

I fucking loved this girl.

Paul handed her the next clue. She opened the envelope and grinned like a lunatic. There was a shitload of twenties inside. Twenty-four hundred dollars worth to be exact, with a note saying *Share Me!* She loved helping people, and I figured this would make her happy. I was right. She practically bounced out the door. Brett was having a heart attack. His hand was on the gun the entire time. She was going from person to person and giving out money to those that looked like they could use it. She even got a couple hugs, which she accepted graciously. They were mostly from women, but my heart swelled that she was able to let them close to her.

Her next clue was attached to a telephone pole. It said *Pick Me!* We walked down the street and around the corner to Doggy Delight where we met Maggie. We walked in and as soon as she got "the look" I knew I did well. Maggie had Bella all ready and waiting with two bright pink bows in her hair. Bella was a miniature Yorkshire terrier. She was black with some brown around her face. She had a bedazzled collar and pink nails. Who knew that they made nail polish specifically for dogs? I didn't, but as soon as I found out I knew Aubrey would want it.

"You bought me a baby!" She cooed.

I nodded.

Maggie handed over Bella. This was Kevin's mission. I was the one that decided to get the dog, but he picked her out and helped me name her. We decided on Bella since Bellissimo was my nickname for Aubrey. He already had all of the supplies back at the hotel. All I did was get the proper clearance to keep her there. I could tell she was in love. Maggie rolled around Bella's new pink pet stroller, and Aubrey squealed. She placed Bella inside and zipped it up. She hugged Maggie, and we left.

"How did I do?" I asked.

"Seriously? This is the best birthday ever! You put so much thought into everything. You picked all my favorite things too. Thank you Jake." She beamed, and it was all the assurance I needed. Now, I needed to think of a way to top this next year.

"I already told you baby, there's nothing too good for you. I wanted to keep going, but the boys cut me off." I put my arm around her as she pushed the damn dog in the stroller.

Aubrey

One week later…

"Who's the cutest baby in the whole, wide world?" I cooed.

"I am." Blake said.

"Fuck you, I am." Derek said pushing Blake.

"I was talking to the dog you morons." I teased.

I absolutely adored Bella. Jake came back into the room after going to change his pants since Bella peed on him. I cuddled her closely as he came to kiss my head. I put her in a little baby sling that I wrapped around me. It was something you would put an actual baby in, but she loved it, so that's how I carried her around. We were sitting backstage at the last show before we headed LA. We were in San Francisco. I was really not feeling good today. We were scheduled to see Jake's doctor tomorrow to see if there was something I could do to get a little relief. I knew he was worried about me, but pain was something I was used to dealing with by now.

"You're lucky I love you so much, and I know how much you love that damn dog because otherwise she would be gone." He smiled.

I laughed. Bella slept next to me every night and constantly licked his face. It was adorable. He was such a good daddy to her.

He took her out for walks and made sure she was taken care of, especially when I wasn't feeling well. Which lately had been almost every day. I was feeling extremely run down and looking forward to getting some rest after this weekend. Since I wasn't feeling well, I opted to stay in the dressing room during the show tonight. I kissed Jake and told him to have a good show. He told me earlier that I could stay at the hotel, but I didn't want to stay there. I belonged here, with him. I hugged Bella tightly in her little cocoon and closed my eyes for a couple minutes. When I opened my eyes, I was being moved. I couldn't believe that I slept through the entire set.

"Jake, put me down." I scolded playfully.

"No can do." Was the reply.

"Come on, I'm gonna throw up!"

He moved me so that he was carrying me bridal style. Brett was holding Bella like a baby and tickling her belly. I knew I slept like the dead, but I was surprised they were able to take her from me without me waking up. I started laughing because for being such a big, tough guy he was a real softy. Jake helped me into the limo, and Brett handed me Bella. We were heading straight to the airport tonight. I snuggled into Jake and closed my eyes again. He woke me up when we got to the airfield. I clambered sleepily onto the plane. Mark looked at me concerned. I brushed it off and ran to the bathroom to throw up. Jake came up behind me and held my hair.

"You're the best hair holder ever born." I cooed.

"Baby, are you sure you feel okay? You're looking pretty pale."

"I'm fine, just sleepy. I'll be fine once we get home."

"We're still going to the doctor tomorrow." He said sternly.

I nodded and got settled in for the short flight. When we touched down, Brett did a quick security check of the surrounding area before letting us in the car. When we arrived at Jake's, he demanded to go inside before we did and check the entire place. He said, "better to be too safe than sorry," especially since he who shall not be named was in town. He checked everything and gave us the all clear. Jake carried in our luggage and helped me upstairs. I showered and climbed into bed. Jake was still out taking Bella for her walk. A couple minutes later Bella curled up in my side, and I felt Jake slid in next to me. I drifted off hoping to sleep off whatever was making me feel so sick.

The next morning I woke up and got ready to go to the doctor. I felt even more miserable today. Jake helped me get dressed in a sweat suit and led me down to the kitchen. He tried to convince me to eat something, but I knew I couldn't stomach anything without wanting to throw up. He relented and led me into the Range Rover helping me get inside. We drove down the street and pulled onto the 405 right into prime LA traffic. We arrived at a swanky office building an hour later. Jake filled out the paperwork, and we were immediately ushered back to an exam room. A few moments later a petite doctor came in.

"Hi Jake. You must be Aubrey." I nodded. "I'm Dr. Suzy Scott. My husband is Jake's doctor, but they thought you might be more comfortable with a female."

"Thanks."

"I see here that you've been diagnosed with kidney stones. I'd like to run some fresh labs so I can get a better assessment. Has anything else been bothering you?"

"No. I just feel nauseous all the time."

"Alright. Quick prick." She stuck the needle into my arm and drew some blood.

She handed me a cup for a urine sample. She left with both and told us to hang tight until the results came back. Jake was pacing a hole in the floor while we waited for her to come back. She came in a little while later with a paper in her hand.

"We got your blood work back, and I want to confirm something. She had me lay back on the table. She rolled my shirt up and squirted some warm liquid around my belly button. She took the ultrasound wand and started running it across my abdomen.

"First, it looks like the kidney stones have dissipated. I don't think that's where your symptoms are coming from." She moved the wand again. "Your blood work came back showing elevated levels of HCG, the pregnancy hormone. Looks like you two are going to be parents. They didn't check last time because the kidney stones showed up right away. It would have been too early to tell anyway."

I felt like I could faint. I was excited, but nervous at the same time. It was really happening. Jake was grinning from ear to ear. The doctor moved the machine closer so we could see better. She pushed my pants down lower and placed the probe over where the baby was. It looked like a little sack, but it was hard to make anything out. She took a couple screen shots and looked at me, then Jake.

"Looks like it's twins." The doctor smiled.

"Twins?" I squeaked.

"Yes!" Jake jumped up from his chair knocking it over in the process. "When I do things I do it right the first time! Balls to the wall, baby. Balls to the motherfucking wall!"

"Jake!" I scolded.

"Sorry." He apologized and picked his chair up so he could sit back down.

"It's really hard to get an exact due date yet, but I would say that you're about five to six weeks along. You should start taking prenatal vitamins right away." She hit print and handed us a couple ultrasound pictures.

"She has been taking them for about that long." Jake stated proudly.

"Good. I'll write you a prescription for them as well."

She pulled out her pad and wrote the prescription. She handed it to me, and I accepted it with a shaky hand.

"Congratulations guys."

"Thank you." I said finding my voice.

She handed me a towel and walked out of the room.

"We're going to be parents!" Jake beamed leaning in to kiss me. "To twins." He smirked.

"Twins…" I smiled, but I was screaming on the inside.

I was in *complete* shock.

Jake helped me off the table and out to the car. He wanted to know if I needed anything on the way. He specifically asked if I wanted pickles or ice cream. I couldn't help but laugh. He said even though you weren't supposed to say anything until after the first trimester that we had to let my parents know. He also said we would need to take a weekend trip to Smithville to look at the property so we could break ground ASAP. I agreed. He picked up his phone and called them on the Bluetooth. My mom answered right away.

"Hi mom." Jake said proudly.

He started calling her that about a month ago when we got engaged.

"Hey sweetie. How are you guys doing? How's LA?"

"It's great actually. Aubrey and I have some news. Is Tim there?"

"Yeah. Let me get him." She yelled at him to come over. "Okay, you're on speaker."

"Are you sitting?"

"What happened? Is Aubrey okay?" Tim yelled.

"I'm fine!" I yelled.

"Oh, okay. What's this news?"

"You're going to be grandparents."

My mom shrieked, and I could only imagine her face. She was undoubtedly jumping up and down. My dad was probably imagining how the whole thing happened and probably wanted to choke Jake, even though he loved him.

"That's wonderful news!" She yelled excitedly.

"That's not the best part. It's twins!"

"Twins?" My dad choked.

> *Exactly my feelings dad…*

"Two, dos, double." Jake laughed.

"Oh, we're just thrilled for you guys." My mom said.

"Thanks. We're going to be planning a trip out soon. I'd like to have a house ready by the time the babies arrive."

"Congratulations. We love you both very much."

"We love you too! It's still early, so keep it low key for now."

"Of course. Take care of my baby, Jake."

"I fully intend to." He vowed.

      We pulled back into the garage and Jake insisted on helping me to bed. I cuddled Bella while he rubbed my feet and did research some research on the computer. I was letting the news sink in. I knew that I was excited, but the thought of twins literally scared the shit out of me. What about when he was on tour? I would have two babies to take care of instead of one. Double everything. At least we wouldn't have to worry about money. I already knew I wouldn't want a nanny. Hopefully my mom would lend a hand when Jake couldn't. I wanted to mentally slap myself because I was Aubrey Thompson, well almost Aubrey Parker, and I was strong dammit. I could do anything I put my mind to, especially with Jake's help. He was glowing.

"Whatcha thinking?" He asked.

"Twins." I joked.

"I know. It's so crazy. Hey, it's your fault. You're the one that always says I go balls to the wall with everything, this is no exception." He teased. "I am beyond excited baby. I can't wait to go on this amazing journey with you. We're going to be the most kick ass parents a kid could ever have. Plus, we're still young so we will have the energy to chase after them no problem. You already know I don't require a lot of sleep, so I'll be good for night feedings. Though it says here that breastfeeding is the best choice. Maybe you can pump during the day so I can have enough for nighttime feedings. We have a while to figure all of it out. Maybe we can ask Brett. He's the only dad I know, other than yours, and chances are his skills are rusty."

"There's no one else on the planet that I would want to do this with other than you." I said honestly. "I hope I still fit in my dress."

"Since we just have the Radioactive show left maybe you should just stay here. I know you like to come to the shows, and I love having you there, but I'm worried about you over exerting yourself. It's not just you anymore."

He placed his hand on my stomach and leaned in to kiss me.

"Maybe you're right. Now go get me some In-N-Out burger and a giant chocolate shake."

"Anything for my baby momma." He grinned.

"I'm going to try and take a little nap." I yawned.

I strapped Bella to me in her little cocoon, so she wouldn't run off and poop somewhere while Jake was out. We snuggled up to take a nap. Jake kissed my hair and left the room. I closed my eyes and dreamed about what our little babies were going to look like. I woke up when I was being scooped up. I yelled at Jake to put me down. I had a serious love/hate thing with him constantly picking me up like a ragdoll. I was going to say something when realization hit me. It wasn't Jake.

I stayed completely still as I processed the information and placed the voice. I needed to plan an escape. I tried to move my hands, but they were secured with something. *How the fuck did my hands get tied?* I put my hands on Bella to keep her from falling out of her pouch. I searched my surroundings. Somehow we were already out the back door, and it was dark. I tried to fight him off with my legs, but I was too weak. He tossed me into the back of his car and sped into the night. *How did he find me?*

My heart was hammering in my chest. My first thought was about the babies I was now carrying. He slammed on the gas and drove into the night. I tried to open the door, but it was locked from the inside. I told myself to keep calm. We finally came to a stop about twenty minutes away at a Motel 6 right off the main highway. He dragged me roughly into a room around the back of the hotel. I wanted to scream, but nothing would come out. There were no witnesses, no one to help me. He was going to finish what he started six years ago, except this time he was going to kill me.

When he opened the door the room, I gasped. It looked like a torture chamber. There were candles flickering and the dresser was lined with an assortment of shiny metal knives. I felt my panic start to rise. My mind automatically drifted to Jake. I couldn't leave him. I was a survivor, not a victim. I decided that I was going to act like a willing participant. I remembered the last time and how the more I fought, the more he liked it. He saw me as weak, and I wasn't, not anymore. I just needed to find a way to get the upper hand. He came up behind me and touched my neck with his finger. I flinched.

"How does it feel knowing you're going to die tonight?" He bit down hard on my shoulder blade. I screamed. He turned me around and backhanded me.

"Bre-bre, I missed you." He whispered into my hair.

"I wish I could say the same. I haven't missed you at all." I spat.

"Awe, don't be like that. I was going to wait until this weekend but since your fiancé knows that I'm the replacement in Blood to Bleed he would have kept you away. I've been dreaming of this for too fucking long." He licked his lips. "I wasted two years in that hole for you and I didn't even get anything out of it. That's going to change tonight." He growled.

I couldn't even be mad at Jake for withholding pertinent information about Jeremy. He knew I would regress if I found out. Hell, I wanted to regress right now for crying out loud. I closed my eyes and sucked in a deep breath. I needed to hold on to my strength. I rubbed the top of Bella's furry head and tried to think of a way out of the hand restraints. Jeremy was looking at me with a sinister grin. It completely freaked me the fuck out. He walked over to the dresser and picked up a knife. I felt pain sear my chest. Jake would find me; he had to. I just had to hope that he could get someone here in time.

I could hold on that long, right?

CHAPTER TWELVE

Time Won't Let Me Go

Jake

I was literally on cloud nine when I pulled back into the garage. I got Aubrey a bacon cheeseburger with extra pickles and the biggest chocolate shake that I could get. I had a feeling I was going to be making lots of trips like this over the next several months. Call me a masochist, but I was actually looking forward to it. I grabbed the bag and headed up to the bedroom. The bed was empty. I checked the bathroom and prayed she wasn't sick again. She wasn't in there either. It wasn't a huge place, so it didn't take me long to realize that she wasn't there. Neither was the dog. Her sneakers and flip-flops were both sitting by the door. I pulled out my phone to call her. She never went anywhere without her phone. I heard it ringing upstairs. That's when I just knew something bad happened.

I frantically called the police and then Brett. He had the brilliant idea of checking Bella's microchip to get a GPS location. *That's why I pay him six-figures a year to babysit my ass.* I knew deep down that it had to be Jeremy. I had no idea how he could have found her, let alone gotten inside. Then it dawned on me... I forget to set the fucking alarm on my way out before. A million

249

thoughts were racing through my head as I waited for Brett to call me back with the location. Was she okay? Were the babies okay? Was she hurt? I was deliriously worried. I was worried about how this would set her progress back, and the stress it would cause down the road.

I checked my security cameras, which of course were down because I didn't set the fucking alarm! I ran my hands through my hair and paced the floor. I was busy tormenting myself until the phone finally rang. Brett said as soon as the police had the microchip information they got a hit. He gave me the address and said he was already on his way there.

"If you get there first wait for me. Don't do anything stupid Jake." He said sternly.

Fat fucking chance. Stupid was my middle name right now. I hung up on him.

If that asshole touched even one hair on her fucking head, I was going to kill him. I decided the quickest way to get there was if I took my bike. I threw my helmet on without even bothering to secure the strap. I revved the engine and sped out of the driveway. Traffic was still kind of thick and I didn't have time for that shit right now. I started weaving in and out of cars, riding on the shoulder and running red lights. I just needed to get to the address that Brett gave me. It was to a Motel 6 that bordered the city. I knew the roundabout location since I did some volunteering down there not too long ago. I made the twenty-minute trip in ten and undoubtedly broke every traffic law, at least twice. This place was in a really bad section of town, but I grew up in a ghetto.

A couple shady looking folks stared at me as I approached the office. I glared at them menacingly, and they quickly looked away. I knew the chance of my bike being chopped for parts was stellar. I didn't give a shit right now. They could have it for all I care. All I needed was for Aubrey to be safe. I waltzed into the office like I owned the place. We didn't have a room number yet, so that was priority one. I looked at the greasy slob eating Cheetos behind the desk. He was typing away on his computer and laughing about something. He looked up at me with a pair of thick, black-framed glasses and started choking. I noticed that he was wearing a two sizes too small Battlescars t-shirt.

Great, a fan-man...

"Jake Parker." He stuttered.

"I need a room number, and I need it *now!*" I barked.

"Su-sure." He mumbled.

"It may be under Jeremy Roberts. He's in his mid to late twenties, dark hair, and crazy eyes. I'm sure you know who I'm talking about." I growled. He was nervously clutching a key ring with his disgusting orange fingers. What kind of place didn't have electronic key cards nowadays? He was so jittery that he was having a hard time trying to get the right one. "Sometime today!" I snapped.

I felt bad for acting like such an asshole, especially since it wasn't my normal MO. I made a mental note to send him a proper sized t-shirt when this was over with.

"Room 212, it's around back." He stuttered and handed me the key.

I pushed out the door and took off in a sprint.

I sent a quick text to Brett with the room number. He was going to kill me, but there was no way in hell that I was waiting for him, or the cops to get here. I was rounding the corner when I heard sirens off in the distance. At least I knew they were getting close. I slowed to a jog when I finally reached the back part of the hotel. I needed to stealthily maneuver my way along the wall toward the room without attracting any unwanted attention. I looked at the room number closest to me. It was 259. Their room was on the complete other side from where I was.

I was trying to be as quick as possible, but it was like everything was happening in slow motion. It was like seeing a mirage in a desert, so close yet so far. I was only four-doors away when police finally pulled up. They turned their sirens off before pulling into the parking lot. Brett careened into the parking lot right behind them. He was out of the car and on top of me before I could even register what happened. The big lug knocked the wind right out of me. Undoubtedly on purpose to render me useless, hence keeping me safe. My brain just wouldn't fucking work. I said the first thing that popped into my head.

"She's pregnant." I cried.

Brett's face contorted. As a dad himself I knew he understood what I was feeling. He jumped off of me and kicked the door clear off its hinges. I heard wood and metal splinter. The next thing I heard was Aubrey's blood curdling scream. My heart was beating out of my chest. It was a horrifyingly beautiful sound. At least I knew she was still breathing. A storm of officers followed in behind with guns drawn. I stumbled to get back on my feet. I watched Brett come running out of the room carrying Aubrey. Her trembling hands were bound together. She was hysterically crying and clutching Bella who was still in her pouch. She was going into shock. Brett moved us away from the door and closer to safety. He placed her on her feet and pulled a knife from his pocket to cut the cable ties. Her wrists were bleeding from the deep lacerations she must have got from try to free herself.

Everything happened so quickly. I heard the police yelling at Jeremy to drop his weapon. Then I heard gunshots being fired. Aubrey flinched at the sound and Bella yelped. I started looking her over. I looked down and noticed that her shirt had been ripped at the shoulder. Parts of her skin were red, and I noticed a bite mark near her neck. My heart dropped when I saw blood was starting to seep through the pouch. *Her stomach was bleeding.* She started looking pale. She looked like she was about to fall over. I put my arms around her and moved so that she was sitting on the ground.

"Aubrey. It's going to be okay. Everything is going to be okay." I tried to sound strong, but I knew my voice gave me away.

I ran my hand through her hair and kissed the top of her head. She was staring ahead blankly. She was in 'robot mode.' I was so worried about her. It was really difficult to watch her during her episodes knowing there wasn't anything that I could do. The paramedics rushed over and started assessing her. They pulled her pouch off and inspected at the stab wound on her abdomen. I wanted to cry, the babies... I took Bella from them and hugged her. She licked my face and yelped. I was never more grateful for her unhealthy obsession with the fucking dog. That microchip saved Aubrey's life. That's when I realized that Bella was bleeding too. I looked her over and saw that there was a lot of blood coming from right above her hind leg. I handed her over to Brett and told him to get her to a vet right away. If something happened to that dog Aubrey, okay me included, would be devastated. He nodded and took off towards his truck. The paramedics loaded Aubrey onto a stretcher and ran toward the ambulance.

"Jake!" She cried.

"I'm right here baby. I'm not going anywhere." I tried to reassure her while running to keep up with them.

I climbed in behind them and took Aubrey's hand in mine. I was clutching to her for dear life. They closed the door and started an IV. One of the medics was wrapping her wrists in gauze. She moved her hand to her abdomen and started sobbing.

"She's pregnant." I told the woman medic who was assessing her.

She nodded in understanding. I felt sick to my stomach with the thought of losing even one of our babies. Her bottom lip was trembling, and I felt so helpless. I wanted nothing more than for her and our babies to be safe. I wished that I was on the damn stretcher for once. When we arrived at the hospital, they ushered us in through the emergency entrance. A team of doctors were already there waiting. I was fucking livid when they told me that I needed to stay outside the room. They closed the curtain so that I couldn't even see what was going on. I anxiously paced the floor as I waited for news. Twenty minutes later a nurse came out and told me that it was okay for me to go in the room.

"Hey baby, are you doing okay?" I asked her.

She nodded solemnly.

"She's going to be just fine. We had to give her three stitches in the abdomen. She told us that she had the dog in a sling. I can tell you from my standpoint that the dog saved her life. Otherwise, the knife would have gone straight through. It would have undoubtedly terminated the pregnancy and possibly killed her. You're a very lucky girl, Aubrey Thompson." The doctor said. "We're going to admit you for observation as a precaution. Get some rest and we'll move you up to your room shortly."

"Thank you." I said earnestly and shaking his hand.

He nodded and left the room.

"Aubrey, he said that you and the babies are going to be fine. Why do you look so sad?"

"Bella." She wept.

"Brett's at the vet with her right now. They're going to do everything they can to make sure she's fine. Baby, she saved your life."

"I know, but she's my baby too." I watched tears slide down her pale cheeks.

I used my fingertips to wipe her tears away. I placed her hand in mine and waited for news. I knew that I should call Tim and let him know what happened, but I wanted to get the rest of the details first. We waited for over an hour before they came to move Aubrey to another room. Once she was situated the nurse gave her a mild sedative to help her sleep. I started to protest until she said that it was safe for the babies. It didn't take her long to fall asleep. I sat with my phone clutched in my hand and waited for it to ring.

Forty minutes later there was a knock at the door. I looked up and saw a detective standing there with another officer.

"Can we come in?" He asked.

"Actually I'd prefer to talk in the hallway? I don't want to disturb her." I motioned to Aubrey.

"That's fine."

I stood up and walked out into the hallway. We stood right outside the door so I could keep an eye on her.

"Mr. Parker, as you are already aware, Ms. Thompson had a restraining order against Mr. Roberts. This evening he kidnapped her with the intent of doing something extremely sinister. Luckily, with your quick thinking about the microchip we were able to avoid this being a homicide investigation." I felt bile rise in my throat at the thought. "Unfortunately, well not really, our officers had to use deadly force to take Mr. Roberts down to prevent further incident. I want you to rest assure that our department will do everything in its power to wrap up this investigation quickly so that you can put it behind you. We were aware of this case when you brought it to our attention last month, but we weren't aware that you and you're fiancée were back in town."

"We actually weren't due back for a couple more days. Aubrey hasn't been feeling well lately, so we ended up cutting our trip short so that she could come home and rest. We just found out earlier today that we're going to be parents, to twins."

"Congratulations. Please let us know if we can be of any further assistance. We will need a statement from Ms. Thompson, when she's feeling up to it as well. Oh, and your bike is gone…"

He handed me a card with his contact information.

"Yeah, I figured as much. I'll be in touch." I told him shaking my head. I knew that was going to happen.

I went back into the room and sat next to Aubrey again. She was mumbling peacefully in her sleep with her hand on her stomach. I put my hand on top of hers and was beyond grateful that both of our babies were okay. I was still trying to work through what happened tonight. It felt like an eternity while I waited for my phone to ring. Finally, it did. It was Brett.

"Hello." I answered quietly.

"Bella's going to be fine." He said in a rush. "I don't really understand vet lingo, but from what I did understand the knife didn't penetrate anything vital. She's one lucky dog, especially since it went completely through. They just finished the surgery, and she's in recovery now."

"Thank God!" I yelled.

Aubrey stirred and I told myself to calm the fuck down.

"Brett, thank you for everything. Seriously." I said sincerely.

"I was just doing my job." He stated.

"Brett you put your life in danger to protect Aubrey tonight. You put your ass on the line every time you go anywhere with me. I just want you to know that I appreciate it, and you."

"I love you like a brother, Jake. Over the past few months, Aubrey's become like a sister to me. The change I see in both of you is nothing short of a miracle. I'm serious." He started laughing.

"I know. It's pretty crazy." I couldn't help but laugh too.

It really was some sort of kismet that brought us together. We were like two lost souls wandering the world and then *bam!*

"So about what you said earlier, that Aubrey's pregnant. Is it true?"

"Yeah, we just found out this morning. She's literally only like five or six weeks along, and it's twins."

I could hear him chuckling on the other end of the phone. Why does everyone think the fact that we're having twins is so hilarious?

"Twins, huh? Figures. Either way you guys are going to be rock star parents."

"We're sure as hell going to try. The doctor said if it weren't for Bella that we would have lost the babies and possibly Aubrey. She saved all of them."

"Bet you don't think that stupid cocoon thing is so stupid anymore, do you?"

"I'll need you to go pick up a new one before she gets released." I teased.

"I'm on it. I'll be over there in a little while to check on things. Do you want me to call Vin in the meantime?"

"No, we're good. Why don't you just go home and spend some time with Ri and Kayley? I've got things under control here. I'll see you in the morning."

"Call me if you change your mind and I'll be right there."

"Thanks again, Brett."

"Anytime Jake, anytime."

I disconnected Brett's call and scrolled through my contacts. I pulled up Tim's number and hovered my thumb over the send button. It was after one in the morning their time. I thought about waiting until morning, but I put the call off long enough already. It rang quite a few times before he finally answered. I knew I woke him up. I told him everything that happened and that Jeremy was out of the picture, permanently. I explained that Aubrey, the babies and Bella were all going to be fine. He wanted to come out, but I assured him that I had things under control. I told him we would be there in a week anyway. He reluctantly agreed. I promised him that I would keep him up to date on any changes and to go back to bed. It felt like Texas déjà vu all over again. The hospital. Aubrey in bed, at least this time she wasn't in a coma. I put my head down on the bed and tried to catch some zzz's.

Aubrey

I woke up completely befuddled. I blinked a couple times before the realization of what happened hit me. It came at me head on, like a freight train. I started freaking out. Jake lifted his head and looked at me with wide eyes. He stood up and sat next to me in bed. I was still rattled from last night. Jeremy. Knives. Bella. Gunshots. I was having a difficult time categorizing it all. I quickly remembered the babies and forced myself to relax. I looked at Jake again. He had worry etched all over his handsome face. I reached out my hand that didn't have IV's and touched his cheek.

"He can't hurt you anymore baby." He whispered.

I knew he was telling me that Jeremy was dead. I already knew and a majority of me felt an enormous wave of relief. The other part of me felt guilty for feeling that way because he was still someone's son. He was obviously very mentally disturbed. I wasn't excusing his actions by any means because I would wear the scars that he gave me for the rest of my life. I'm sure that karma takes calls in the afterlife as well. My next thought was my puppy.

"What about Bella?" I asked.

I was expecting the worse because she was so tiny, and he thrust that knife at me with such force. The conviction in his eyes will probably haunt me for the rest of my life. He wasn't kidding when he said he wanted to kill me. I felt horrible that Bella had to bear the brunt of the attack, especially because she was completely defenseless. I guess in hindsight it was a good thing since the outcome could have been much graver, but I still wanted her to be okay. She was my first baby.

"She's going to be fine. They said that the knife missed all major organs. They expect her to make a full recovery."

"Thank goodness." I breathed a sigh of relief.

"How do you feel baby?" He eyed me apprehensively.

"I'm a little sore. I'm feeling confused. But, I'm okay."

I tried to sit up some more so I could get comfortable. Jake reached around and helped me. He told me exactly what the cops told him. He said that we needed to meet with the detective to discuss my side of events. I told him just to make the call so we could get it over with. He called Brett first because he wanted him to be here too. After he made the phone calls he lifted up my hospital gown to look at my stitches. I knew exactly what he was feeling. Last night when I felt like I might lose the babies it all became clear. It was meant to be, they were meant to be. Life doesn't throw you more than you can handle. *It likes to test though.* Brett came into the room with some bagels and coffee. Just the smell of the coffee turned my stomach. He laughed and quickly ran them out into the hallway.

"Ri had the same problem when she was pregnant with Kayley." He smiled.

He reached into the bag and handed me a bagel with cream cheese. It tasted stupendous. It tasted like the forbidden fruit. I was popping the last bite into my mouth when the police showed up.

"Ms. Thompson, I'm Detective Johnny Cruz, and this is Officer Ryan Consuelo." He said as he came into the room.

They pulled up chairs next to the bed, and the detective pulled out a notebook.

"Can you tell me what you remember from last night?" He asked softly.

"We had gone to the doctors earlier and what we thought was kidney stones turned out to be babies. I remember going to take a nap because I was feeling really tired. I hadn't been able to keep food down for most of the day, so I sent Jake to go get me some.

When I woke up I was being carried. At first I thought it was Jake because he's notorious for tossing me over his shoulder and carrying me around like that." I looked at him, and he smirked. "Except it wasn't Jake, it was Jeremy. He somehow managed to bond my hands while I was sleeping. He threw me into the back of a car and drove to the hotel. He dragged me inside, and the dresser was lined with candles and knives. My instincts were to fight, but the last time I was attacked by him the more I fought the more he liked it. I decided to act like a willing participant and see what happened. I remember him asking me, 'How does it feel knowing you're going to die tonight?' The next thing I knew he picked the biggest knife and taunted me with it. As soon as he heard activity outside he stabbed me with it. Brett came into the room right after that, or I'm certain that he would have kept stabbing. Brett used some kind of ninja move on Jeremy knocking him down. He was distracted long enough for Brett to grab me and run back out the door. Then we ended up here."

The detective reached into his pocket and produced an evidence envelope.

"Does this look familiar?" He held it out.

I felt all of the air rush out of my lungs.

"That's her ring." Jake stammered.

We both looked down at my hand at the same time and saw that my replacement was still in place. It was *him,* he was the one that attacked me in Texas! Jake looked absolutely enraged. Brett walked out of the room and came back in a couple seconds later.

"That fucking asshole!" Jake roared.

"Jake." I scolded. "We couldn't have known that it was him. Relax."

"I can't even let myself think what almost happened in Texas."

"That fucking snake!" Brett yelled.

"What snake?" The detective asked.

"You should talk to Ian Voss." Brett scoffed.

"From Blood to Bleed?" The officer asked.

"The very same. I'm sure that you're familiar with the ongoing feud. Well, it's pretty much one sided, but Ian has had it out for Jake from the beginning. He would know that something like this could potentially ruin him. Think about all the cancelled tour dates they had, plus it threw Jake off his game. He still managed to put on an epic show each time, but his thoughts were always with Aubrey. It was very disconcerting for Jake."

Holy fuck! I didn't even think about that.

"It all makes sense." Jake said.

"We're going to have a talk with him right now. I'm sure he's in town since you are all set to play that show on Saturday. Thank you for your time, Ms. Thompson."

I nodded. They left and closed the door behind them. Jake came over and kissed me.

"I can't wait to add a Parker to that name." He grinned and winked.

Jake and Brett went and huddled in the corner like a couple hens. They were whispering so that I couldn't hear them. A nurse came in and checked my vitals. She said she would put in the discharge papers so that we could go home. I wanted to go home and sleep, but not before I got my bacon cheeseburger with extra pickles. Jake kicked Brett out so he could help me get dressed. We signed out, and I got the customary wheel chair ride. I hoped that the next time I had to do one of these would be for a much happier occasion. Jake helped me into Brett's Escalade.

I didn't even need to tell them to stop to get me food. Brett pulled into the first In-N-Out that we passed. I sat happily in the back next to Jake and devoured my food. He called the vet, and they told us they wanted to keep Bella for a couple more days. They wanted to make sure that everything was okay, but said she was doing great. I wanted to protest, but I just wanted her to get better. Jake promised me that the second they said she could come home that we would go and get her.

Three days later we were walking out of the vet with my baby Bella. She was happy to see me, but not as happy as I was to see her. Her little tail was wagging a million miles an hour. They even gave her a fresh coat of pink nail polish while she was there. Jake helped me into the truck and closed the door behind me. I pet Bella's fluffy head and gave her lots of kisses as we headed home.

The Radioactive show was tomorrow. Jake was still too anxious to leave me home alone after everything that happened, so Bella and I were going to the show after all. They still didn't have enough evidence to prove Ian had any connection to Jeremy either. Jake also hired his other bodyguard Vin to come babysit me.

I made him make a pit stop to get me some burritos on the way home. My appetite was either ravenous or non-existent these days. Right now I was starving. I wolfed down my food in the most unladylike fashion and practically growled at Jake to give me the rest of his. He just smirked and handed it over. He pulled another one out from next to him. *That sneaky bastard.* We pulled back into the garage and headed up to the bedroom. Just that little bit of running around left me utterly exhausted. I climbed into bed, and Jake offered to walk Bella for me so that I could rest. I turned on the TV and started watching reruns of The Golden Girls. That show always cracked me up. When Jake came back after checking the alarm three times to make sure it was armed, we decided we would fly back to Ohio on Sunday to start looking at property. We needed to go soon because my dad was having a stroke all week since he was worried about me. I agreed and closed my eyes.

When I woke up it was morning. I managed to sleep almost fourteen hours. I turned my face and Bella started licking my nose. I pet her head and sat up. That's when I smelled it… bacon! I felt like Super Woman flying down the stairs. Jake looked over at me and grinned like a lunatic. I rolled my eyes and walked over to the plate on the counter. He made French toast and lots of bacon. He took my hand and led me over to the table, pulling out my chair. I sat down, and he placed the plate down in front of me. I savored each morsel. Poor Jake was going to have a miserable couple of months ahead because food was much higher than sex on the hierarchal desires right now. I finished my breakfast and got up to put the plate in the dishwasher. He took it from me and sat me back down.

"Rest is really important right now. I'm going to wait on you hand and foot, my lady. I already talked to all the guys this morning, and we've agreed that we are going to record a new album. But, we're going to do it in Ohio."

"Huh?" I asked confused.

"When we build the house I'm going to incorporate a studio in the basement. That way it will save me from having to make a lot of trips back and forth. I've already got it all figured out. The guys agreed that it would be nice to get out of LA for a bit too. Do you think Smithville can handle Battlescars?" He teased.

"I think we'll all manage just fine. You don't have to do that though. I understand your work, and I know that you love what you do. I don't want to take you away from that."

"You're not taking anything, baby. If anything you're giving me much more than I could ever have hoped for. I love you so much Aubrey Thompson, almost Parker."

I couldn't help. it I turned into an emotional blubbering mess. These pregnancy hormones were taking me on a damn roller coaster.

"I love you too, Jake Parker."

CHAPTER THIRTEEN

Radioactive

Jake

I showered and got ready for the show. I dressed in a pair of gray cargo shorts and a black t-shirt. I was just finishing tucking my laces into my boots when Aubrey walked into the room. She took my breath away. She looked awesome in a pair of camo capris and a black tank top. She was always sexy as hell, but lately she's just fucking unbelievable! I was looking forward to getting this last show under my belt so we could focus on the future. I walked over to her and kissed her deeply. I reached into my back pocket and handed her a surprise that I found at the store other day.

"Where has this been all my life?" She squealed excitedly. "Whoever thought of making bacon flavored lip gloss is my hero." She hugged it tightly.

I kissed the top of her head and laughed. She elbowed me playfully in the rib.

"Do not make fun of me, Jake Parker! I happen to be carrying not one, but two babies around for you right now. If I want to eat bacon 24/7 then you're just going to have to deal with it. Capiche?

"Yes, ma'am." I teased.

"Good. Do you think we can get bacon cheeseburgers on the way to the show? Because that sounds sooo good right now."

"I'm sure we can figure something out. We don't want Brett and Vin to see what an angry bear you become when you haven't eaten in a couple hours. On second thought, maybe we should pick up a bunch of stuff so you can snack while we're there. It's going to be a long day, and I don't want you leaving, for any reason. Capiche?"

She growled, and the dog followed. I handed her Bella's sling, and we headed downstairs to wait.

"Come on, we have fifteen minutes before they get here."

I pulled her over to sit on my lap and rubbed her shoulders. The doorbell rang, and I went to open it while Aubrey scooped Bella up. I set the alarm and double-checked to make sure that I locked the door. We climbed into the Escalade. I introduced Aubrey to Vin. I told Brett that he better stop and get Aubrey food, pronto. Especially if he knew what was good for him. He laughed and agreed that if we all wanted to keep our man parts we do as the pregnant lady says.

She leaned on my shoulder and snuggled closely with Bella on her lap. Every time I looked at that dog I saw much more than a dog, she was my little angel. I hated thinking about that night. It was hard to believe that it all happened less than a week ago. It was fresh and far behind at the same time. Brett pulled into

Ray's Burger House and ordered Aubrey and array of selections, including her bacon cheeseburger. He handed her the bag, which she happily accepted. She finished her last bite just as we were pulling into the venue. Vin had strict orders not to leave her alone, even for a second.

We were escorted in through the stage door and over to a dressing room that was set up for our band. All the other guys were already in there when we arrived. Kevin got up right away and ushered Aubrey to take his seat. He was such a mother hen sometimes. He was asking how she was feeling, yada yada. He reached into his backpack and pulled out a gift bag. He handed it to her. It was a guide to a healthy pregnancy and a couple boxes of herbal tea. He was all into that health conscious stuff. Aubrey thanked him and gave him a hug. *What a kiss ass!* Blake and Derek surprised me too. They were all being super sensitive to Aubrey and Bella. I cocked an eyebrow at Blake.

"What?" He asked bemused.

"Nothing. I was just wondering if I'm going to have to start buying you tampons next."

"Shut up dickhead." He teased.

"Ah, he's still in there somewhere." I joked.

"Please, we were all worried about her. I still can't wrap my head around the fact that you're going to be somebody's dad. That's some freaky shit right there." Derek shook his head as if trying to comprehend what he just said.

Aubrey laughed.

"About that… it's twins." I stated proudly.

All heads snapped to me. Blake looked like he was going to pass out. Derek was white as a ghost. Kevin just shook his head and whispered what sounded like 'figures.'

"That's right. My boys can swim." I said proudly.

"And she didn't kill you when she found out?" Derek laughed and looked at her. "Aubrey you deserve a fucking medal or something."

"I would have totally had your sack cut off right then and there." Blake yelled.

"Oh I thought about it." Aubrey grinned and winked at me.

I shook my head. "What is this pick on Jake day?"

"No, that's every day." Blake laughed.

I shook my head and walked to stand next to Aubrey. She started skimming through the book that Kevin gave her. She was asking him a lot of questions about the information in the book. Then we talked about the upcoming move to Ohio and the wedding, which was only two weeks away! Blake and Derek couldn't wait to meet Granny Jean. I could only imagine what choice words she was going to have for them and their shenanigans.

I couldn't wait to figure out where we were going to build. I wanted to build something big so we wouldn't have to move again, *and* so I would keep having an excuse to knock Aubrey up. *Can you say football team?* I also wanted to have enough space for when company came. I already knew that I wanted to build a small guesthouse since I wanted the guys to have a place to stay when we were recording. I definitely want something secluded and plan to put a gate around the entire premises. Maybe we could incorporate a moat. How fucking cool would that be?

My ideas were flowing like crazy when they came to tell us it was time to go on. Aubrey was going to stand off the side of the stage with Vin and Brett, who were both packing .40 calibers. I took her hands and helped her to her feet. We walked hand and hand over to the stage. I did a quick survey of our surroundings and relinquished her to them, but not before getting my pre-show kiss.

Aubrey

I was standing off to the side of the stage holding Bella. I watched as Jake approached the middle of the stage. I had Brett to my right and Vin to my left. They were both huge. Vin was probably around my age and Jake said he was really into boxing.

He was about the same height as Brett with bulging muscles. I noticed his gun peeking out from his jacket. I looked over at Brett who winked. I knew in that moment I'd been *Jaked.* I knew Jake was worried about Ian, but seriously the guy is like my size and probably even skinnier. I could take him down no problem if I had to, and I'm positive that Brett could obliterate him with his pinkie. Jake picked up the mic. I looked at him with his Mohawk with pink tips. I was crazy in love with that boy.

"Ladies and gentleman LET ME HEAR YOU!" He yelled.

The sound that followed reverberated from everywhere.

"How's everybody doing tonight? We're going to start with a song that will be on our next album once we get into the studio. It's called, 'Life Starts Now' and it's dedicated to my incredible fiancée. I love you baby!"

I knew that they had been playing around with some new songs, but I had no idea that they actually had a full song with music and everything. The song was basically about letting go of the past and embracing the future. I watched the show feeling bittersweet about the whole thing. I reflected over the past three and a half months. It was so surreal. It almost seemed like Jake was sent to me to help me heal. When we met I was scared. I thought I was protecting myself by shutting him out. Somehow he managed to worm himself into my world and right into my heart. He was jumping around on the stage like a crazy person. The crowd was completely enthralled by him. I was in awe like always. Finally, when they finished up their set, he tossed his towel and walked over to me. He scooped me right up, and I wrapped my legs around his waist. I handed Bella over to Brett in order to save her from being dropped or smothered. Jake leaned down and kissed me dripping sweat on my face in the process. I wouldn't have it any other way. I tried to get down, but he wouldn't let me. He started walking back toward the dressing room with the guards flanking. He stopped midstride.

"Hey asshole, nice stunt you tried pulling. I really appreciate it fuck-face." He yelled.

I turned to see that he was talking to Ian. Bella started barking like crazy. His dark hair was combed over to the side. He smirked at Jake and I felt him tense up. I moved my head and licked his neck in an attempt to try and distract him. I didn't want him to get into a fight with Ian because he definitely wasn't worth it. They were locked into some staring contest. Jake wasn't responding how I had hoped. I bit down on his earlobe gently. That got his attention, but he still stood unmoving.

"Jake, just go." I pleaded. I knew he wanted to listen to me but his pride, manly-hood, etc. just wouldn't let him move. "It's not going to change anything. Just let karma take care of it. What comes around goes around…"

"You're going to let your woman boss you around like that, Parker?"

Jake started shaking. I leaned into his ear to whisper.

"Baby, you're all sweaty, and I really *need* you right now… Let's go home. Please." I ended with a low moan.

That did it. He started walking toward the back door. I looked over my shoulder and saw Vin full on body check Ian. Blake and Derek emerged from somewhere and saw the tail end of things. Blake looked murderous. Derek looked enraged. I watched as Blake walked up to Ian and punched him right in the throat. Kevin appeared next.

"I was thinking blunt force trauma to the voice box might make your voice less annoying. You're a spineless, dickless, piece of shit." Blake spit in his face and stormed off kicking over a garbage can in the process.

"I don't know how you look at yourself in the mirror." Kevin scoffed. "Is Jake Parker really that much of a threat to you that you needed to stoop low enough to hire her stalker?"

Jake stopped and turned around. Ian looked like a deer caught in the headlights.

"I didn't know he was her stalker until the police told me the other day. Jeremy said that they used to date, but I didn't know anything else that happened. I think Jeremy had this whole thing planned out from the beginning." He stammered. "Mark left mid-tour with no notice right after the Texas show, and we needed a new bassist. He practically appeared out of thin air. He was really good, so we took him on as a replacement knowing that it would get back to Jake."

Derek's fists were curled so tight I could clearly see every tendon in his hand. If looks could kill, Ian would have been dead right where he was standing.

"The tour is over, and we're not going to have any reason to see each other again. I may seem all laidback and mellow, but if you as much breathe in our direction I will personally take you out. Do you understand?" Kevin bellowed.

I've never seen him angry before. He was actually intimidating. Ian nodded anxiously.

"Good, now go change your underwear." He barked.

I looked down and saw the front of Ian's pants were wet. He'd pissed himself. That's when I knew there was no way in hell that he could have known about Jeremy's sinister plans. Ian was all bark and no bite, despite what he wanted other people to think. I pulled on Jake's hair to bring his attention back to me. He looked lovingly at me. I moved so that I could peck his lips. We continued kissing as he walked until we got safely into the car. Brett handed me back Bella, and she licked Jake's face and wagged her tail. I told them to stop and get me a banana milkshake on the way home. I sipped it happily. When we got home, Brett insisted on taking precautions and checked the entire place before giving the okay for us to go inside. We headed straight to the bedroom with the intention of packing for Ohio since we were leaving in the morning. The second that Jake lifted his shirt over his head I was too sidetracked to do anything, other than him. I walked over and put my arms around him breathing in his cologne. My sense of smell was heightened from the pregnancy and he smelled even better than before. I looked up at him with lust filled eyes.

"I need you." I whispered.

I didn't need to say anything else. We made quick work of the rest of our clothes. He kissed me, devouring me. He lifted me up, wrapping my legs around his waist and walked over to the wall to shut off the alarm. He carried me over to the sliding glass door and opened it up leading me outside to one of the lounge chairs. He carefully placed me down and kissed down my neck, my breasts, and my stomach stopping to pay extra attention to where the babies are before ending up at my core. He lifted my legs around his shoulder blades and licked a long swipe up my moist heat paying special attention to my swollen nub. It only took a couple of circular motions with his talented tongue before I was writhing underneath him.

He lifted his head looking at me contently. He nudged his angry erection at my entrance slowly pushing forward until he filled me completely. When we were like this it made me feel whole. He rocked in and out to the rhythm of the crashing waves. I ran my fingers through his hair, looking into his handsome face. My heart swelled with the love that I had for him. He was pushing me closer and closer to my orgasm. When it came it was the seeing stars, glorious kind. I felt him thicken and fill me. I never wanted this moment to end. He picked me back up and carried me inside to the bathroom. He sat me on the vanity and cleaned me up before placing me in bed. I turned on my side and closed my eyes feeling euphoric.

~~~~~~~~~

We found a nice piece of property not too far from my parents. It was ten acres, and we could start building right away. Jake made arrangements to meet with an architect today, so that's where we were headed. He had all of these elaborate plans that he wanted to incorporate. I wanted a kitchen, a bedroom and a bathroom. Those were my must haves. We pulled up to the office and Jake came to help me out of the car as if I was incompetent of opening my own door.

When we walked inside and were greeted by Nick, the architect. He led us into his office where he had a large touch screen set up with some plans already drafted. Jake looked like a kid in a candy shop. We talked about our wants and our needs. I let Jake handle the money because I didn't even want to know what the whole thing was going to cost. It would probably end up giving me nightmares. By the time we left the plans were already underway. I talked Jake down from twelve bedrooms to eight. I tried for five but was vetoed by both parties. Instead, the guesthouse was going to have five, and its own studio. I was actually really impressed with some of the ideas Jake came up with.

We stopped on the way back to my parents and picked up some sandwiches for lunch. Today was also the day that we were putting the final touches on our wedding plans. We didn't have much time left before the big day. We needed to get anyone that didn't already have their airfare a plane ticket, make sure they had arrangements to pick them up from the airport and transport them to the ranch. I was excited and nervous. I was really hoping that I would like Ron and vice versa. He seemed like such a special person for Jake, and it was extremely important to me that we got along. I know he looked up to him as a mentor, but Ron seemed to have taken the father figure role in his life. Once everything was squared away, I went to go lay down because I was exhausted. I demanded that Jake come and cuddle with me while I napped. I always slept better when he was there.

"Jake, did you remember you skirt this morning?" My dad teased and rolled his eyes.

"Shut up old man. We all know that Aubrey wears the pants in this relationship." Jake grinned.

"Don't you forget it!" I told him teasingly.

Those two were something else together. I was really glad they got along so well, especially since I'm a daddy's girl and I don't see that changing, ever. My dad wholeheartedly loved Jake. They picked on each other mercilessly, and it was rather entertaining to watch. I curled into Jake and closed my eyes.

CHAPTER FOURTEEN

Ranches and Wounds

We arrived at Ron's ranch the week before the wedding. We planned to get there first so that we could have a couple days to get know one another and make sure everything got set up correctly. Jake still hadn't told him about the babies and was bursting at the seams to tell him the news. He had a car waiting for us at the airfield. They loaded the bags in the trunk and Jake gave the driver the address. We drove for over an hour to the middle of nowhere. There was literally nothing around for miles, except for the occasional cactus. Finally, we came right up to a driveway with a gate. The entire place was surrounded by a fence. Jake was grinning from ear to ear. He pushed in a code, and the gate opened. I sucked in a deep breath trying to quell my nerves. He rubbed my hand reassuringly. Jake grabbed our luggage and fished a key ring from his pocket. He opened the door and called out for Ron. A man came around the corner in a wheel chair. He had snow-white hair and a black cowboy hat on. He smiled the brightest, whitest smile I'd ever seen. Jake put Bella on the floor, and she ran off to explore.

"Jake, my boy. You're here." He beamed. Jake leaned down to embrace him. "I've missed you son." He patted Jakes back.

My heart swelled and I felt the tears coming on. *Damn pregnancy hormones.*

"Pops, I'd like you to meet my beautiful fiancée Aubrey. Aubrey, this is Ron."

"She's a beaut Jake." He looked at me. "It's lovely to meet you, Aubrey."

"You too." I blushed feeling embarrassed.

"Come on, I had Janine set up a spread for you guys before she left. We can sit and catch up. Well I'm already sitting, but you get the idea." He joked.

Ron had such a warm aura about him. You could tell that he was without a doubt a good-hearted person, and I immediately felt comfortable. I also felt a huge wave of relief. I looked around the house. It had an open floor plan and was decorated mostly in earth tones. We went over to the kitchen. Jake pulled a chair out from the table for me to sit down. I sat, and Jake went over to make some plates of food.

"Glad to see you still got your manners boy. I might be in a chair, but I'll still find a way to kick your ass." He eyeballed him. Jake smirked and laughed. "So tell me about yourself, Aubrey."

"There's not too much to tell. I'm from Ohio, and I work as a stewardess for my dad's small airline." Jake cleared his throat.

"Used to baby. You used to work as a stewardess." He smirked.

"Whatever." I rolled my eyes at him and turned back to Ron. "I'm an only child and would like to say that I come from a good family. That's about it." I said bashfully.

"She's modest. I like that in a woman, Jake." He looked at me and winked. I smiled back. "I am so happy that you two are here. Thank you for having the wedding here, it means a lot to me."

"Pops, I wouldn't have it any other way. You know that."

"I know son."

Jake placed plates down in front of us and took a seat next to me. I started picking at my food. One of the cheeses smelled, and it was making me feel really nauseous. I got a lump in my throat. I was trying my best to conceal it, but I had to push the plate away before I threw up. Jake noticed and smirked.

"Pops we have some news… We were going to wait until tonight to tell you."

"Spit it out, boy." Ron laughed. He lifted his fork to put a piece of melon in his mouth.

"You're going to be a grandpa." Jake beamed.

"Seriously?" Ron asked skeptically.

"Absolutely." Jake reached in his back pocket and pulled out his wallet.

He took out the ultrasound picture and pushed it over to Ron. He picked it up and looked at it with tears in his eyes. It was emotional just watching it, and I started to tear up along with him.

"Aubrey, I don't know if Jake told you this or not, but I was never able to have children of my own. I was married to the love of my life. Unfortunately, some years ago she was tragically killed by a drunk driver. We were already in our forties when it happened, and I never remarried. Instead, I ended up putting everything I had into giving back. It was either that, or suicide. I started working with a youth mentoring group, and that's how I met Jake. He was such a lost boy when I met him. Scrawny little thing he was." He wiped his eyes with a handkerchief and took a long sip of water. "Years later I tried to adopt him. They didn't see it as a fit environment because I was a single, middle-aged man. Regardless, I think of him as my son. I made sure no matter where he was that I spent as much time as possible with him. Then one day when I brought Jake to my house he walked over and picked up my old guitar. You see, when I was a youngster in the seventies I used to jam with a group of guys. I saw he had musical talent and made sure that he got lessons and had whatever he needed to thrive. The rest is history." He said proudly.

I was a full on blubbering mess.

"Th-that's wonderful." I sobbed.

Jake reached over and rubbed my back.

"It was much more than that, and you know it." Jake told him.

"Just because you were dealt a shit hand doesn't mean you had to play it. You're a smart kid, and you've made me proud, son."

"Thanks Pops."

I could see that Jake was starting to get emotional.

"It's twins." Jake laughed trying to change the subject.

"Of course it is." Ron shook his head laughing.

We headed outside to see where the wedding was going to take place. It was beautifully landscaped. There was a fountain a little ways out where we would be saying our vows. I could envision the whole thing already. My parents, Granny Jean and Piper would be here in a couple days along with Mark. Mama Bee and Rosie were coming in to prepare all the food. Penelope was coming with her mom and dad. She was so excited when Jake asked her to be our flower girl and the doctors said it was fine. Blake, Derek, Kevin and Kevin's girlfriend Bryn were coming in on Wednesday night. Brett, Ri and Kayley were coming in last minute since Jake sent them on an end of tour vacation. That was it for the guest list since we wanted to keep it as small as possible with just the people that mattered most to us.

Jake excused himself to answer his phone. He had a brief conversation with the foreman from the construction company he hired to oversee the build. They were supposed to be starting on digging the foundation for the new house tomorrow. My parents were thrilled we would be living so close, especially with the babies coming. We sat outside in the fresh air for most of the day. At dinner, we ate barbecued chicken around the fire. The sky was so clear that you could see every star in the sky. We said goodnight to Ron and retreated to Jake's room. He led me down to the other side of the house where his room was and opened the door.

The room was very much Jake's style. The walls were painted a bright blue. It had a queen size wooden bed with a rust colored comforter. There was a dresser against one wall and a giant flat screen hanging on the other. He put our luggage down and led me into the bathroom. There was a sunken tub in the actual floor. I grinned at him. He turned on the faucet and pulled my shirt over my head. He kissed his way down the throat.

"I adore you." He whispered in my ear.

He pulled his shirt over his head and helped me slid out of my shorts. I stepped down into the lukewarm water. He slipped in next to me. I moved over so that I was straddling his lap. I looked into his eyes. I was feeling completely captured in his trance. He lifted his hand to the side of my face. I leaned into it. We were both completely lost in the moment.

I loved being skin to skin with him. It almost made us feel like we were one. I lifted up and slowly slid down onto his hardness. I kissed him passionately and started moving, slowly and deliberately. He wrapped his arms around me and held me close the entire time. We found our release together, and it was such a powerful moment for me. After everything we've been through in such a short time, we were here. We were going to get married and had a growing family on the way. Jake kept kissing me, refusing to let me off of him. Finally, he helped me out of the tub and dried me off, kissing where the babies were.

When I woke up the next morning, I hurried to get dressed. We had to go into town to obtain our marriage license. I picked out a yellow sundress with white flowers and threw on a pair of flip-flops. I added a yellow flower clip into my hair and walked to the kitchen. Jake was drinking a cup of coffee with Ron and laughing. As soon as he noticed me he came over to kiss me good morning. I said hi to Ron and poured a glass of orange juice. Jake already had my vitamin ready and popped it in my mouth.

We ate breakfast together before heading to town. We walked into the court and filled out all the necessary paperwork. They said we could pick it up in two days. Jake helped me back into Ron's Chevy pick-up truck and started going in the opposite direction from where we came from. We drove for fifteen minutes before Jake came to a stop in front of a run-down apartment building.

"This is where I grew up." He said solemnly.

I looked around at the dilapidated, gray building covered in graffiti. My heart sank thinking that a kid actually had to grow up in a place like this. Not just any kid, but Jake. I knew he was born into a set of circumstances beyond his control, but it still hurt. You could clearly see that this place was shady, even during the daytime. I could only imagine what it looked like at night. He leaned on the steering wheel and looked at the building that was once his home. I think he was looking for some sort of closure. I reached over and put my hand in his. I interlaced our fingers, and he brought our hands to his lips and kissed mine. He took one last look before we drove away.

He said he wanted to make one last stop before we went back to the ranch. He stopped at a stand on the side of the road and picked up a bouquet of flowers. We drove to the other side of town and pulled into a cemetery. He kept going until we were almost at the end before he stopped. He got out with flowers in hand. He walked around to my side and opened the door. I climbed out and took his hand. He led me down the path. We stopped at a pink headstone. It was his mom's.

Crystal M. Parker
May the angels lead you home
11/3/1970-12/22/1997

I did the math in my head. She had been gone sixteen years, which was how old she was when she had Jake. She was almost his age now when she died and would have been forty-three. I looked at the date of death. She died right before Christmas. As usual he knew what I was thinking.

"She died right before Christmas. I didn't even know what Christmas was other than what I saw on TV and what the kids in class used to talk about. They used to get really excited about it, but I never had one Christmas as a little kid. She would make me pancakes as long as she wasn't too strung out. My first real Christmas was with Ron when I was twelve. He got me this shiny, red Gibson guitar. I'll never forget it. He gave me a couple beginner's books and helped me learn all the cords. When I was ready, he showed me how to write music. Someone broke into my and Blake's apartment when we first moved to LA and stole it. I literally searched everywhere for months to see if I could find it. I checked every pawn shop in LA but never found it."

He kneeled down and placed the flowers in front of the headstone. I knew even though he didn't have a lot of pleasant memories with her he still loved her. A child's love is unconditional. Unfortunately, some parents don't deserve it. I think she wanted better. She just didn't have the skills to achieve it. She loved the drugs more. I think that's the main reason why Jake just funded a rehab center for mothers with young children near Phoenix. He was hoping it be open by year-end. It's going to be a safe place with a playground and lots of support for the mothers. It's going to be named The Crystal Parker House in her memory. His main goal is going to be getting the people that want the help out of their situation and give them coping skills to build a better life. I loved his humanity. He always thought there was more to do and said that was the main perk of being really famous. If you attached your name to something it would get done.

I watched as he paid his respects. I wanted to say something to comfort him, but I was at a loss for words. I never liked the word 'sorry' when it came to instances like this. It seemed to lack meaning. Instead, I placed my hand on his shoulder showing my support. He placed his hand over mine. He looked deep in thought.

"I don't know you if you can hear me or not. I know I haven't really come here much, but I want you to know I'm okay. I don't hate you. If anything things worked out the way they were intended to. I wish that you were able to turn yourself around, but I'm going to try and help others like you in your honor." He wiped a tear from his eye. "I'm getting married in a couple days to the strongest girl I've ever met. Her name is Aubrey, and she's amazing. I don't know that we would have met if things were different and I wouldn't want to have a life without her. I'm going to be a dad in a few months, too. I won't make the same mistakes that you did. I'm going to be the best dad I can for my kids. More importantly they're going to know how much I fucking love them.

I know you loved me in your own way, at least I think that you did. I don't know when I'll be able to come back, but I just wanted to let you know that I forgive you."

I wiped the tears from my face with my free hand. He had been carrying around that burden for a long time, and he was finally able to let it go. We didn't talk too much about the past because it was of little consequence anymore. I let him know about Jeremy, and we never talked about it again after that. I was grateful he understood and never pushed me to talk about it again. I'm sure there will always be triggers that set me off. But, for the most part I have been able to get back to a normal life. He's taught me what a gentle loving touch is, and I know that he would never hurt me. I think it's the same thing with his mom, but he's been holding on to that burden for a lot longer. He had to deal with the situation for a lot longer than I did, essentially his entire childhood.

I wondered what life would have been like had I we never met. What if he had a normal childhood with normal parents? Would he be the same person that he is today? Would he still be the lead singer of Battlescars or would he be doing something else? I thought the same thing about if that night with Jeremy never happened. How would my life have been different? Then I realized it doesn't matter because our pasts were exactly that. We have each other now and that's all that matters.

Jake

We were at the airfield waiting for Aubrey's family to land. We officially picked up our marriage license on the way here. I can't believe it's only a couple days away! I looked over at my beautiful bride to be and smiled. Aubrey and Ron were getting along awesome, and he adored her. I knew he would. We had a chance to talk last night after Aubrey went to sleep. It brought me back to when I was a teenager, and he would lecture me relentlessly about the way of the world. I would look at him like he was a crazy, old man, but I would listen to him anyway. It turns out he was right about 99… make that 100% of what he told me. I thanked him for being the dad I never had and for all of the opportunities he afforded me, from my first guitar and lessons, to giving me the money to move to LA and follow my dream and everything in between.

I was lucky to be surrounded by such selfless people, Aubrey included. She was always thinking about others before herself, which would be one of her best qualities as a mother. Nothing is going to be about us anymore because we're going to have little people to worry about. I can't wait until she starts getting a bump. Her dress arrived last night. She was hoping it was still going to fit because she gained two pounds since the original fitting. I offered to help her into it, but she said it was bad luck and that she would wait for her mom and Piper to help. I was looking forward to introducing Tim to Ron and vice versa.

I watched as the small plane landed on the tarmac. I got out to help Tim load the luggage into the truck. Once everything was loaded up we had to cram everyone inside. We had Tim, Caroline, Piper and Mark in the back and Aubrey and Granny Jean were up front with me. Luckily it was a roomy truck. I started the ignition and headed back to the ranch.

Aubrey was animatedly talking with her mom and Piper about the wedding plans and how she wanted everything set up. She was so excited, and it was contagious. I would have been excited anyway, but seeing her like this just pushed it up a couple notches. Granny Jean was bitching about wanting to stop at a reservation so she could get cheap cigarettes. Tim and Mark looked like they were surrounded by too much estrogen and needed a beer, or several. When we pulled into the ranch, everyone practically jumped out of the truck, except Aubrey.

"I love you." She grinned and pulled my face to hers.

"I love you more." I whispered before kissing her like a madman.

There was a knock on the window. Tim stood outside the window holding his wrist up and tapping on his watch. Aubrey turned bright red and started giggling. I shook my head and kissed her one last time before opening the door.

"We're waiting." He teased.

I grabbed a couple suitcases and led them to the front door. I held it open so they could all go inside. Ron rolled into the foyer with a huge grin on his face. I put the suitcases down and did introductions. Aubrey and I showed everyone to their rooms and told them to get cleaned up for dinner. We were going to do a BBQ out back tonight since I was cooking. We told them to meet us in the living room in an hour.

Aubrey grabbed my hand and led me back to our room. She closed the door and locked it. She pushed me back until I was on the bed. She leaned in and started kissing me again. She was purposely rubbing her ass against my crotch making me hard enough to crush diamonds. She had a short, little skirt today, so I moved her panties aside and started caressing her gently. She moaned in my mouth a couple times before I moved so that she was on her back. I unzipped my pants and felt bad for not taking my pants off, but it was an afternoon quickie after all. I slowly sank into her. I slowly built a rhythm. Her hands grasped handfuls of the comforter before grabbing onto my ass and making me move at her pace. I felt her detonate around me, and I knew that I couldn't hold out much longer. She leaned up and whispered in my ear.

"Fuck me, Jake!" She purred. "Please…you're always so gentle with me. I want you to fuck me hard and fast. *Please.*" She pleaded.

Just her talking like that was enough to make me lose it. At first I didn't want to because I was worried about the babies, but we talked to the doctor and I did my own research. It all said it was perfectly fine. So I reared back and slammed into her. I picked up the pace and if her moaning was any clue she liked it, a lot. *I've created a monster.* I continued to thrust into her, and I could tell she was close again. Three more thrusts and I felt her like a vice grip squeezing me. My balls tightened, and I found my release deep inside her.

"Holy shit! That was amazing…" She grinned.

"It's always amazing as long as it's with you, baby. I love you."

Every time with her seemed better than the last, except for our first time. I don't count that because it goes down in history as being the best night of my life so far, bar none. I held her close for a couple minutes before running to the bathroom to get a washcloth. I went back into the bedroom and cleaned her up. Seeing her spread out on the bed like that just made me want her again. I looked at my watch. We went at it for almost forty-five minutes and everyone would be waiting for us. I helped her to her feet and led her to the living room before I changed my mind.

Thankfully we were all the way at the other end of the house so no one could hear us. I think even though we're getting married and Aubrey's already pregnant that Tim would want to kick my ass. I'm probably going to have all daughters just for karma's sake. In fact, we should probably just name our first Karma and save everyone the trouble, they can just say Karma did it. I've been trying to pay restitution in the form of good deeds for a long time, but I can't even imagine how many broken hearts I led to...

We arrived the same time as Piper did.

"Oh my God, you guys just totally did it!" She shrieked.

"Shut up." Aubrey whisper yelled. "At least I'm getting some." She smirked.

"You've got me there." She teased.

We walked into the kitchen and gathered all of the ingredients for dinner and set everything up outside. I started the grill while Aubrey went to get Ron up from his nap. Piper was setting the table. Everyone else came out a couple minutes later. I put on Ron's *Kiss the Chef* apron and threw some burgers on the grill. I handed Tim and Mark a much needed beer from the built in fridge and popped the caps. Granny Jean was sitting off to the side with Ron drinking her whiskey sours and smoking a Lucky Strike. Those two hit it off right away, probably because they both had a quick-witted charm about them. Aubrey was talking with her mom and Piper. I made the food and looked at my happy extended family. I was beyond grateful.

"Do you want some help, honey?" Caroline asked.

"Caroline, grilling is a man's job. Ain't that right, Jake." Tim teased.

"Whatever he says." I laughed shaking my head.

Son-in-law rule #1: Always side with the father in law.

"That a boy." He clapped me on the shoulder.

The girls just cracked up.

"Timothy Andrew Thompson, you behave yourself or I'm gonna come over and spank you." Granny Jean yelled from across the way. "I might be almost eighty years old, but I'll still take you over my knee."

Ron looked at her thoughtfully. I know that look…

I put everything on plates and set it on the table. Everyone dug in, and I even got some compliments on my grilling skills. Okay, just Aubrey commended me, but she counts too. We sat around talking into the night. I started a fire in the fire pit and went inside to get the S'mores supplies. I handed everyone a skewer and a handful of marshmallows. I roasted Aubrey's to perfection and handed it to her. I noticed Ron staring at me. When I looked at him, he nodded his head letting me know he thought I was doing a good job. His approval meant more to me than anything. I only hoped I could be half the man that he is one day. Around eleven everyone turned in for the night. We needed to be up on the early side since we had venue people coming to do some pre-wedding set up.

The next morning I got up before dawn and went to the kitchen. I set up the coffee pot so that it would be ready when everyone else got up. I grabbed some fruit out of the fridge and cut it up to snack on. Then I decided to try my hand at making a breakfast casserole. I was almost finished when Ron wheeled into the room. He looked at me and smirked.

"Whatcha doing?" He asked.

"Trying to make breakfast." I laughed.

I finished sprinkling some cheddar cheese over the top and put it into the oven.

"Looks like you did a good job. Let's just hope it tastes as good as it looks." He teased.

"We can only hope." I took a seat at the table.

"Jake, the difference I see in you from the last time you were here is nothing short of amazing. You're like an entirely new person. I know you've always been uncomfortable with hearing about your self worth, but dammit boy I'm not getting any younger, and I don't know how many more opportunities I'll have. I'm going to tell it to you straight. You deserve everything you've got going on right now. I've watched you learn, struggle, fall and pick yourself back up. I've watched you succeed and fly to new heights, but this is what life's all about. I'm so happy that I'm here to see it. I'm humbled that you've chosen and allowed me to be a father figure for you. If I had a son you're exactly who I would have wanted."

He pulled a handkerchief out of his pocket and wiped his eyes. I went over and hugged him. I got emotional too.

"If I could have had anyone to be my dad I would have picked you too. You've shown me how to be a man. Even through my mistakes you never criticized me. You only offered advice when I asked for it or when you thought I truly needed it. I will *never* be able to repay you for what you've given me. I love you Pops."

"I love you too, son. I'm glad we got this chance."

"Me too."

The timer went off for the casserole, and I took it out of the oven. It was a southwest egg bake sort of thing. It had cheese, eggs, peppers, onions and sausage, and I pushed a can of biscuits down in the bottom of the pan for good measure. It smelled good. I poured us each a cup of coffee and cut up the casserole. I walked over and placed the plate down hoping to get a stamp of approval from the old man. He cut a small piece off with his fork and sniffed it before putting it in his mouth. He nodded in approval, and I tried a bite. It was actually pretty good. I was proud of myself. Tim was the next one to come to the kitchen. He was another early riser. He grabbed a mug of coffee and sat at the table.

"Did you make that?" He asked skeptically.

"He did, and it's actually edible." Ron teased.

"Well what the hell are you waiting for? Go get me some and no I will not kiss the damn chef." He laughed.

I put the dirty dishes in the dishwasher and made him a plate. I brought it over to him and waited for his response.

"I'll be damned, the boy can cook."

I grinned happily.

Pretty soon everyone, except Aubrey, was up. They all seemed to enjoy my casserole too. I excused myself to go wake my girl up. I opened the door and saw she had somehow sprawled herself across the entire bed. I walked over and sat on the empty part of the bed. I moved her hair out of her face and shook her lightly. She scrunched her face and swatted at me.

"Go away." She mumbled.

"It's time to get up, baby. Everyone else already ate and everything."

She bolted upright.

"You ate without me?" She shrieked. "I'm starving. Did you make bacon?"

"No, sausage." She pouted. "Come on, I'll go cook you some bacon."

I led her to the kitchen.

"Nice of you to join us this morning, princess." Tim chimed.

"Talk to the hand 'cause this princess is grouchy until she has breakfast."

The whole room erupted into laughter. I turned the skillet on and prepped to make her some French toast and bacon since it was her favorite. I worked at warped speed and managed to have it in front of her within five minutes. She took the fork from me and stabbed the first piece of bread and put it to her mouth. She quickly scarfed everything down and smiled. I brought her a glass of orange juice and her vitamins. She tossed them in her mouth and swallowed.

The boys and I were off to go get fitted for some suits today. There was this awesome tailor not too far from here that said he could have them ready by Saturday. The girls were going to stay here and do girly things. I planned a surprise for them. I knew Aubrey would enjoy it and I thought the others would too, except maybe Granny Jean. We climbed into the truck and headed out.

Aubrey

"Alright let's see this dress." Piper chimed excitedly.

I walked over to the closet and pulled out the garment bag. I unzipped it and did the big reveal. Piper jumped up and down excitedly. My mom said she loved it, but that she wished it were white. Granny Jean asked if I was changing my name to Morticia. I stripped down so I could finally try it on. I was just about in when the doorbell rang. I hobbled over to the door clutching the dress to my chest. I wondered if someone arrived earlier than expected. I wasn't worried about opening the door since you needed to have the gate code in order to get in. The only people that had it were Ron and the guests.

It was two women dressed in uniforms. They said that they were from Lotus Spa and that they were here to give us a day of pampering. I invited them in and told them we needed a couple minutes. We quickly tied the dress, and I looked in the mirror. It fit perfectly and looked wonderful. I took it off and hung it back on the hanger and stuck in back in the closet.

We walked back into the room, and they had brought in a couple of massage tables along with a couple boxes. They asked where to set everything up, and my mom suggested outside by the patio. Piper and I had our massages first while my mom and Granny Jean got their nails and toes painted. It felt really nice. It was yet another thing I thought I would never be able to enjoy. I rolled over and got a chocolate facial next. I was buffed and polished by the time the boys arrived back. Jake was carrying a bag. He held it out to me and gave me a kiss.

"Did you like your surprise?" He asked.

"It was very thoughtful and we all thoroughly enjoyed it. Thank you." I hugged him. "I missed you. Did you get your errands done?"

"Sure did, wait until you see me on our wedding day." He grinned happily. "That bag you're holding contains a piece of triple chocolate cheesecake with a chocolate ganache topping, and homemade chocolate whipped cream." I clutched the bag and jumped on him wrapping my legs around his waist.

"You are the best almost husband ever!" I kissed him biting his lip before I pulled away. I leaned in and whispered in his ear. "You are totally getting laid later."

I felt him get a semi and laughed. He refused to put me down and carried me into the kitchen. He grabbed a fork and sat down, so I was on his lap. I opened the bag and pulled out my cake. It looked like an orgasm on a plate, the Picasso of cakes. I almost didn't even want to eat it. Who am I kidding? I had my fork stabbed in it in the blink of an eye. I put it to my mouth and moaned. It somehow managed to taste even better than it looked if that was even possible. The only thing that could have made it better was if it had chocolate covered bacon bits on top. I should totally call and see if they could make that for me. I bet Jake could convince them to do it.

"Can we get one of these with chocolate covered bacon?" I asked with my mouth full.

He chuckled into my hair and tried to pretend like he wasn't. He pulled out his phone and looked up the number.

"Hi I was just there and bought a piece of your triple chocolate cheesecake. I was wondering if it would be possible to have one made with chocolate covered bacon on top?" He waited. "Yes that's me." He laughed. "Thanks. I'll be there tomorrow to pick it up." He turned to look at me. "The chef said absolutely."

"I love you like a fat kid loves cake." I kissed him.

I fed him the last bite because sharing is caring.

"I think you might be onto something with the bacon." He teased.

We went and joined everyone else. We spent the last night before the rest of our company was set to arrive relaxing around the fire.

CHAPTER FIFTEEN

Do I?

The whole place had turned into chaos since everyone arrived. Blake and Derek were in love with Granny Jean and made it a point to sit next to her at every meal. Derek asked her if he could move in with her when they moved to Ohio.

"Do I look like a motel?" She asked.

"No, you look like a grandma." He teased.

"Don't be a smart ass." She playfully whacked him in the back of the head.

"Aubrey, I'm totally stealing your Granny."

I shook my head and laughed. I was helping Mama Bee and Rosie peel corn on the cob. Jake came up and kissed my cheek. He leaned in to whisper.

"Have you seen Piper?"

I shook my head no. As a matter of fact, I haven't seen her in a while.

"Is she with Blake?" I asked.

"That scoundrel." He walked away mumbling something under his breath.

A little while later both Piper and Blake came into the room. They were looking chummy. I wondered if they might start something up, especially since Blake would be Ohio bound soon. We've talked enough that she knew his reputation and that he wasn't exactly the settling down type. The doorbell rang, and I got up to answer it knowing that we were only expecting one last group today.

It was Penelope and her family. I leaned down and hugged her. I couldn't wait for her to see the dress I had Lulu make for her. I greeted her parents, Lucy and Paul. Jake walked in and took them to do introductions. I used the opportunity to steal Penelope for a couple minutes. I led her down to my room and pulled the dress out. I took her hand and led her back to the living room because I wanted her mom to see her reaction too. She politely excused herself, and we went into the kitchen. I unzipped the bag and took it out. Her entire face lit and she squeaked loudly. It was a hot pink Cinderella style dress with rhinestones and glitter. It had extra layers of tulle to make it extra poofy. She ran her little fingers over the fabric and hugged me tightly.

"What do you say Penelope?" Lucy asked.

"Thank you Aubrey. It's just like a real princess dress."

I handed the bag to Lucy so she could put it in their room. She thanked me too. Penelope ran in to the living room and jumped on Jake.

"Jakey!"

"Princess Penelope, I missed you. How's my girl?"

"I'm fabulous. Did you know that Queen Aubrey got me a dress? It's the most beautiful dress I've ever seen in my whole entire life!"

"Is it now? Queen Aubrey has good taste. That's why she's marrying me." He looked at me and winked. The room laughed.

Jake showed them to their room and helped carry their stuff. Mama Bee and Rosie called dinnertime. Tonight they made a pot roast, mashed potatoes, corn on the cob and some of Mama's famous biscuits. Whatever they did to the pot roast made it even better than my mom's recipe. It was mouthwatering. I savored every last bite. After dinner, we were going to meet Kevin and Bryn for ice cream with the boys and Piper. Kevin wanted to take her around the city. Since they didn't eat meat, he found a vegan restaurant to try. Mama offered to cook them something else, but he said they were fine.

I noticed some thick, sexual tension between Piper and Blake. It was only a matter of time before they realized they were a match in BDSM heaven. Piper was into some weird stuff, at least it was weird to me. I had a feeling it would be right up Blake's alley. We all climbed into the truck and headed to down. We pulled into Cones and Such and ordered ice cream. Jake paid for everyone.

They even had a kind that Kevin could have. Jake pulled me onto his lap.

"Look at those two." I laughed.

"I give it until the end of the night."

At that moment, a drop of ice cream dripped onto Piper's chest. Blake leaned over and licked it off. They initiated some sort of staring contest.

"I'm going to bang you so hard we should probably exchange insurance information." She rasped.

"Gladly." He winked.

The two of them engaged in a full-blown public make out session. Jake kept throwing things at them to make them separate, but they weren't breaking. He tossed Blake the keys, and he caught them midair.

"Don't get the seats dirty." He cringed.

"I have no idea how you dealt with them for over three months." Bryn laughed.

"Puh-lese, she kept us in line. She loved every minute of it. Didn't you Aub's." Derek smirked.

"It wasn't nearly as bad as I thought it was going to be." I admitted. "Plus I get a husband out of the deal." I kissed him lightly.

"Are you guys all ready for tomorrow?" She asked.

"As ready as we're going to be."

"I'm really happy for you both." Kevin said earnestly.

"Thanks Kev."

We finished our dessert and made sure that the truck wasn't rocking before opening the door. They were both smirking, and I just knew...

When we got home, we said our good night's and went to bed. We weren't conforming to the traditional "not seeing the bride the night before." We didn't want to be apart, especially if we were going to be separated for most of the day tomorrow. I curled into Jake and closed my eyes. It was my last night as Aubrey Thompson.

The next morning I opened my eyes and saw the blue sky out the window. I stood up and stretched. Jake wasn't in bed, but there was a pink rose on his pillow with a red box next to it. I picked up the rose and smelled it. I lifted the lid to the box. Nestled inside was a necklace with a row of gray Tahiti pearls and a diamond clasp. They would look amazing with my dress. I was starting to get choked up by his thoughtfulness when he walked into the room with a tray of breakfast. He smiled and put the tray on the end table.

"Do you like them?"

"I love them. You have no idea how perfect they are. Thank you Jake."

"Today's the big day. I'm not supposed to be in here right now per the womens' orders, but I at least need one kiss to get me through the day."

He placed his hand on the side of my face and captured my lips. He pulled away way too soon. I pouted, but he shook his head no. I think he knew that we would both end up getting carried away, which was exactly what I wanted right now. I needed some relief. He sensed it and dropped his hand. He rubbed me gently until I found my release. I wanted to return the favor, but he kissed me and quickly stepped out of my reach.

"I'll see you at the alter, baby." He winked.

"Yeah, see you later." I grumbled.

Thankfully the wedding was in the early afternoon, and I wouldn't have to wait too long. I had no patience as it was. Especially when it came to something I was looking forward to. I ate my breakfast and hopped in the shower. I dressed in one of Jake's button downs. I walked toward the living room to find my mom. I saw Jake in the other room and heard him groan. My mom was sitting on the couch reading the paper. I leaned over the couch and gave her a hug. I made sure I bent over so that he could see my panties.

"No fair." He yelled before disappearing.

Stick that in your pipe and smoke it. I laughed.

"Are you all ready for today?" She asked.

"Definitely. The hairdressers should be here soon. We should gather everyone up that wants their hair done and go to my room since we have a bigger bathroom."

We left to gather all the women. I had one last surprise for Penelope too. Since she said she loved my pink hair we had the salon make her a pink wig to wear. It was going to match her dress, and I knew she was going to love it. Once we had everyone assembled we set up in my room. My dad brought in a couple chairs. He said that he and Ron had everything under control outside.

A little while later the hair and make-up crew arrived. They started with my mom and Granny Jean first. When they were done, they took Piper and Penelope. Her face when she saw the wig was priceless. When they had it in place, they did Lucy's hair next. She tried to decline, but we all insisted. I was last. They got to work pulling the hair up and securing it in curls. When the final finishes were done I looked in the mirror and gasped. I looked spectacular.

They did an awesome pink and black smokey eye, and pale pink lips. My hair looked awesome. It was very 1950's pin up. I knew Jake was going to love it. They even managed to make the curls in the front look like a heart. The last thing to do was pin in my netted veil. They cleaned up and left. Everyone else left to go get dressed. My mom and Piper were coming back to help me get into my dress once they were finished. I picked up my string of pearls and fastened them into place. I was bouncing in place until they came back. My mom handed me my bouquet of pink roses wrapped in black satin ribbon.

I went and pulled my dress out of the closet and laid it on the bed. My mom looked beautiful in a silver dress with cap sleeves and a pair of matching shoes. Piper had on a hot pink tutu dress and black pumps. Granny Jean was dressed in a knee length leopard print dress. She had a thing for leopard print for as long as I can remember and for being eighty she rocked it.

"Since your pearls are your something new we each brought you something to finish the rest."

Piper handed me a blue garter as my something blue. Granny handed me something old. It was my grandpa's pocket watch. My mom handed me her topaz ring for my something borrowed. It was a twenty-year anniversary present from my dad, and she never took it off. I slid it onto my right hand. We unzipped the garment bag and lifted the dress out. I unbuttoned the shirt and tossed it on the floor. I stood there in my all black lingerie and stepped into my dress. Piper laced up the corset making sure to leave it a little loose, so we didn't hurt the babies.

My mom helped me into my shoes. I picked out bejeweled flats instead of heels because I didn't want to risk falling on my face or being embarrassed. I took one last look in the mirror. Just as we were finishing the final touches, my dad knocked on the door. He looked dapper in his black suit and crisp white shirt. He had on a hot pink tie. It made me smile. They each kissed me as they left the room.

"You look beautiful, princess." He looked my dress over. "I can't believe my baby is getting married." He started to get choked up.

"Don't start, or I'm going to totally lose it. I'm emotional enough because of the pregnancy hormones." I fanned my face and tried to keep the tears at bay.

He held his arm out, and I looped my arm with his. We walked out of the bedroom and down the hallway. We stopped right before we reached the patio. I sucked in a deep breath to quell my nerves and stepped outside. The backyard looked magical. There were three rows of white chairs with pink and black bows tied to the backs. I noticed that Brett and Ri made it last minute. Jake made plans to send them to Disney World as a gift for being awesome. This was the only week that Kayley was off. Penelope was sitting with Kayley holding Bella looking adorable in her dress and pink hair.

Everyone turned to look at me. I just focused on Jake at the end. He was in a black suit with a hot pink shirt and black tie. I laughed when I saw he was wearing his untied boots. He claimed they were good luck and wore them year round. I stepped one foot in front of the other until I reached him. My dad kissed my cheek and went to take a seat next to my mom. Kevin was officiating the ceremony since he took a class online and was probably the only person that would take our kind of wedding seriously. Jake took my hand and smiled brightly.

"We are gathered here today in front of family and friends to witness the marriage between Aubrey and Jake. I've known Jake for about eight years, give or take, and he's grown to be like a brother to me. Over the past few years, I've watched him walk around missing something. Love. That is until he met Aubrey. She was exactly what he needed, and whether she wanted to admit it at the time he was exactly what she needed too. Together they have started creating an amazing future together. A life that most people would envy. I am honored that you guys chose me to perform your ceremony. Your marriage resembles a pair of sheers. Joined they cannot be separated, often moving in opposite directions, yet punishing anyone who comes between them. This is especially true when it comes to these two. I would never want to be the one to try and keep them apart." He laughed. "Instead of traditional vows they have chosen to write their own. Jake you start."

"Aubrey, my Bellissimo, my love. I write songs for a living and I had a hard time putting into words just exactly how much you mean to me. When we met you were like a tornado. You knocked me right on my ass and wouldn't put up with any of my crap. I told myself on the plane ride to New York that I knew you were worth it. I was right. It was that same time that I wanted to win your heart. I had to work so hard to get you to acknowledge that I existed at all. I'm so glad you found a reason to believe in me because you showed me what it was like to live again. I was living a shell of a life before you came along. I got up and went through the motions not feeling anything. You make me feel again. You don't take any of my shit, and if I get out of line you smack me back in my place. I truly love you more than I can ever express and I promise to spend my life showing you exactly that. You're my smart-ass, eye-rolling partner in crime. You're with me every moment I breathe. Until I die I will sing our names in unison. I love you baby." He leaned in and pecked my lips lightly.

"No kissing until the end." Kevin playfully reprimanded. "Aubrey, it's your turn."

"Jake, when I met you I was a scared girl putting on a tough front. I spent years pushing people away because I didn't want to get hurt. You were so patient and understanding about everything even when I shut you out, which I did, *a lot.* But, you pursued me anyway and managed to make me feel both safe and loved. You helped me let my guard down and learn to live again. I've been able to experience things that I didn't think were ever possible for me. Well you know why… but you have given me the strength. You've helped me heal. You make me want to be a better person. I knew it was no sacrifice to let you in. I love the fact that you're passionate, even if you do go balls to the wall with everything. I need that in my life because I'm the exact opposite. We counterbalance each other. You're everything I could ever want in a husband and so much more. I can't wait to go on this journey and experience all this life has to offer with you by my side. I love you." I managed to get it all out without having a breakdown.

"Can I have the rings please?" Kevin asked.

Penelope handed Bella to Kayley and brought up the rings. I got Jake a black carbide ring since it seemed fitting for him. Kevin handed my ring to Jake. He took my hand and slid the ring onto my finger. It was a band of rose gold surrounded by diamonds.

"Aubrey, I give you this ring with my promise to always be faithful to you. I promise to love you unconditionally in good times and in bad. I promise to be what you need when you need it. I promise all these things to you for as long as we both shall live."

Kevin handed me Jake's ring.

"Jake, I give you this ring with a promise to always love you and be there for you no matter what. I promise to be your faithful, loving and kick your ass when you need it. I solemnly vow this for as long as we both shall live."

"Without further ado I now pronounce you Mr. and Mrs. Jake Parker. You may now kiss your bride."

Jake took his left hand that now had his wedding band and placed it on my cheek. He leaned in and kissed me. It started out all sweet and innocent until the tongues started dancing. Kevin cleared his throat and Jake swatted at him.

"There are children present." Granny yelled.

We reluctantly pulled away from one another. Everyone stood and clapped. The photographer we hired was busy snapping away. Everyone walked over to where the little reception had been set up. Everything was done in black and pink. Mama Bee and Rosie were busy taking the lids off the trays. I looked around at everyone that came. We were so lucky to have such great family and extended family. I think the word "friends" was too lacking for what they were to us. Ron wheeled over, and we both leaned down and gave him a hug. He said to save him a dance later.

We made our way through and greeted everyone before getting some food. They totally outdid themselves. We had chicken Parmesan, four different kinds of pasta, meatballs, sausage and peppers and lots of chocolate cake. I tried to sit down in my own chair, but Jake pulled me onto his lap. Blake started the music. Penelope and Kayley were twirling out on the dance floor that had been set up. They became fast friends, and it was adorable to watch. We went to the dance floor. Jake and I had our first official dance with Adcle's *Make You Feel My Love.* We danced nose to nose as Jake sang the song to me. It was so romantic. When we were done, I danced with my dad, Ron, and the boys. Jake danced with my mom, Granny Jean and Penelope. We walked over to the cake table and cut the first piece. Jake fed me the first bite. I bit down on his thumb as he was pulling out of my mouth. He looked at me with wide eyes. I knew exactly what reaction I was going to get. I placed his piece in his mouth and then smeared the frosting all over his face earning a hooting laugh from Derek.

"I'm going to get you for that later, Mrs. Parker."

"I'm banking on it, Mr. Parker."

"Is it time to go yet?"

"Go? Where are we going?" I asked perplexed.

"On our honeymoon, silly. You didn't think I'd forget that little detail, did you?"

I shook my head because I completely forgot that little detail.

"We're off to Tahiti for two weeks. I hired a personal shopper to buy you an entire wardrobe for the trip. Everything is already packed and ready to go."

"You sneak." I swatted at his chest laughing.

"Well... can we go?" He raised an eyebrow.

"Aren't there rules against bailing on your own wedding?" I laughed.

"No. We've been socializing for hours. Come on, let's start making the rounds." He tugged on my hand.

We did exactly that. We said goodbye to each person. Everyone wished us luck and a great honeymoon. I went inside to change into more comfortable clothes since we were going to be travelling. Jake said the car was waiting out front to take us to the airport. We would be flying first class instead of private. He was hoping to avoid getting mauled and was glad I was going to be there to keep the bitches at bay. We yelled one last final farewell before heading to the car.

We arrived at the airport and made it through security and customs without as much as one heckler. We went to the first class lounge since Jake insisted it was safer than sitting with the general population. They called our flight. We boarded the plane and started our adventure.

When we arrived in Tahiti, we were set up in a little villa right on the beach. We had our own private section of waterfront with no one else around. The sand was white, and the water was crystal clear. I changed into my bathing suit, and Jake did the same. I jumped on his back, and he took off in a run toward the water. He stepped into the refreshing warm water. I felt it splashing up on my feet. He dunked down, so we were submerged from the waist down. He pulled me around, so I was facing him. I leaned in and kissed him passionately. He held me tightly as he sat in the ocean. The water was lapping against my back. We were trying to be discreet in case we had any unwanted visitors or a paparazzi with a long lens. I undid the Velcro to his swim shorts as he slid my bottoms to the side. I moved until we were lined up. I gently lowered myself onto his hardness. We rocked back and forth with the waves until we found our release completely in sync.

We spent the rest of the honeymoon relaxing and eating. We did do a little sightseeing and some activities, but spent most of the time in our little villa wrapped up in sheets. It was refreshing to be able to go out and not worry about being spotted though. It was almost like being normal again. I was starting to feel a lot better too. The nausea was almost completely gone, and I was starting to get some of my energy back.

Tonight was going to be our last night on the island. I was looking forward to going home. As nice as it was to be away there is nothing like your own bed. We decided we were going to go to

LA first and spend some time there. Then we would be off to Ohio so that we could check on how the building process was coming along. My dad was there a lot keeping an eye on things.

We were all surprised how quickly it was coming together. It should be though since we had three different full time construction crews there to ensure it was done on time. I was almost at the end of my first trimester already and time didn't seem to be slowing down. I just hoped that it would be ready in time. I also had my Piper and the boys working on a mission for me to surprise Jake.

I was under the umbrella stretched out in a lounge chair watching Jake make sand castles like a five year old. He looked over at me and grinned. I shook my head at him and laughed. He stood and walked to the ocean to clean the sand off his hands. He took off in a jog toward me.

"How's my baby momma? Do you need me to get you anything?"

"I'm good. You can go back to creating your village." I teased.

He leaned in and kissed me and took off to play in the sand some more.

We packed up the rest of our stuff and headed back to LA.

CHAPTER SIXTEEN

The Crow & The Butterfly

5 ½ months later…

Jake

I rolled over and practically fell out of bed. Between Aubrey and Bella I was lucky if I was able to sleep in bed the at all. We've been staying at her parent's house waiting for our house to be finished. Her queen size bed wasn't cutting it anymore since her bump was so big. I ended up spending a lot of nights sleeping on the couch lately. I fucking loved her pregnant belly though. We stopped being able to fly back and forth to LA about a month ago because the doctor said it was too risky, especially carrying twins. We went to the doctor yesterday for a check-up, and they said that she could literally go into labor at any time. Her c-section was scheduled for next week already. We found out what we were having a couple months ago and finally managed to agree on baby names. My vote for Karma Jean got vetoed.

I was looking forward to getting settled into the new house. We were really going to have to work double time to get settled in, and I wasn't going to let Aubrey do any work at all. All of the furniture is expected to be there at some point today. We were planning on going over there later to make sure it looks good before we move the rest of the boxes in. I got up and climbed out of bed. I grabbed my notebook and pen so I could try and write some more stuff for the new album since sleep was out of the question. I had been feeling so inspired lately that I filled up over three notebooks with lyrics. I headed to the kitchen to make some coffee. I took a seat at the table while it was percolating.

"Morning." Tim said walking into the room.

"Morning." I replied.

"You get kicked out of bed again?"

"No, but I would have fallen out if she moved another inch." I laughed.

"You're a better man than I am. I would have moved into a hotel or something." He joked.

"I'm used to not sleeping, and I'm good to go with just a few hours. Probably a good thing, since I have a feeling that sleep will become a luxury come next week."

He poured us each a cup of coffee and sat at the table. I decided to go shower and get ready so when Aubrey woke up we could get going. I went into the bathroom and started shaving when I felt Aubrey and her bump come up behind me.

"Morning handsome." She croaked.

"Good morning, beautiful. How are you feeling?"

"Like I swallowed a bowling ball, a watermelon and the USS Enterprise." She laughed.

"You look awesome Aubrey. I mean it."

I did mean it. After the first trimester, she cut a lot of the junk food out of her diet since it was bad for the babies. She only ate bacon occasionally and even started walking more. She didn't even gain that much for carrying twins. I would have thought she looked banging regardless because to me she was the prettiest girl on the face of the earth. She just smirked at me. I wiped the rest of the shaving cream off my face and leaned in to kiss her.

"Are you ready to go see the house today?" I asked.

"Yes! I feel like a sardine in this house now." She pouted.

I hopped in the shower and by the time I got out she was all ready to go. She took my hand and pulled me out to her car. She was still keeping her car even though I bought her a white Range Rover since it would be easier with the babies. I opened the door and helped her climb in. She was so damn stubborn. I wish she would just take the truck, but she loved her little car. I got into the driver's seat and drove exactly seven minutes down the road until we reached the house. We had the entire house surrounded by white privacy fencing. I even managed to incorporate a moat around the property. We drove over the little bridge and up to the gate. I punched in the code, and it opened. I drove around the first half of the circle. In the middle of the driveway was an exact replica of Ron's fountain. The same one we got married in front of. The house had slate gray vinyl siding with a stone front. We had lots and lots of windows too. I helped Aubrey out of the car and opened the door.

The entryway floor was black tile and the walls were painted a pale gray. There was a small table set up with a mirror hanging above it. It had a bowl on it for our keys. Off to the right, was our family room and the left was our kitchen and dining room. The bottom of the house was built so that all the rooms were connected like a square. The living room was painted a burnt orange color that Aubrey picked out. I wasn't sure about it at first, but once it was painted I loved it. We had a stone fireplace in there and a large bay window. My 70" TV was already mounted and looked spectacular.

The dining room was painted navy blue and had white wainscoting. We picked out an antique crystal chandelier to hang in there. The kitchen was everything that Aubrey wanted and more. She decided on all white cabinets with dark granite countertops, while the walls were painted the same blue as my bedroom in LA. I got her all top of the line stainless steel appliances and these really cool vintage lights to hang above the breakfast bar.

We walked into the den off the kitchen. The den was painted a soft shade of beige. We would most likely use this as a playroom for when the babies got a little bigger. My office was going to be one of the rooms off the den. This was Aubrey's top-secret project. I wasn't allowed to know which room it was yet. The buzzer sounded letting us know we had company. I walked to the front door and pulled the camera up on the screen. I saw the furniture delivery truck and hit the button to let them in.

Aubrey was wandering around, looking for something to clean. Poor thing was nesting like crazy. I unlocked the other side of the door to make the entranceway bigger and led them inside. They brought in the dining room furniture first. Aubrey picked out a white table and navy blue upholstered chairs to match. Next was the living room furniture. It was an oversized beige loveseat, couch and two recliners. They brought in a mocha colored coffee table and put it in the center. They carried in the stools for the breakfast bar and my desk. I tried to show them where to put it, but Aubrey stopped me. I looked at her confused. She grabbed my shirt and pulled me into the living room and made me sit on the new couch. She told me no peeking and left to do more nesting.

The last of the furniture was all going in the bedrooms upstairs. The second truck for the guesthouse pulled in shortly after they were done unloading. They drove around back and got to work. Aubrey came back and led me back to my office. She put her hands over my eyes and scooted me forward pushing her bump into my back. She stepped around in front of me and pulled her hands away.

HOLY FUCKING SHIT!!!

"Are you serious?" I felt like crying.

She nodded and started crying. I leaned in and kissed her before going to inspect it. I couldn't even imagine how much trouble she must have gone through to find it. It was one of the most thoughtful things anyone has ever done for me. Mounted behind my desk was my first red Gibson guitar. I knew it was the same one because the scuffs were in the same spots. I walked around the desk and ran my fingers over it. I couldn't even believe it.

"Thank you." I said sincerely.

"You're welcome. I knew how much it meant to you, and I wanted you to have it back. It wasn't easy to find. I had some help, but ultimately it was me that tracked it down." She said proudly.

If it weren't for her being eight and a half months pregnant, I would have thrown her over my shoulder and carried her upstairs to have my way with her. Instead, I was going to have to take her hand and led her to the bedroom like a gentleman. We did have a new mattress to check out after all. We headed up the stairs and down the hallway. At the end of the hallway, there were doors on either side. Those would be the nurseries. Our room was at the very end behind a set of double doors. I pushed down the handle and opened the door. Our room was painted a sage green, and we picked out the same driftwood style furniture I have in LA since we both really liked it. She pulled me over to the bed and pushed me down. She pulled up her maxi style dress and climbed on top of me. I thought I was going to have my way with her, but it turned out to be the other way around.

"I'm going to check out my closet." She beamed when she was done.

I made sure she had room for all of her clothes, shoes and whatever other kind of stuff she had. I also had a couple things picked out for her. I got her a nice, new piece of jewelry because I wasn't going to buy her clothes until after the babies were born. However, I did buy her a Juicy Couture diaper bag because the lady at the store said that girls like them. I went and peeked into the nurseries to make sure they got the right furniture in each room. Everything looked perfect. I heard my name being called. I walked in to see Aubrey in the bathroom.

"Took you long enough. I came in here to pee, and I'm pretty sure my water just broke."

Shit! I've been mentally preparing myself for this day for months already. I took a moment to collect my thoughts. I thought back to our birthing classes and tried to remember what they taught us.

"Do you have any pain?"

"No, but we're going to need to call Dr. Robinson so she can meet us at the hospital. C-section, remember?"

"Right. I'm on it."

I pulled my phone out and called the doctor feeling completely discombobulated. Next I called Caroline. I asked her if she could meet us at the hospital and bring the overnight bag. I asked her to take the Range Rover since that was the car with the infant seats in it. She was going to leave in a couple minutes. I took one of the towels from the linen closet for the car seat. I helped Aubrey up and couldn't help but smile. After the longest nine months of my life, it was finally happening. I let myself relax. I helped her down the stairs and back out to the car. I locked the door and set the alarm before pulling out and heading to the hospital.

We arrived fifteen minutes later. Aubrey already preregistered, so it was just a matter of letting them know we were here. A nurse came down from labor and delivery and brought us up to the third floor. She helped Aubrey change into a hospital gown started an IV. She paged the anesthesiologist per our doctor's orders. A couple minutes later Caroline came in with Granny Jean in tow. She said Tim was on his way and should be here soon. I held her hand as the doctor came in to administer the epidural. Our doctor came in to let us know she was going to get scrubbed in. She handed me a pair of scrubs to change into. I fished our camera out of the overnight bag and went in the bathroom to change.

It's really happening. I'm going to be someone's dad...

After I changed I folded my clothes and put them in a neat pile. I hurried back into the room, and Tim was there. Aubrey said she was fine, nervous and excited. They came to tell us it was time to go. I kissed Aubrey and told her I would see her in a couple minutes. I hated the thought of leaving her. A nurse took me to where I could wash my hands. She instructed me to wait in the hallway until they were ready. I was anxiously pacing the hallway until she came and told me I could go in. I walked right over and sat in a stool next to Aubrey. There was a blue sheet draped in front of her. The doctor asked if she could feel anything. She said she couldn't. I held her hand and stood up so I could watch.

I watched as the scalpel moved across her skin. I watched as the doctor reached in and pulled out a set of feet and then the rest of the baby. I heard crying and I started crying myself. A nurse came over and brought the baby to the table. The doctor quickly reached in and pulled out the second baby. I heard the crying again, and Aubrey told me to go check on the babies. I reluctantly moved since I didn't want to leave her side, but I wanted to see our babies.

I walked over to baby 'A' first. Our son, Jameson George Parker. He weighed 7 lbs. 1 oz. and was 20 inches long. He had a full head of dark brown hair. I took a couple pictures and walked over to the next table to see our daughter. Violet Kate Parker. She weighed in at 6 lbs. 12 oz. and was 19 inches long. She had light brown hair and opened her blue eyes. My heart melted. She was only minutes old and already had me wrapped around her little finger. I snapped a couple more pictures and stood there in complete awe. They were both doing wonderfully. Once Jameson was cleaned the nurse handed him over to me. I carefully cradled him in my arms and walked him over to Aubrey. I sat down and leaned so that she could kiss his forehead.

"He's perfect." She cried.

"Just like his momma." I said. "Violet's getting cleaned off now, but she's doing really well too. She has your nose and lips, thank God." I laughed.

She giggled and grimaced. They were putting in the final staples to close up the incision. One of the nurses came over and switched babies. I held Violet up to show Aubrey. She kissed Violet's little nose and told her she loved her. The nurse stood there with Jameson next to Violet.

"I'd sacrifice my beating heart before I'd lose either of you." I told them.

They wanted to take them to the nursery so they could move Aubrey to recovery. I told Aubrey I would meet her there since we decided we wanted to make sure they got there safely.

Tim, Caroline, and Granny Jean were outside waiting as they pushed the bassinets into the hallway. They peeked in and saw their grandchildren for the first time. Caroline was completely overcome with emotion. Tim clapped me on the back and told me that 'I done good.' I told him that I didn't do anything except for the fun part, which earned me a smack in the back of the head.

"Always the smart ass, isn't he. I guess I'm officially an old coot now since I'm a great-grandma." She laughed peeking at the babies.

Caroline said she was going to stand by the window and watch them get checked over. We headed down the hallway to the nursery. I wish I could clone myself so that one of me could stay here and the other one could be with Aubrey. The nurse said as soon as they were done they would bring them to our room. I unwillingly left them and went to go find Aubrey. I had to force myself not to turn around a handful of times. She was in her room when I got there. I leaned in and kissed her.

"Do you feel okay?" I asked her.

"Yeah. I'm a little uncomfortable, but nothing unbearable."

"You're amazing. Seriously baby, you're the strongest person I know."

She smiled sleepily at me.

"I can't believe they're finally here. They're perfect." She mumbled.

"Yes they are. Why don't you close your eyes for a couple minutes? I'll get you up when they bring the babies in."

"'Kay."

She closed her eyes and fell right asleep. I would imagine the whole thing was really rough on her body. She had to be exhausted. I walked into the hallway and called Ron. He answered the phone right away.

"Hey Gramps." I said.

"Did she have the babies already?"

"Yes, less than an hour ago. Her water broke at the house this morning, we came straight to the hospital, and they took her right in."

I could hear him getting choked up on the other end. He was planning on taking a flight out and staying with us for a little while so he could meet them. He said he would call and make the arrangements right away. Next I called Brett and the guys. They all said to send pictures, and that they would see us in a couple weeks. Piper was my last call. She shrieked so loudly that I had to hold the phone away from my ear. She said she was on her way and would see us soon. Tim was walking down the hallway when I was hanging up. He was grinning from ear to ear.

"I can't believe I'm a grandpa." He shook his head. "How's my princess doing?"

"She's good. She's sleeping. I'll get her up when they bring the babies in, but she needs some rest to recover."

It was a full hour before they wheeled the babies into the room. Aubrey was struggling to sit up. I went to help her and saw in her face that she was in pain. As soon as I handed her Jameson her whole face lit up. Caroline went to sit on the bed next to her. Aubrey held him closely and rubbed her nose on his. I picked up Violet and kissed her head before handing her to Granny Jean. She handed her off to Tim when she was done. They were just leaving to go home when Piper came in. She practically bounced into the room and over to the babies. She picked up Jameson first and cooed at him. She claimed that she wanted one, and that since we had two we should share. It turns out that she was a total baby hog. She didn't end up staying too long since Aubrey needed to rest, but vowed that she would be back tomorrow.

Aubrey was nursing Violet when Jameson started. I could see this was going to be a challenge with both of them wanting to eat at the same time. We turned them so they could both eat at the same time. Poor Aubrey had turned into a human milk machine. She looked up at me and smiled. I couldn't help laughing at the sight in front of me. I burped Violet while Jameson finished. We were going to have a method down in no time. Aubrey scooted over so I could slide in next to her. Here, we were with our perfect little family.

Two days later we arrived home to our new house with the babies in tow. I opened the door and helped Aubrey inside. Caroline set a room up for her downstairs so she wouldn't have to do the stairs until after her staples were removed. I brought in both infant carriers and set them down on the floor. Bella came running over to see what all the excitement was about. I couldn't help but thinking without her, they might not be here at all. She was sniffing them and laid down right in front of the carriers like a little protector. We fed Jameson first, and I brought him up to his room to sleep.

His nursery was rock star themed, of course. It was painted gray and red. I hung pictures of guitars on the walls. We had a black glider chair set up in the corner. He had a black crib and changing table. His sheets were white and had little records on them. I carefully placed him down in the crib and made sure the baby monitor camera was on. I headed back downstairs to get Violet. Violet's room was a carbon copy of Aubrey's room at her parents. It was hot pink with white wainscoting. She had a white crib and changing table. Her glider chair was hot pink, and she had zebra patterned curtains and sheets. I looked down at her and read the onesie she had on. It said, 'look what my daddy did.' I smiled. I double checked her camera and went to go sit with Aubrey for a couple minutes. Bella was sleeping in the middle of the hallway since she couldn't decide which baby's room she wanted to be in.

I went into the kitchen and made us a couple sandwiches. I put them on a tray and carried them into the living room. I handed Aubrey her plate, and she thanked me. We enjoyed eight minutes of silence before Violet started crying. I went up to check on her. She had a total diaper blowout. I carried her over to the changing table and put a new diaper on. I put her pacifier in her mouth, and she was back out in minutes. The rest of the night was pretty much the same. Maybe Bella was onto something with sleeping in the middle of the floor. They were being really fussy, and Aubrey called her mom to see if she had any advice. She said because they have been together in the womb for such a long time they probably wanted to be near each other. I went and moved them so that they were together, and it was lights out. *Unbelievable!*

Aubrey

One month later...

A month has gone since the babies were born. They were actually really easygoing for being newborns. They ate, slept and pooped. A lot. I had turned into a 24-hour diner, and life has never been better. Jake was wonderful. He made sure that everyone was taken care of and though I didn't really like to bottle-feed he would do it sometimes at night so I could get a little more sleep. My mom was over almost every single day cooking and helping out how she could. I was so thankful that she was nearby. The boys were scheduled to fly in today to start working on the new album. Jake wanted to push it off for another month or two, but I told him it was fine and that they should start now. I also knew there was mounting pressure from the record company. He pulled his guitar out and started strumming a lullaby.

We just got the babies to sleep when the buzzer went off. It was the boys. I hit the button and let them in. They came in through the front door bearing giant stuffed animals. They bought Violet a giraffe and Jameson a monkey. They also brought a bottle of champagne. We took it into the kitchen and pulled out some glasses. Jake popped the cork and poured it. Everyone took a glass and clinked.

"To some of my best friends, congratulations." Kevin saluted.

"I still can't believe that Jake's somebody's dad." Derek said shaking his head.

He still cracked me up when he did that.

"Is Piper coming over?" Blake asked.

"I'm not sure…" I said trying to avoid the subject.

After the wedding, they went their separate ways. Piper was being stubborn and hasn't talked to Blake since. Blake has been trying to pursue her to no avail. It was hard being on the other side of the country. He really tried, though it was several failed attempts. He sent her flowers, shoes, sketch books and really fancy art supplies. I knew he was still pining hard for her, but I didn't really want to get in the middle of things with them because they were both my friends. They were adults and could figure it out on their own. Really, I thought the whole thing was a colossal misunderstanding, but I was biting my tongue.

"You have to get her to talk to me, Aubs." He pleaded. "I miss her like crazy. It was like those couple days with her ruined me for all other women. I haven't even slept with anyone since. I can't even you know…"

Derek started cracking up. "You can't get it up, can you?"

"Shut up asshole." Blake grumbled.

"Blake's got a crush." Derek goaded, and Blake glared at him.

We finished our champagne, and they headed back to see the guesthouse. The babies woke up a little while later. We bathed, changed and fed the babies before putting them back to bed. They would be good for at least a couple hours. Jake and I went into our room. I was feeling good and really missed that connection between us. He was so set on waiting the full eight weeks, but I wasn't about to let that happen. I undid my wrap dress and kicked it at him.

Jake's head snapped back, and I knew that I had his undivided attention. He walked over to me and ran his fingertips along my collarbone making me shiver. He moved them over my tattoos, right over my scar. It's taken me a long time to realize that no one can go through life without a scar or two. I've chosen to turn my scars into stars, figuratively. He's helped me learn to accept them and heal from the inside out. I looked into his blue eyes and felt completely awestruck.

"I love you, Mrs. Parker." He smiled.

"I love you too, Mr. Parker." I leaned in and kissed his nose.

The key to finding lasting love is to find someone who loves you, battlescars and all.

THE END

Be on the look out for Piper and Blake's story coming Summer 2013

Follow me on Facebook @
www.facebook.com/sophiemonroewrites for updates!

Official Battlescars Playlist:

30 Second to Mars- I'll Attack

Finger Eleven- Living in a Dream

The Brixton Riot- It's Been Too Long

Lit- Partner In Crime

Nonpoint- Everybody Down

Angus & Julia Stone- Big Jet Plane

Lostprophets- Can't Catch Tomorrow

Hinder- Heaven Sent

Journey- Don't Stop Believin'

Papa Roach- Alive (N' Out of Control)

The Gaslight Anthem- Blue Dahlia

Metallica- Turn the Page

Age of Daze (Days) – Afflicted

Made in the USA
Charleston, SC
30 May 2013